THE ELEMENTAL COLLECTIVE

AN ELEMENTAL PALADINS SPIN-OFF SERIES

MONTANA ASH

THE ELEMENTAL COLLECTIVE:

VOLUME ONE

An Elemental Paladins spin-off series

BY

MONTANA ASH

Published by **Paladin Publishing**

The Elemental Collective: Volume One

Copyright © 2020 by **Montana Ash**

All rights reserved

This is a work of fiction. Names, characters, businesses, places, events, and incidents are either the products of the author's imagination or used in a fictitious manner. Any resemblance to actual persons, living or dead, or actual events is purely coincidental.

This book or any portion thereof may not be reproduced or used in any manner whatsoever without the express written permission of Montana Ash, except for the use of brief quotations embodied in critical articles and reviews.

Cover design by: **Jennifer Munswami**, J.M Rising Horse Creations

Formatting by: **Sariah Skye**

A NOTE FROM MONTANA

Dear, Readers

This is just a reminder that The Elemental Collective: Volume One is a collection of novellas and short stories. It is a direct spin-off from the Elemental Paladins series (completed seven book series). If you have not read the Elemental Paladins, this collection will be super spoilery for that series. I highly suggest reading them in order. I wish you all happy reading and fun within the pages xxx

BOOK ONE

MORDECAI

PROLOGUE

In Otherworld (10 weeks ago)

Dana laughed, shaking her head as her son-in-law face-planted onto the wooden floor. The look of stunned joy followed swiftly by dawning horror was a sight to behold, and she took as much delight in it as his family did. As the others laughed and joked, stepping around the fallen soldier, Dana couldn't really blame him. The thought of another Max in the world was daunting even to her. Though she shouldn't really be observing, she found she was unable to look away from the rapturous joy on her daughter's face. The gentle, protective hand on her womb cradling the delicate young soul within, had tears rushing to the forefront and Dana blinked rapidly to dispel them. Now was a time for happiness. Her daughter had returned to her family.

Dana watched as Darius unceremoniously slapped his Captain awake and Ryker bolted upright, the name of his love the first sound on his lips. Dana sighed, watching as Ryker's and Max's souls literally reached out to each other. Theirs was a one in a billion love to be sure.

Although, looking around at all the happily matched couples, she decided that the one in a billion chance was occurring at an alarming rate within the wooden and stone walls.

Despite her best intentions, Dana sought out Mordecai – the father of her child. The guardian and keeper of death was immersed within the festivities for once, instead of standing on the sidelines – his four trusted and noble companions still loyally by his side. As she watched, she saw Mordecai's deep, green eyes travel to his daughter where they lingered, hungrily tracing her features as if he were afraid she would disappear from his sight. Dana pressed a hand to her stomach, feeling it churn and rebel. It always acted so whenever she thought about the grievous wrong she had committed. Even so, the urge to reach out and smooth away the lines of stress present on Mordecai's face was overwhelming.

Unable to help herself, she passed her hand through the veil and ever so lightly, brushed the back of her hand over his forehead. Mordecai's frown deepened, and he reached up, his hand passing untouching through hers without pause. She knew he didn't feel her – he couldn't when she was between worlds like she was now. But the way he straightened and looked around suspiciously made her wonder if he could somehow feel her watching him. It certainly wouldn't be the first time she had done so.

Despite the futility of her desires, she longed to feel Mordecai's strong arms wrapped around her once more. She yearned to see his cool, green eyes warm as they stared down at her, his muscular body trapping hers in a cocoon of heat and lust. But she knew what she would see if their eyes were ever to truly meet now; hate. She exhaled shakily, pressing the heels of her palms against her eyes, physically forcing the tears back. She had no right to cry and deserved everything Mordecai said, felt, and thought about her. She had betrayed him in the worst possible way. Yes, she had asked permission and gained consent to do what she did that night so many years ago in Germany. But the consent was dubious at best because she had not divulged all the facts. And she knew they certainly would have made a difference to the man. Mordecai would never have agreed to the night of incredible sex had he been fully aware of the outcome. By the Gods, she would never have agreed either.

In the early hours after the Great Massacre, with so many of her guardians slaughtered, nature's balance so horribly skewed, and the Earth crying in mourning, Dana's senses were so raw that every breath was agony. The voices of her warriors calling for her aid had been deafening. But she could do nothing. As omniscient as everyone believed Gods to be, they were still limited by the laws of nature and governed by the laws of their kind. She could no more enter the Earth plane and fight battles for her wardens and paladins than she could become human. She was what she was. But that didn't mean there weren't loopholes.

On that day, one man's pain had pierced her shields more than others. One voice had called to her and resonated within her so clearly, that she had spun where she stood in Otherworld, thinking him beside her. The voice had been beautifully accented with the echoes of the Scots, but had been brutally painful and full of curses. Breaking her own self-decreed rule to never pass through the veil again, she had swiftly pushed aside the figurative curtain and sent her body to the time and place of Mordecai, Liege of Valhalla. The man had been everything his voice had conjured; a mighty Scotsman warrior, imbued righteously with the element of Death – and in so much physical and emotional pain Dana had promptly fallen to her knees upon first laying eyes on him.

After quickly picking herself up and listening to a few more of his half-drunken accusations and recriminations, she had boldly approached him with no forethought as to where the night would end. Mordecai's offhanded remark about creating something to cure the chade infection had sparked an idea. Yes; she *could* create a weapon – a tool – that would act as a cure for the disease wiping out her precious wardens. Little did she know, that tool would one day be her beloved daughter, known affectionately as Max. Dana had in fact named her daughter for what she would become; the great one.

Titania.

That night, Dana knew she would be creating life – it's what she did – she was a Creator. But never having carried and birthed anything from her physical body before, she had been ignorant of the feelings it would inspire. From the very first moment she felt the stirrings of life in her womb, she knew she had made a grave mistake. Not about conceiving her daughter – never that. But that her daughter had been made solely to serve a purpose. Dana knew what it would cost Titania – Max, rather – to rid the world of the taint evolution had wrought and had considered aborting her initial plans innumerable times. She had even once resolved herself to let the wardens and paladins die out, for that was exactly where their path had been headed. The loss of nature's guardians and their knightly protectors would have meant the total extinction of every living organism on the planet. But looking at her precious daughter as she laughed and played in the Eden Gardens in Otherworld, Dana had been prepared to let the world descend into oblivion. It had been Max who had insisted on fulfilling her purpose.

Dana sighed, thinking of Max's inner strength and wondering for the millionth time how she had managed to raise such an awe-inspiring woman. Max had just been entering the first blushes of womanhood when Dana had felt another cataclysmic shift in the balance. Emmanuel and his deranged parents had begun to make greater strides in their evil plan, consuming more and more vitality and infecting more and more wardens. The poor rangers were inundated with chades and the Councils seemed oblivious – or they had simply given up.

Thinking of it now, Dana knew Max had been correct in her initial assessment and judgement of their government and society. It had degraded into complacency and had placed inappropriate emphasis on warden hierarchy and the caste system. At the time of the power shift, Max had insisted she be allowed to enter the Earth plane and begin her task of healing the lost souls. Dana had cried rivers of tears and clung to her flesh and blood child so hard that Max had needed to pry her off. Max had then given her one of her now well-known, righteous speeches leaving Dana feeling like she was the child and her daughter was the wise crone. Unable to deny Max anything, in the end, Dana had kissed Max on her forehead and bestowed her blessings.

Passage from one plane to the next was not necessarily a difficult task, but it was governed by rules and the laws of nature. Souls had no trouble passing through the veil between worlds. But physical bodies? That was another act of physics entirely. Dana had no such issues because she was a pure goddess, but Max, on the other hand, was a mix of mortality and divinity. She was a custodian of the flesh, and though she had been able to successfully cross, maintaining the physical body of a young woman on the cusp of adulthood, the passing had some unforeseen consequences.

Amnesia.

Dana had been absolutely horrified and had been about to pass through the veil and retrieve her when a piece of paper near the metaphysical barrier had caught her eye. There, in her daughter's neat handwriting, were the words; *Don't you dare!!!* Max had apparently foreseen the complication even though Dana herself had not. Dana shook her head, mouth quirking when she thought about the note and sketchbook Max had left for herself this time. Her daughter was nothing if not prepared. Dana had obeyed Max's wishes and had left her alone and afraid in a foreign world with naught but the clothes on her back. She had trusted her daughter to know what she was doing and where she was destined to end up.

Observing the joy and happiness of Max with her family now, and the revolutionary healing of the chades, Dana still couldn't honestly say that she did the right thing or that she would do it all over again had she seen the outcome. Though she didn't need to wonder what her stubborn daughter thought. Max had told her in no uncertain terms what her opinion was upon her return to Otherworld just weeks prior. The moment Max had crossed the veil in her pure soul form, her memories as Titania had returned and Dana had an armful of laughing, sobbing energy. Their happy reunion had lasted a blissful matter of minutes until Max had let loose a string of creative curses and demands to know what was going on. After that, Dana had been forced to endure three weeks of whining, cursing, and pouting until Max had been able to reform her physical form. Dana had been under no illusion that Max would return to Earth the moment she was physically able to, but they had both been surprised and overwhelmed to learn of the presence of the tiny being nestled contentedly in Max's womb. Though Dana was able to essentially birth souls in the form of Custodians, she did not get to choose where those souls were housed. That was the responsibility of a different deity. Besides, Dana had refused to create any more Custodians after the last of her creations was taken against its will.

Naturally, the discovery of her own daughter made Max even more determined to return and Dana had aided her as much as she was able to. Unfortunately, all the preparation in the world still had not been enough to prevent the resulting memory loss. Human bodies simply weren't supposed to cross the veil. Dana had watched on tenterhooks as Max found her way yet again and although she was overjoyed at the scene in front of her right now, she was even more gratified to hear Max call Mordecai *dad* and ask him what he thought of being a grandfather.

Dana laughed out loud as Mordecai noticeably paled. Seems that small fact had escaped him. To be fair, he responded to the good-natured ribbing from his Order and Ryker well, even smiling a time or two before finally threatening them all with bodily harm. *I wish he would threaten my body again,* Dana thought without meaning to. She immediately flushed, though there was no one to see her embarrassment. Mordecai had been her first – and last – lover. The title of Great Mother was more symbolic than literal. Yes, she had birthed the first souls and the first seeds of nature, but like her fellow gods and goddesses, procreation had not involved sex. Even with Mordecai being exceptionally drunk and herself aware of the purpose of the act, it had still been the most incredible night of her life. She could well understand why humans placed so much emphasis on sex. Too bad she was doomed never to experience it again.

Her sigh this time was big enough to displace the air minutely, and Max's head popped up, eyes searching keenly. When they looked directly through where the veil was hovering in the doorway, Max gave her a small grin and a wave, even though Dana knew she couldn't actually see the shimmering, pearlescent curtain. It was invisible and impervious to all – other than pure divinity. Still, Max was sensitive enough and astute enough to know Dana was there.

The small gesture from Max had Dana slumping in relief. When Max had said she remembered everything, Dana didn't know if that included herself or not. Thankfully, it appeared to and she wondered when Max would see fit to tell the others about her trip to Otherworld and what she remembered of her time growing up as Titania, the beloved daughter of Mother Nature.

Max raised her eyebrows and patted her stomach one last time before turning her attention back to Beyden and Jasminka. Dana was glad the two had resolved their feelings for each other, knowing they had been destined to meet even before their births. But sometimes destiny wasn't enough, and choices accompanied by actions often forged new paths. She was relieved to see these two had not travelled down different roads because Max was going to need them – need all of them. Or rather, Max's daughter was.

Max had only been partially correct when she had said her babe was a goddess. The little girl was half life paladin and half custodian in corporeal form. The resulting child – Dana's granddaughter – was destined to be the first of her kind.

A Spirit Goddess.

The time would come when Dana would reveal the full potential of her grandchild, but that time was not now. Now, there was a society to rebuild and a government to re-establish, and one last paladin whose own destiny was about to come knocking on the door.

CHAPTER ONE

10 WEEKS LATER ...

"Have you talked to mum yet?"

Mordecai paused in the act of making his first cup of coffee for the day. He wasn't a man with many vices, but he could admit to being heavily dependent upon the bitter, caffeinated goodness that was coffee. It had evolved a lot over the years – the brewing of it as well as the flavours – but its desired effect remained the same, no matter the century. Fuel. Motivation. Love. Yes, he loved coffee. But it was a testament to how much he loved something more when he put his half-filled mug down on the kitchen counter and turned to the woman behind him.

Five-foot-three inches of pure miracle, with startling turquoise eyes and a mouth – that was more often than not – quirked into a genuine and mischievous smile. He felt himself blinking rapidly and spinning back to his neglected coffee without answering because looking at her still hurt so bad. It also brought joy and happiness in equal measure, but the pain was ever-present as well. He wondered if that was ever going to change – or, more to the point – if he ever *wanted* it to change.

'Stop being a miserable old martyr.'

Mordecai scowled, ignoring the voice as he filled his mug to the brim with plain, black coffee. He didn't add milk or sugar or fancy syrup like most of the soft yuppies of the world today. No, he took it black and straight. His thoughts led to even more amusement bouncing around inside his head and even more teasing.

'Soft yuppies? You're showing your age, my liege.'

'Fuck off,' was Mordecai's swift internal reply to his usually softspoken and mature second in command. Four variations of male laughter flowed through the Order link and Mordecai felt his lips twitch. Once upon a time, Bastien – along with Aiden, Tobias, and Madigan – would never have dared tease him in such a way. Paladins were long seen as glorified servants as well as bodyguards and battery packs. Mordecai had never held true to such ideas and thankfully, the natural bond he shared with his Order had allowed them all to settle into a comfortable rhythm sooner rather than later. And now, sixteen-hundred years later, they were friends and brothers. Although, Mordecai often felt those words didn't do their bond justice. There would be no Mordecai without the Order of Valhalla.

'Aww, we love you too, boss,' Tobias crooned through the link, even as he slapped Mordecai on the back and sought out his own mug.

Mordecai watched his coffee lap against the rim of the mug before it settled once more. "You're lucky that didn't spill, cowboy," he murmured, his voice low and dangerous.

Tobias merely rolled his eyes, as completely fearless as always, before he proceeded to add no less than five teaspoons of sugar to his own coffee. Just watching the horrifying act made Mordecai want to gag, and he cupped both hands around his own brew in a protective gesture.

"Dad? How long do you think you can ignore me?"

Mordecai spun back around because he wouldn't ignore Max for all the lives on the planet. Not ever again. "I'm not ignoring you."

Max squinted those expressive eyes of hers, "No – you're just ignoring my mother."

Mordecai felt his eye twitch, but he resisted the urge to rub it. That would just earn him more ribbing from his Order. Plus, it would be like an acknowledgement that the Great Mother got under his skin. *Which she absolutely, unequivocally did not,* he assured himself.

"Pfft, you keep telling yourself that," Madigan chimed in, out loud this time as he set about making himself some breakfast.

"Will you all fuck off out of my head for five fucking minutes?!" Mordecai snarled, glaring in the direction of his knights, who were now all lined up like a bunch of trained monkeys along the kitchen island. They had all made themselves very much at home in Ryker's lovely log house by the sea. It was tight quarters – even in such a huge house – but Mordecai didn't mind. He would live in a hovel if it afforded him the chance to get to know the daughter he had once lost.

Ryker sauntered over to Max, wrapping an arm around her waist. "Now we know where Max gets her filthy mouth from."

"I thought you loved my filthy mouth?" Max smirked up at her man.

Ryker's eyes widened and he quickly looked at Mordecai, who merely raised his eyebrows, daring the younger paladin to say something salacious about his daughter. "Why do you insist on trying to get me killed? I want to be around to meet my daughter, you know," came Ryker's eventual response.

Max pulled Ryker down for a chaste kiss on the lips. "I think it's so cute that you're afraid of my father."

Ryker pulled back, frowning. "I'm not afraid of your father. He wishes I was afraid of him."

Mordecai simply straightened from where he was leaning against the counter, beyond amused when Ryker took an involuntary step back. His own smirk was met with a fierce scowl and a silently mouthed *'go fuck yourself'* from the younger man. Mordecai covered his smile by taking a healthy swallow of his coffee. He really did like the grumpy, violent life paladin that was his daughter's soulmate. In fact, he couldn't have chosen a better partner for Max himself. Not that he would ever admit that. No, he would go to his grave before ever saying so out loud.

"Seriously, dad, you can't ignore her forever. She's sticking around this time," Max paused, looking sadly uncertain as she bit her bottom lip. "At least, I hope she is."

Her Order was quick to rally around her with murmurs of assurance, Beyden hugging her from behind. "Hey, she said she would stay, right? Pop in and out or something?" he reminded his friend and liege.

Max sighed, slumping back against Beyden. "Yes. She did."

Beyden scrubbed his large hand over her hair, making it even messier, saying, "Then she will."

Jasminka rolled her eyes as she passed her lover and best friend on the way to the coffee machine. The human doctor literally shoved Mordecai to the side with her hip so she had room to make her own cup. "Bey, you're so sweet and perky. It's barely eight in the morning. I don't have the stomach for that yet. I almost preferred it when your soul was being eaten by the darkness." She cast Mordecai a conspiratorial wink, "At least then I could have my cup of coffee in peace."

Mordecai grinned at the doctor, appreciating her level of ease with him, as well as her love and respect for coffee. She had never once been intimidated by him and it made him respect her even more – on top of the fact that she had been a true friend to his daughter when she had been sick and alone.

"If you don't want him, I'll take him." Max snarked back at Jazz, holding Beyden tightly to her.

Jazz grunted, drinking down her coffee in one breath like a true veteran. "You already have your own giant. What would you do with another one?"

"Really? Do you even need to ask?" Max retorted, causing Beyden to blush and step back, and Ryker to growl.

Sexual jokes were commonplace within the group, and whilst Mordecai liked to believe he had a sense of humour, he didn't really like to listen to sexual banter from his daughter. "I'm leaving," he muttered.

Max stepped into his path, her belly now leading the way at twenty weeks along. "I don't think so. Mum has been around for six weeks now and you two still haven't talked."

Mordecai knew how long it had been. The infernal woman had simply poofed herself into the kitchen one day like it was no big deal. After playing matchmaker with the latest couple to fall victim of the love-bug, that is. It had been two and a half months since Celeste had first shown up, and six weeks since the news of her son – and Axel's – had been revealed. Since then, Axel and Celeste looked to be forging a new future together and were well on the way to being sickeningly in love again. Just like the rest of the house. *It was nauseating,* Mordecai silently grumped. Not that he wasn't happy for Axel and Celeste to be reunited and for Spiro to have his father in his life for the first time. But being surrounded by so many happy couples was like shining a huge spotlight onto his own very lonely, very loveless existence. He was grateful for his Order, and while his mission in life for the past fifty-odd years had been to seek out his daughter, he hadn't realised just how much he was missing until he set foot in the Aurora Order's 'camp'.

There was warmth and fun, love and life – things he had given no priority to in, well, ever. But all that was irrelevant because although he had seen and done pretty much everything there was to see and do at least three times in his long life, he had never been in love. Not once. The closest he had ever come was an almost violently strong initial attraction, followed by explosive chemistry, and then a bone-deep hate for five decades. And even his stubborn arse knew that shit wasn't healthy.

"I don't know why you're avoiding her anyway. Kind of pointless, don't you think?" Axel chimed in, ushering Celeste to a chair.

Mordecai gritted his teeth. "I am not avoiding her."

Axel looked over to him, his blue eyes a mixture of pity and amusement. "Well, good. Avoidance is futile. The woman is basically the source of all living things. I bet she knows everything about you. Including whether you're a lefty or a righty."

Mordecai frowned. "I'm right-handed. That's obvious."

"No, man. Not what hand you write with – I mean the way you tuck your dick," Axel explained.

Mordecai choked on his next – and last – mouthful of coffee. "What?!"

"Axel!" Darius yelled at the same time – his tone scandalised. "That is no way to speak to a warden. Plus, your son is sitting right there."

All eyes turned to the teenage boy who was grinning and stuffing his face with pop tarts.

Axel rolled his eyes, "I thought Mordecai was family now? Besides, Spiro has a dick too." Spiro laughed even as Axel turned to Celeste with a sheepish look. "Is dick a word I'm not supposed to use in front of Spiro? This fatherhood thing has so many rules!"

"Dick is fine," Spiro said.

"Dick is *not* fine," Celeste said at the same time as her son.

"Ah, ah, ah," the teenager wagged his finger at his mother. "You said it was fine to use when referring to the anatomy. Dick direction is anatomical."

Several snickers could be heard throughout the room as Celeste looked around helplessly. She made eye contact with all the women before responding; "See? He's a mini-Axel. I'm so glad I have you all for back-up now."

"There, there, sweetie. We got you," Diana crooned, hugging the new IDC's Fire Warden in a one-armed hug.

"Anyway," Axel looked at Mordecai once more. "My point is, that woman knows everything. Including –"

"Including my dick direction," Mordecai cut in, dryly. "Uh-huh."

"Is that even a thing? A dick direction?" Madigan asked.

"You're over sixteen-hundred years old and you don't know what direction you hang?" Lark asked, looking askance at Mordecai's paladin. "I, for one, tuck to the left."

"Hey, me too!" Axel exclaimed.

"Huh. What about you, Beyden?" Lark turned to his friend, who was very red in the cheeks.

"I'm not – I don't –" Beyden looked helplessly at Jazz who simply held up her right hand. Beyden sighed, the sound filled with resignation as he muttered, "Right."

"Darius is a righty too." Diana revealed, ignoring her man's gasp as she continued, "But I think it just kind of falls naturally that way because his left testicle is bigger than his right one."

"Diana!" Darius cried.

"What? You make it kind of hard to hide when you wax down there, honey," came Diana's swift response.

"Don't worry, bro. My left teste is slightly bigger than my right as well, so I tend to tuck to the left to give my right ball more room. Maybe it's a genetic thing?" Dex mused.

"How did this become my life?" Mordecai murmured – more to himself than his Order.

"Oh, please," Aiden said, from beside him. "You love it."

Mordecai grunted, scowling in the direction of his daughter's Order. "They're a bunch of morons."

"That Order is one of the best you've ever seen in all your long years," Bastien pointed out quietly.

"With some of the best soldiers you've ever met," Tobias added on.

"And the most loyal," Aiden chimed in.

Madigan smiled, watching the antics with affection. "Certainly the most loving."

Mordecai merely grunted, the non-verbal agreement causing his Order to grin. It was true, he mused to himself. He had never met an Order more in tune with each other – nor an Order that fit so well. Other than his own of course, but that bond was forged over a thousand years. The one in front of him was yet to hit two years. *Some things are just meant to be,* he mused, silently. Refocusing on the conversation, he was horrified to tune back in just in time to hear Max's comment.

"Well, Ryker kind of has to coil his like a snake. Remember the tanto sword comparison?"

"Dear Gods!" Mordecai gagged.

Ryker smirked, "Don't be jealous, daddy-o."

Mordecai pinned Ryker with a frosty glare. "Firstly, never call me daddy-o again. Secondly, I'm not jealous." He then tried really hard to erase the memory of that one time he had seen Ryker naked after Max had disappeared. But for some reason, it just kept popping into his head. "Sweet Mother. I am out of here," he grumbled.

"So soon?" Ryker teased, his dark eyes glinting with evil. "Aren't you going to share with the class?"

Mordecai made sure his voice was pitched to lethal as he responded. "The day I discuss my dick with any of you is the day I sprout pink fairy wings and blow glitter out of my arse." *Besides,* he thought to himself, *I have no idea what side I tuck my dick on.* Quickly followed by; *How could I not know?!*

"You tuck to the left."

It wasn't the smug female voice that startled him so much as the way her warm breath in his ear caused his whole body to tremble. He resolutely kept his stare straight ahead as Dana casually walked past him and enveloped Max in a warm hug. The warmth she left in her wake, combined with the feminine, floral scent had his body rioting and this time he didn't bother announcing his departure. He simply walked out.

CHAPTER TWO

"I see I've chased your father off again," Dana said tiredly to Max.

Max huffed, "If I didn't know any better, I'd say you two actually enjoyed annoying each other."

"Lucky you know better," Dana answered lightly.

"That's just it – I *do* know better. You're both miserable," Max stated, before reaching for Dana and offering another hug.

Dana hugged Max back as hard as she dared considering the bump getting in the way. Smiling, Dana pulled back and patted said bump, "Hello, sweet baby." Her granddaughter gave the faintest of kicks to her flattened palm, but Dana felt the hidden strength nonetheless. Her unborn granddaughter's path was becoming clearer, and Dana was becoming increasingly nervous. Not about what fate had in store for her – but about what her parents would think about it. Looking up, she saw Ryker's dark gaze lovingly latched onto Max's profile before it rested on Max's protruding stomach. That was when the love morphed into a combination of pride and an almost violent protectiveness. Dana knew it was Ryker whom she was going to have to battle when the truth came out. Setting aside the worrying thoughts for the moment, Dana gave Max a final pat before kissing Ryker on the cheek.

"Hi, uh, Dana," Ryker said, looking flushed.

Dana laughed lightly. "You did it. You called me by my name. And the world didn't end." She teased because it had taken weeks and weeks of her asking him – and the rest of the household – to call her Dana and not some form of the Great Mother. She understood their reticence. It was not every day one came face to face with a God or Goddess. But she desperately wanted to be viewed as a member of the family instead of a deity.

"Ha, yeah," Ryker agreed before his eyes pinned her. "It's *not* going to end, is it?"

Max rolled her eyes and moved over to the large dining table, sitting down and gathering food onto her plate. "Of course, it's not. I – will you let me do that?" she grumped in exasperation as Darius took her plate and filled it up for her, just as Lark passed her a glass of orange juice.

Darius pinned Max with his hazel eyes, stating, "Liege. Pregnant liege."

Max grumbled, but Dana noted that she did not argue further. It made her happy to see how far Max had come with her Order and understanding her place in it. Not having been raised in the world of wardens and paladins, Max had been so independent when she had first arrived that the thought of being aided – let alone waited on – was abhorrent to her. She'd had to rely on herself for so long that the idea of accepting help was a foreign concept. The thought saddened Dana and had guilt, anger, and shame rearing their ugly heads once more. She was trying so hard to let it all go – as per Max's request – but it was much easier said than done. And it certainly didn't help that a particular Death Warden kept reminding her of all her failures. As if reading the direction of her thoughts, Aiden turned to her and smiled.

"Bas and Madi say Mordecai is in the gym beating the shit out of a punching bag if you want to go talk to him?"

"I do not think so," Dana replied. She very much approved of Mordecai's Captain, as well as the rest of his Order. The bond between them was startlingly strong. And although it was exactly the type of relationship Dana had envisaged when she had first helped craft paladins and wardens, she felt slightly envious of it also.

"Seriously, my lady," Tobias began. "He is the walking, talking, physical manifestation of the word *stubborn*. He will wither and die before he starts a conversation with you willingly. I know because he told us so. Several times. And that shit just isn't healthy. So …" Tobias gestured in the direction of the gym, "please, will you just …?"

Dana opened her mouth to reject the idea once more, only to snap her mouth shut when she realised everyone in the room was staring at her in silence. "Wow, this isn't half creepy," she murmured.

Ivy – whom Dana enjoyed very much – spoke up. "Dana, take my advice. You cannot win against these people. They will keep at you until you buckle under their smiles and their warmth and their affection. They are insidious with their love – like a virus. Do yourself a favour and do whatever the fuck they say. It will save you – and everyone else – a whole bunch of time."

"Is that so?" Dana asked, unsure whether to be amused or terrified. She glanced around the room at the still silent and staring occupants "And what is it you are all saying?"

"Go talk to Mordecai!" came the almost simultaneous yell.

Dana winced, wondering if she and Mordecai really had been that annoying to those around them. She had only popped in a couple of times a week for a few hours at a time – all she was permitted to at this point due to the consequences of her visits. And each time she had pointedly ignored the father of her child. Either that, or she had pointedly irritated him, she thought, smiling to herself. It wasn't really her fault though – the man was ridiculously easy to get a rise out of.

Clearing her throat, Dana straightened her spine, "You know, I think I will talk to him. Thank you for your suggestion." A series of snickers and rude snorts met her ears, making her smile.

"My lady, we will accompany you," Tobias offered her his arm, every bit the charming gentleman.

Dana waggled her finger at him even as she accepted his arm. "That babyface and charming smile do not fool me, Tobias."

"I have no idea what you mean," he grinned down at her.

Aiden took up position on her other side and they led her from the house to the large building that housed the gym and indoor pool. "You know exactly what I mean. You are a lady's man. But you will not trap me."

"I'm not trying to. My liege did that fifty years ago," came Tobias's reply.

Dana stopped walking. "He did no such thing. *I* trapped *him*."

Tobias shook his head, gently pulling her along once more. "Whatever you need to tell yourself."

Dana frowned but said no more. She was becoming increasingly nervous as the knights led her to speak to the man she hadn't had a real conversation with since making a baby with him. *And isn't that ludicrous?* Dana thought to herself. Touching her unbound hair, she wondered if she looked okay. Glancing down, she then fingered the material of her emerald green blouse before smoothing her hands over her dark jeans. She had chosen the outfit because it was so different from what she usually wore in Otherworld. There, she was known to wear flowing gowns and robes and go barefoot. Yes, it was a little cliché, but it was also very comfortable and practical. On this side though, she could admit to liking the trend that was skinny jeans or leggings and loose, flowing shirts. As such, whenever she could, she crafted such clothes in varying colours and designs. One of the habits she brought with her from Otherworld, however, was going barefoot. She had a mental need, as well as a physical one, to be close to nature. Having some part of her skin being in contact with nature at all times fulfilled that need. Even as she walked, she could feel the heartbeat of the earth beneath her feet, and it gave her courage as well as comfort.

"You look great," Aiden said, presently.

"I'm sorry, what?" Dana asked.

Aiden gestured to where she was still tugging on her shirt. "Your clothes; they're fine. More than fine. That green brings out your eyes and those jeans make your legs look impossibly long – even though you're a short-shit like Max." He winked when he said the last part. "You look beautiful."

"Oh, well ... I ... thank you," she stuttered, feeling flustered.

Aidan laughed, the sound rich. "You really have no idea how appealing you are, do you? It's one of the things that drew Mordecai to you in that bar all those years ago."

Dana was unsure how to respond to that, because no – she had no idea how appealing she was as a woman because she had never had the opportunity to just *be* a woman. Other than for a few short hours long ago, that was. Shaking off her thoughts, she shored up her courage and was about to open the door to the gym when Aiden spoke once more.

"Dana ..." Aiden began, waiting for her to pause and look at him. "Don't let him heap all the blame on you, okay? He is a grown-arse man who has been making his own decisions – as well as his own successes and failures – for hundreds of years. His choice was his alone. You did not make him do anything. Remember that."

Dana drew in a deep breath, "I shall try."

Aiden nodded and Tobias added, "Oh, and Dana? Feel free to remind him of that fact too, huh?"

Dana cast them a wry look. "I may be the Great Mother, but even I cannot combat male stubbornness."

She heard them laughing as they followed her at a discreet distance, stopping with the other two members of their Order off to the side. Dana continued on, but soon found herself rooted to the spot when her eyes landed on Mordecai. He was stripped from the waist up, his muscled torso glistening with sweat as he beat the living hell out of a punching bag. Thankfully, he was wearing boxing gloves, otherwise she was sure his knuckles would have been torn to shreds due to the force he was exerting. Although the motivations behind his frenetic movements were troubling, Dana could not deny the result was pleasing.

"Are you just here to watch the show? Or did you have something to say?" Mordecai asked, pausing in his punches but not turning around.

Dana kept her mouth shut, wanting to see his face when they had their first real conversation. The stubborn man kept his back to her, shaking his head and muttering to himself when she continued to stand in silence. His back expanded as he dragged in a couple of deep breaths and Dana found her eyes tracking several rivulets of sweat as they ran down his spine and into the waistband of his low-riding trackpants. Her eyes were the only part of her that moved when he abruptly spun around and she found herself following the dark line of hair that sprouted from his groin and made a delightful path up to his bellybutton. His corrugated stomach moved in time with his still harsh breathing and his pecs flexed as he shook out his arms and hands. Overall, Dana thought – mouth completely dry – Mordecai was *supremely* male.

Mordecai must have realised the direction of her thoughts because he became still, those cold green eyes narrowing on her even as tension began to rise – and not the usual kind that was present between them. No, this was a *sexual* tension. It was lust, desire – and any other word that could be used to describe the fact that Dana wanted to scratch him up. *And maybe bite him a little too,* she mused, her mouth kicking up at the corners. Mordecai's frown deepened and he swore, marching over to a bench where he hastily pulled on his discarded shirt. To say she was disappointed would be an understatement. So, instead of starting the conversation in a mature way that could lead to a thoughtful discussion, she blurted out; "I do not know why you are bothering with a shirt. It's nothing I haven't seen before."

Mordecai's mouth lifted in a sneer. "One night with me fifty years ago isn't enough for you to know anything about my body, oh Great Mother. Don't flatter yourself."

"And you suppose I'm referring to that night? And not all the nights since then?" Dana baited.

Mordecai strode over, his long legs eating up the distance in seconds. "So, you admit to spying on me? I knew it! I knew I could feel eyes on me! Have you been watching me all these years? Like some kind of goddess-pervert?"

Dana winced internally. She really should have known better than to tease a wild animal. Yes, she had been spying on him – for a very long time. But no, she really did not want him to think she was some kind of creeper who watched him when he showered ... or dressed ...

or sometimes pleasured himself. Dana groaned out loud, dropping her head into her hands, *by the gods. I really* am *a pervert!*

"Dana, are you listening to me?" Mordecai demanded.

Dana raised her head. "My apologies, Warden. I should not have said that. I did not come here to pick a fight with you."

Mordecai snorted rudely. "Then you're wasting your time. Because all I want to do is fight with you. I want to yell at you. I want to make sure you are as miserable as I have been all these years, knowing I had a daughter destined to save the world and not be able to help her. Not be able to find her. Not be able to *love* her!" he shouted.

Guilt and shame slammed into her, and she opened her mouth, hoping for a small chance to explain. But it was not to be, because Mordecai was apparently taking his first opportunity of a one-on-one with her to do precisely what he said; fight with her, yell at her, ensure her misery.

"You get off on watching, is that it, Dana?" His deep voice was deadly as he moved with predatory grace toward her. "You have nothing better to do with your eternity than to perch on your little windowsill in Otherworld and watch as your creations ruin each other and desecrate their domains? You get your kicks from watching your own flesh and blood flounder in a world that was not only foreign to her, but also poisonous to her? Is that it, huh? Answer me!" he shouted, practically in her face.

Dana's good humour – as well as her limited patience – fled in the face of his hostility and she allowed her fingertips to spark with pure power as she responded, "You forget your place. I do not answer to you, Warden. Step back."

Their gazes clashed and locked for a tense few seconds before Mordecai looked at the hands which had coloured vapour swirling over them. Dana knew it looked almost like rainbow fog, but one touch of the swirling mist could bring down mountains.

Mordecai eventually shook his head, a sardonic smile curving his mouth as he took a single step back. "Typical. Put on your Goddess hat when you don't like the questions. Or is it the answers you're so afraid of?"

Dana extinguished her powers with a single thought, flushing when she realised what he said was true. She wanted to talk to Mordecai as *Dana* – as the mother of his child. Not as the creator of pretty much everything. How had her intentions gotten lost in mere seconds? Because the man pushed every button she had without even knowing it, she admitted. He was her weakness – and her biggest threat. And he had no idea. She wondered what he would do if he ever found out. "I apologise. That was instinct. I came here to talk –"

"And if I don't want to talk to someone like you?" he interrupted.

Dana grit her teeth, striving for calm. "Someone like me? You don't know anything about me."

Mordecai shook his head, his top lip curling in disgust. "I don't *want* to know anything about you. You conceived and gave birth to a child only to sacrifice it. You are a selfish, manipulative bitch."

With every word he spoke, he took a step forward, forcing Dana to take a step back to maintain some space between them. A black cloud, speckled with gold, began to take shape around him and Dana knew he was losing control of his Death magic. To everyone else – including death wardens – the elemental magic felt cold, heavy and depressing. It was also painful and capable of tearing open old wounds and causing nightmares. Dana was only able to see the physical manifestation of Mordecai's powers because she was – at its root – its maker. The magic would not hurt her, but it revealed just how emotional Mordecai was that he was losing control of it. Especially in such close proximity to Max and her family. Aiden, Tobias, Bastien, and Madigan swarmed around Mordecai, putting their hands on him and placing their bodies between him and her. Much to her surprise, Mordecai shook them off.

"How could you, Dana? Seriously, how could you sit behind your precious curtain and do nothing?" Mordecai asked, pain in every syllable. The black cloud was still present, but it was stationary.

"A curtain?" Dana choked out, furious herself now because Mordecai kept harping on about the veil and her apparent wilful idleness. "You ignorant fool, you have no idea –" she barely cut herself off before revealing too much.

"Veil, curtain, window – it doesn't make any difference what you call it. The end result is the same; you sitting idly by and watching as your own daughter went through hell," Mordecai interjected. He pulled himself up – and pulled his magic back – shoving past his paladins before stalking toward the door. Just as he reached it, he threw back over his shoulder, "Good chat." And then he was gone, slamming the door and leaving a deafening silence. And an even greater gaping hole in their relationship. One Dana was sure she had no hope of repairing.

CHAPTER THREE

Mordecai was so furious he was shaking. He hadn't been at all prepared to come face to face with Dana. After hearing the teasing innuendo in the house, he had thought to beat some of the tension away. It was why, when he turned and saw Dana standing there looking gorgeous and soft and inviting, that he had immediately gone on the defensive. Nothing he had said was untrue, and he believed it was all warranted. But there was a sharp ache in his chest when he thought about the hurt on her face when he had flung his words at her. It felt almost like regret, and that was something he did not need more of. He had enough regret to last him a lifetime. Still, the more he paced back and forth along the shoreline of the now freezing cold ocean, the more he began to feel like shit. And the more something akin to panic began to set in. His chest began to feel tight, and his breath became hard to drag in. Clutching a hand to his throat, he began to hyperventilate.

"Hey, whoa there, bro. Take it easy," Aiden's voice reached his ears, and before he knew it, there were four pairs of hands touching him, rubbing his back, patting his chest and stroking his arms. Soothing words and logic met his ears in a steady stream until he was able to breathe normally again and the tightness receded from his chest.

"What the fuck was that?" Mordecai demanded.

"I would say that was one big panic attack," Madigan offered.

Mordecai shook his head, "Impossible. I've never had a panic attack in my life."

"Well, I guess you don't consider wars, famines, nightmares, and deaths to be panic-worthy. But talking smack to Mother Nature and your baby-momma is a whole new level," Bastien volunteered.

Mordecai refused to let that niggle of regret back in. "She deserved it," he muttered.

"Maybe she did," Aiden agreed. "And I have no doubt she would agree with you. Because that woman is carrying just as much guilt as you are. But I don't think that's the point."

"No?" Mordecai challenged.

Aiden shook his head, "No. The point is, do you feel better after getting all that off your chest? You've been carrying that around for years. How do you feel?"

Mordecai slammed his mouth shut, refusing to answer as he stalked up and down the sand. His sanctimonious, self-righteous, arsehole brothers merely watched him with knowing looks as he practically created a ditch in the beach with his movements. "Oh, shut the fuck up. All of you," he barked, unable to bear their smirks any longer.

"We didn't say anything," Tobias said, innocently.

"Fuck you," Mordecai grumbled again.

His Order laughed, Tobias commenting, "You do know *fuck you* is always your default when you don't want to admit we're right."

Mordecai was about to say *fuck you* again but figured it was redundant at this point. Instead, he stopped walking and put his hands on his hips. "What the fuck am I supposed to do now?"

"Apologise," all four paladins said at the same time.

"Other than that," Mordecai retorted, knowing he wasn't ready to apologise for his words.

"Then apologise for your behaviour," Madigan said, reading his thoughts. "If you're not sorry for your words, you should be sorry for your actions. You were like a toddler throwing a tantrum, except you're a large muscular, six-foot-five man. How do you think a tiny woman felt being yelled at and towered over like that? Do you think that is an acceptable way to treat a woman?"

"No …" Mordecai mumbled, now thoroughly ashamed of himself. Nobody could bring him back to earth and call him out on his shit like his Order.

"And what would you do if you saw a man speaking to a woman like that?" Madigan pressed.

"I'd kick his arse," he admitted.

"That's right. You'd feed him his balls," Aiden confirmed, crossing his arms over his chest. "You know there's only one thing for you to do now, right?"

Mordecai sighed, running his hands through his black hair. "Apologise for my appalling behaviour."

"That's right," Tobias paused, "and maybe go and feed Dana *your* balls. I don't think she'd mind."

Mordecai's mouth fell open in shock before he realised Tobias was already off and racing. Mordecai swore because of the unfair head start and began chasing the irreverent paladin with the intention of throwing him in the icy seawater. One thing he absolutely did not do was visualise a certain goddess with his balls in her mouth. Nope, he did not do that at all.

～

*D*ana was still shaking a little when she found Max laying in the library with her feet directed at the lit fireplace, a comfy pillow under her head, and speckly dog by her side. Dana took a moment to calm herself, as well as take in the miracle that was before her. Her daughter with her hand lovingly cupped over the mound of her growing stomach. Such a scene was one she could have easily seen through the veil in Otherworld, but having spent some time Earth-side now, it made her realise just how much the veil muffled the experience. Here, she could touch her daughter's hand and feel the warmth of her skin. Here, she could place her hand over her daughter's womb and feel her grandchild kick. It made her never want to return through the veil – which was impossible. She was Mother Nature. She had responsibilities. But did she not also have responsibilities to her child? To her people? Mordecai sure seemed to think so.

"Well, that didn't go as well as I was hoping," Max commented.

Dana shook off her thoughts and walked into the room. She grabbed her own pillow before stretching out next to Max on the floor, giving Zombie a hard scratch behind his ears. "You were listening?"

Max shook her head. "No. I can tell by the look on your face. What happened?"

"Nothing I did not deserve," was all Dana said, not wanting to create a rift between Max and her father. The pair were only just getting comfortable in their relationship and Dana would never jeopardise that.

Max's sigh was loud, long, and filled with frustration. "You two are as bad as each other."

Dana merely hummed in response.

Max propped herself up on an elbow, looking directly at Dana. "When are you going to tell him?"

Dana stared resolutely at the ceiling. "Tell him what?"

"Please," Max drew the word out whilst simultaneously rolling her eyes, "don't play dumb."

Dana shrugged, "He thinks he has it all figured out. Who am I to disabuse him of his assumptions?"

"As I said; you're as bad as he is. At least I don't need to wonder where I got my stubbornness from. It was from both of you. A double whammy," Max muttered.

"Poor Ryker," Dana said, not without amusement. She really did enjoy her son in law very much. And he was definitely easy on the eyes.

Max laughed. "Yes, poor Ryker. But seriously, mum. You don't have the best track record for communication with dear old dad. Don't you think you should try something different this time around? You know, like the truth?"

"I have never once lied to Mordecai," Dana said, quickly.

"No. But you've sure left a lot out. Kind of like the night I was conceived," Max pointed out.

"I do not regret it," Dana said, looking into Max's unique eyes. "I regret a lot of things, including how you were forced to live – the pain, the uncertainty, the fear. But I do not regret you."

Max reached out and took Dana's hand. "Nor should you. I love my life. Truly. My man, my friends, my family, my daughter … what is there to regret? We knew this wasn't going to be easy. But it's been worth it."

Dana's head knew Max sincerely believed that, but her heart still had a hard time with it. Mordecai, on the other hand, clearly wasn't ready to believe it on *any* level. "There is nothing I can tell him that will make him change his mind," she said, finally breaking the comfortable silence that had formed.

"Ah, is that what you're telling yourself? Just no point? I call bull-shit," Max scoffed in her usual blunt fashion. "The reason you won't tell him is because you feel guilty about that night – the night I was made – and every damn night after that too. You believe you deserve his censure and his poor moods and his cruel words. A part of you even revels in them because you think that maybe one day it will make you even. But I have a secret for you, mother …"

Dana swallowed hard as Max trailed off, knowing her daughter's words were correct in every way. She did feel guilty. She did feel shame. She did deserve everything Mordecai threw at her. As crazy as it sounded, the verbal battering was almost like a healing balm rather than a bruise, and she felt less burdened with every frosty look. "What secret?" she finally asked her daughter.

"Your guilt will not lessen over time. It will not be chipped away by ignorant taunts or misplaced anger. That's not how guilt works," Max said.

"No?"

"No," Max sat up. "The only way to be free of guilt is to let it go."

Dana closed her eyes, listening intently but shutting out the face that was a perfect mix of Mordecai and herself. "Let it go?"

Max nudged Dana's shoulder. "Yes. Let it go. Voluntarily and consciously. You are the source of your guilt, and so you must be the one to free yourself from it. I happen to know a little about this. It was how I healed Ryker ... and Darius ... and Dex ..." she added. "You need to *want* to heal. Do you want to heal, mother?"

Dana sighed, the sound carrying love and pain, pride and frustration in equal measures. "I suppose I do. How did I manage to make such a wonderful, wise woman?"

"With the help of a wonderful, wise man," Max responded, leaning down and kissing Dana on the cheek.

Dana sat up as well, taking Max's hand in her own. "Thank you. You are right."

Max grinned, "I usually am."

Dana sputtered out a laugh, "You are incorrigible. You have your father's arrogance."

Max merely winked. "And my mother's strength. Don't forget that."

Dana turned back to the crackling fire, grateful for the reminder, and resolved to clear the air with the father of her child. She would not tell him everything – she could not. But she could perhaps tell him enough so they could *both* start letting go of the guilt that was weighing them both down.

CHAPTER FOUR

Mordecai stood at the edge of Eden and waited for the rest of the newly formed International Domain Council to arrive. They had broken ground on the new headquarters, as well as the new local orphanage just a few days before and they were meeting to discuss what direction to take next. He would have rather had the meeting at the Training Lodge, indoors where there was more cover, but Max had been firm that Eden was going to be the new heart of their society, so they needed to get it beating. And what better way than to start making all the big decisions there? He chuckled a little because of course his daughter was right. Looking around, he could already see the effect the land – with its clean and whole spirit – was having on their people. Chadens, paladins, and wardens alike were working side by side, building and constructing with their bare hands. Together. United. Even before the plague that was the chades, their people had never been so harmonious.

"I can hardly believe it myself," Blu commented, catching Mordecai unawares.

Turning, Mordecai reached out a hand to clasp his good friend's forearm. "Blu, sorry. I didn't see you there. How are you?"

Blu smiled, patting Mordecai on the back and releasing his arm. "I am well, thank you. I seem to feel a little better every time I come here."

"I know what you mean," Mordecai muttered. Given all the death that had occurred on the land, it should by rights be one giant scar – writhing in agony and festering with infection and pain. But his element could find no hint of death whatsoever. It was like no suffering had ever touched the earth here. It was pure.

"Does that mean things are going well on the home front? How are things with Max?" Blu asked, his eyes darting to Mordecai and a small grin kicking up the corners of his mouth. "How are things with our Great Mother?"

Mordecai barely refrained from telling the older warden to go fuck himself. The poorly concealed laugh from Blu told Mordecai that his friend had read him accurately anyway. Blu was one of the few who knew Dana was crossing the veil. After some discussion, they had decided to notify the entire IDC. Max didn't want to start the council with secrets or omitted truths. She had made it clear she wouldn't see the new council follow in the footsteps of the old one. Mordecai agreed with her entirely. As had Dana, who assured them all she wasn't there in secret and the people were permitted to know about her. That was all well and good in theory of course, but telling an entire society that their literal god was walking among them was no small feat. And given the huge upheaval it had seen in the past few months, Mordecai wasn't convinced another doozy like Mother Nature hanging out in his kitchen would be received well. Still, Dawn, Blu, Hyde, and Slate had taken it pretty much in stride when Dana had introduced herself for the first time. In fact, Blu had looked more intrigued than shocked when he had first seen Dana. Something Mordecai had yet to ask him about. And given the other five members of the IDC were making their way over to them – all their paladins dutifully in tow – he figured he wasn't about to get answers just then either.

Mordecai greeted all the wardens, well pleased with how the council was taking shape. Dawn and Dex had been a part of their society for a long time and were loyal, intelligent and trustworthy. Although Celeste was young in warden terms, she was powerful, mature and level-headed and he had no doubts she would also prove to be an asset. Looking over at Hyde where the beast warden was conversing quietly with his two paladins, Mordecai snuck a peek at him with his powers, finding no huge scars or wounds in the man's psyche. He didn't know the man well at all, and although Max assured them all he was a man of worth, Mordecai was still relieved to see Hyde wasn't some kind of psycho. Once upon a time, he would never think to use his powers against his own brethren. It was decidedly impolite, as well as distasteful to his own code of ethics. But having your best friend stab you in the back and attempt genocide kind of changed one's mind.

Speaking of which, he thought, turning to look at Slate. Slate was standing off to the side, nodding politely at something Dawn was saying to him. Slate had been a member of the local council in the area for years, so he was well versed in the politics, rules, and regulations of their society. Unfortunately, he was also known to be somewhat of an arsehole. Mordecai knew for a fact Slate's welcome of Max into their world had been less than stellar. It kind of made him want to punch the earth warden in the face. But the man had won the Trials fair and square and he seemed to have turned over a new leaf. *War will do that to a man,* Mordecai acknowledged. Still, he asked his domain to check Slate out and was unsurprised to find the man in need of lots of healing. But that was no different to many of them – chadens, paladins and wardens alike. For now, he would give Slate the benefit of the doubt.

"Satisfied?" Max asked, nudging him with her elbow.

"For now," Mordecai responded, not bothering to pretend he didn't know what she was talking about. "Well, are we ready to begin?"

"Almost. We're just waiting for one more person …" Max trailed off. "Oh, here she is."

Mordecai didn't need to look in the direction Max was smiling to know who was walking up behind him. Not only did the awed gasps give it away, but his whole body reacted as if she was physically caressing him. The Great Mother herself was making an appearance at their meeting.

'Well now, isn't this going to be interesting?' Aiden said through the Order link.

'You never did get a chance to apologise, did you?' Bastien added, unhelpfully.

'This is going to be awkward,' was Madigan's two cents.

'Hella awkward,' Tobias confirmed. *'But, damn, she looks good, my lord.'*

Mordecai gritted his teeth, *'Will all of you shut the fuck up?!'* He heard a few snickers but his Order wisely shut their mouths – or their thoughts rather. Turning around, he felt himself begin to sweat, because, yes, she looked damn good. She walked the last few metres toward them and flashed him a tentative smile that went straight to his dick. As such, when he spoke, it was without the aid of blood flow to his brain.

"What are you doing here?" The sudden silence caused him to cringe internally. He really didn't intend for that to come out so harshly. Nor so disrespectfully. The woman was just so damn beautiful and he hadn't been expecting her to be there. On top of that, without having the chance to apologise for his actions three days prior, he felt a distinct disadvantage. Dana had stayed around but had avoided him at all costs. Something he didn't blame her for in the slightest. And judging by the pinched look on her face he knew he had fucked up again.

"I asked her here," Max answered, breaking the extremely awkward silence. "I want her to see what we're doing here and give us her opinion."

"Oh, Max. You do not need my opinion about anything here. It is wonderful. You are all doing a spectacular job. I am so proud of all of you," Dana said, looking around and making eye contact with every single warden and paladin surrounding them.

Mordecai saw the way everyone stood a little straighter and how their faces flushed under the praise and focus of Mother Nature herself. It was strange, but he had never felt the urge for that himself. Perhaps because he was too busy being pissed at her to really comprehend that she was indeed a goddess. And before that? Before his anger and disappointment? There had only been lust. Watching as she placed hands on the people around her, smiled and laughed, and made everyone feel at peace and valued, he decided that the anger was dissipating. But the lust? He traced her full breasts, nipped-in rib cage and flared waist with hungry eyes. Oh, the lust was still well and truly there.

"My lady, you honour us," Blu was murmuring as he took her hand in his and kissed the back of it like a true gentleman.

Dana beamed, "The honour is all mine. This place you are all building here, it will be the beating heart of society."

"Thanks to Max," Blu agreed. "Your daughter has wrought such beauty here."

"Pfft," Max responded casually. "The beauty was already here. I simply healed it. And *all* of us are helping it to reach its true potential."

"Yes," Hyde agreed, the quiet man speaking for the first time without being asked a question first. "It is a true garden of Eden – or so I hear."

Dana smiled impishly at the Beast Warden and Mordecai wanted to shave the hairy man bald and rip out his beard. He wondered if the women would find him so appealing then. Laughter, that was poorly masked as a coughing fit from his Order, had him baring his teeth at them.

"Hyde, it is so lovely to see you again. It is true Max named this place after where she was raised for the first few years in Otherworld. Although I must say, you did a fine job with the national park in Alaska too. It is a true sanctuary for nature and its animals," Dana praised.

Hyde smiled, bowing his head a little. "I am glad you think so, my lady."

Dana touched his arm lightly before turning to Max. "Anyway, do not let me stop your important meeting. Pretend I am not here."

Mordecai nearly choked on his own spit as he turned disbelieving eyes to Dana. "Pretend you're not here? You're kidding, right?"

Dana stiffened once more, casting him a dirty look. "If my presence is so distracting, perhaps I will take myself on a tour of Eden then."

Before he could wrestle his big foot out of his mouth, Knox materialised beside him. "Hey. I was hoping to talk to you all about …" he trailed off as he noticed Dana, his grey eyes widening in male appreciation. "Well, hello there. Max, I didn't know you had a sister," Knox's grin was as unrepentant as it was flirtatious. Mordecai wanted to knock his teeth out.

Dana laughed, the sound literally causing all the birds in the trees to sing. "I am not her sister. I am her mother."

Knox laughed, clearly thinking he was being punked. But when no one else laughed with him, he quickly closed his mouth and bent down on one knee. "My lady, I apologise."

"You were simply being you," Dana cut him off, extending a hand to him and helping him to his feet. "And I for one am so very glad you can be *you* once again. After everything you've endured. So very brave, Knox." Dana stood on her toes and pressed a kiss to his cheek. "Perhaps you would like to give me a tour of Eden? Show me what your chadens have accomplished?"

Knox looked suitably stupefied as Dana hooked her arm through his and led him away. After, that is, casting Mordecai a look that should have flayed the skin from his bones. After scowling in her direction for a few moments, he turned to find multiple glares upon him. "What?" he demanded, feeling like shit and not in the mood to be called out for it.

"Man, you have it bad!" Ryker walked over to Mordecai and slapped him on the back. "I thought it was just a whole bunch of rage combined with a whole bunch of lust. But it's more than that, isn't it?"

"I have no idea what you're talking about. And why are you still touching me?" Mordecai growled, shrugging off Ryker's hand where it was still resting on his shoulder. "I can make Max fall out of love with you, you know."

Ryker snorted, "No, you can't."

"No, you can't," Max confirmed. "Besides, I'd worry about my own love life if I were you."

"I don't have a love life. And if I did, it wouldn't involve Dana," Mordecai ground out.

"Why were you such a prick to her then?" Dex questioned.

Mordecai turned a frosty glare on the healed chade. "She took it the wrong way."

"Of course it's the woman's fault," Dawn said, crossing her arms and narrowing her eyes on him.

Mordecai was beginning to sweat. *'What is happening here?'* he asked his Order.

'I believe it's called having a family, sir,' Madigan answered, merrily.

'Oh, fuck off,' was Mordecai's reply. Out loud he said, "Look, I didn't mean it the way it sounded. I just meant it's impossible to ignore her. I mean, she's Mother Nature. A goddess walking the Earth. She's powerful and soulful and –" he quickly shut his mouth before it ran away from him.

"And she's beautiful and intelligent, and sweet and kind and funny," Blu filled in. His eyes were twinkling when he continued, "She's perfect, my friend."

"Perfect for what?" Mordecai muttered.

Blu harrumphed, "If you don't know the answer to that, it's no wonder you're tied up in knots." He turned his back quickly, addressing the rest of the IDC. "Right, let us move on from our clueless friend here, shall we? Let's start with the construction and then move on to the formalities of Orders and the local council."

CHAPTER FIVE

The next several hours were spent formalising the plans for Eden, for the chadens, for the training lodge, and for the Paladin Trials. Many processes that had been in place for hundreds of years were thrown to the wayside and new protocols and policies were implemented. The chadens, with their special abilities still intact after being made whole, were essentially doing all the building of the structures. It came in very handy to be able to manifest as an element and it meant the construction would take a quarter of the time it would take a regular human. It had been decided that Knox and Dex would continue to act as the 'officially unofficial' leaders of the chadens. Nobody wanted to segregate the chadens but they knew they faced unique issues and it made sense to put in place leadership they could relate to. The training lodge would remain as it was – with Max's Order running it and seeing to the training of the new recruits there. There had been a small amount of arguing from her paladins, especially with a babe on the way. But in the end, Max got her way – naturally. She wanted them to keep their sense of self and for them to have a purpose and also a hand in ensuring the next generation was up to scratch. Mordecai agreed with her. Local councils were to become a mixture of paladins, wardens and chadens, ensuring every member of their society was represented and had a voice. Caspian would be appointed the head member of the local council. It would take time to spread word throughout the world, and Mordecai knew they were going to have to send some of the IDC travelling in the coming months. As for the proposed Paladin Council, that was happening too. They were going to take one paladin from each of the training lodges around the world and appoint them to the PC. The local member for their area was a no brainer and Lark was thrilled to get started on organising the others.

Discussion on Order formation and the Paladin Trials had taken longer. Mordecai still firmly believed the Trials were a good thing. Max believed they were archaic and there were other ways to prove one's worth as a soldier. In the end, Max was outvoted, and paladins would still need to prove themselves, both physically and mentally, before they could be placed with an Order. However, the manner in which they were undertaken would change, and be more in line with their society's new ethos. What's more, Orders would now be formed based on an organic bond, whenever possible – just like it had been when Mordecai had formed his Order of Valhalla. Over the years, the need for strength and power – or at least the illusion of it – had become more important to the wardens than a natural bond with their knights. As such, stronger paladins – with a heavy bias to males – were deemed more desirable. It was why paladins like Lark and Beyden had been cast out of society, and why Cali had been viewed as nothing more than a sex toy and battery pack. Mordecai couldn't wait to see such changes come to fruition. But he wasn't stupid. He knew the systemic prejudices running throughout their society would not be abolished overnight. No, it was going to take time. He was already exhausted just thinking about it.

"It will be worth it," the voice was soft but resolute.

Turning from where he had been lost in thought watching the new IDC interacting casually, he nodded at Dana. "I know it will be." He didn't bother to take her to task for apparently reading his thoughts. He was already in enough trouble with her as it was. He cleared his throat, "About earlier –"

"You do not need to explain yourself," Dana interrupted.

"But I –"

"Truly, Warden. It is of no consequence," Dana butt in once again.

"Damnit, woman! Would you shut up and let me finish a sentence?" he practically yelled. Dana snapped her mouth shut and Mordecai looked up to find all eyes on them once again. Ryker gave him a sarcastic double thumbs-up, to which Mordecai flipped him the bird. "Fucking ingrate," he muttered.

"He is wonderful," Dana murmured, looking at Ryker with fondness.

"Yeah, yeah. Anyway, I'm trying to apologise here," Mordecai said.

Dana's eyebrows rose. "Is that what you are trying to do?"

Mordecai huffed, "I know I suck at it, okay? But apparently, you're not so great at accepting them."

Dana's blue-green eyes mapped his face for a moment before she nodded, "Perhaps you are right. Continue," she invited.

He opened his mouth to do just that, but he developed a case of nerves instead. He still felt it was his right to be angry at the woman, but that was no excuse to keep treating her like shit and tearing her down every time he opened his mouth. He was old school in how he felt women should be treated. So then why couldn't he simply open his mouth and say sorry? *Shit,* Mordecai thought. *I'm freaking out. I'm actually freaking out. Pull it together, you pussy!* he scolded himself.

"Do not hurt yourself, Warden," Dana said, dryly.

Mordecai glared at her, torn between feeling amused and aggravated. "I'm sorry, okay? What I said earlier was not supposed to be rude. You're not someone who can be in the background. You're the star of the show – and always will be."

Dana blinked a few times quickly, obviously processing his words. "Well … that is … thank you. Apology accepted."

"Good. Great. As for my behaviour in the gym, that was uncalled for and unacceptable. I am very sorry if I scared you or made you feel threatened in any way. I have never treated a woman like that in my life, let alone a goddess. I humbly apologise." It wasn't hard to say the words this time, likely because every one of them were true. And far overdue.

Dana was looking at the ground, her bare foot making small circles in the lush green grass. Even as he watched, bright yellow flowers began to bloom as if from nowhere and a small ring of simple daisies formed to encircle Dana where she stood. She created life so effortlessly and with such simple beauty that it took his breath away. She appeared lost in thought and didn't even seem to notice what she had wrought. When she continued to keep her head down and not say anything, Mordecai bent down and plucked a single flower. Strangely, it wasn't attached to any stem and when he held it, he felt no death. Usually, as soon as a flower was picked, he could feel the plant begin to die. Sometimes it took hours, and other times days if it was well cared for. But, inevitably, a picked flower was a dying flower. Apparently, that was not the case if it was created with Mother Nature's toe, he thought. Nudging her chin up, he pushed her unruly red hair behind her left ear and tucked the flower there. The contrast of yellow and red was astounding and he wondered what she would look like wearing nothing but yellow lingerie.

Dana's eyes were a little bewildered as they met Mordecai's and she touched the flower with a tentative hand. "Thank you," she said quietly. "Apology accepted." And then she poofed away in a cloud of coloured sparkles.

"Whoa, that was positively fuckin' romantic, Mordecai," Ryker yelled at him.

Spinning around, Mordecai snarled at his son in law, "I'm going to kill you, Ryker!"

Mordecai used the ensuing, undignified chase to cover up the burning of his cheeks. Because, yeah, it did feel fuckin' romantic. And he had no idea what to think about that.

CHAPTER SIX

*D*ana closed her eyes as she leaned back against the wall in the hallway just outside Axel's music room. The fire paladin was currently inside playing a particularly poignant piece on the piano, and Dana was forced to stand and appreciate the beauty of the music as well as the skill of the man playing it. She really liked Axel and was so relieved he and Celeste had come together once more. It was true, she should not have stepped in and created small opportunities for the pair to come together. She did not necessarily break any rules – not like she had with Mordecai all those years ago. Still, Dana had come close to blurring a few guidelines and she was going to have to answer for that. *As soon as I stop dodging my colleagues*, she thought. Tempus and Tanda had not called for her, so she was able to keep on deluding herself that they did not care what she had been doing on Earth the past couple of months. But just because she had not heard from them, did not mean they were unaware. They knew all. Just like she did. Yes, she was going to have to answer for her actions. And soon.

"What are you doing?"

The voice startled her, and she gasped, a hand flying to her chest as she opened her eyes. "Warden," she breathed out. "You startled me. I am not doing anything."

Mordecai scowled at her as he crossed his arms over his burly chest. "Really? Then why are you so jumpy? Are you spying again?"

Dana pushed herself off the wall, indignant rage filling her. "I was not spying!" She had thought after the whole flower deal and the apology the day before, that perhaps there was a truce looming on the horizon. Apparently, she was wrong. "I do not spy! Yes, I watch – that is pretty much my job description these days. But I do not go around spying on my family."

Mordecai blew out a harsh breath, easing up his rigid stance. "I'm sorry. I hate that my immediate thought of you is that you're doing something sneaky or crappy."

Dana felt the words like a punch to the gut. "I hate that too," she told him softly.

"I'm sorry," Mordecai offered again.

"It is what it is," Dana appreciated his honesty, but it still hurt like a bitch.

"Yeah," he agreed, looking pained by the admission as well.

Looking around, she did not see any of his paladins but knew they must not be far away. Even in the safety of the house, Mordecai's knights were always on the job. When he made no effort to move along or speak again, Dana cleared her throat. "I honestly was not spying. I was just listening. Axel plays beautifully."

Mordecai cocked his head to the side as if just noticing the pure sounds floating out of the room next to them. "He does. Especially considering he's self-taught." He shook his head, "Max's order seems to be filled with innately talented paladins."

Dana smiled at that because Max's Order was filled with very special paladins indeed. "Hmmm," was all she offered though, rocking back and forth slowly to the music.

"Would you like to dance?"

Dana felt her mouth fall open in shock and she looked up at Mordecai in surprise. Had the man just asked her to dance?

"The look of abject horror on your face says it all. Forget I said anything," Mordecai snarked, already moving away from her.

"No, wait," she grabbed his arm, turning him around. "It is not that. I would love to dance. I just … I've never danced before."

Mordecai looked down at where she was touching him, and she quickly let him go. He cocked a single eyebrow, disbelief evident in his voice, "Never danced before as in …?"

"As in ever," she admitted.

"But you're old as dirt. Hell, you're older than dirt!" He must have realised what he said because he was quick to apologise, "Shit, I'm sorry. I didn't mean to make you feel –"

"Ancient?" Dana asked, eyes twinkling with mirth. "I suppose I am. But just when would I get a chance to dance? And with whom?"

Mordecai shrugged his heavy shoulders, looking uncomfortable. "I don't know. Don't you have eternity over there? Nothing but time? Seems like plenty of time to learn a hobby or two."

Dana rolled her eyes at his ignorance. "It does not work that way. Yes, I have nothing but time. I am immortal, after all. But I cannot just go and take up a hobby of my choosing. You really have no idea what I am or what I do."

Mordecai's face softened as he considered her more closely. "I'm beginning to see that," he admitted. Then he shocked her further when he held out his right hand. "So … dance?"

Dana looked at the outstretched hand and smiled small. "I guess I should learn how to dance before Max's wedding."

Mordecai went still, "Max is getting married?"

Dana's grin grew, "She is."

"What? When?" Mordecai asked, looking shocked and confused.

"Soon," Dana shrugged, before finally settling her palm in that of Mordecai's. Warm sparks immediately shot up her arm, causing her heartbeat to accelerate, and her eyes darted to his. His green eyes narrowed on her face, tracing her features as if looking for something. Of what, Dana was not sure. But he was voluntarily touching her – and not to throttle her – so she was not going to overanalyse anything.

The music continued to play, the tempo changing to an even slower, softer beat as Mordecai drew her close to his chest. He really was a very tall man, and her head was barely level with his impressive chest. Still, she did not take advantage of the convenience and maintained enough distance between them so their bodies were not in contact. He reached down and grabbed her left hand, placing it high on his shoulder as he drew her a little closer with a hand to her hip. He was still holding her right hand in his as he started to move in what she knew was a traditional waltz. She was so busy concentrating on what her feet were doing and counting the steps in her head that she hadn't noticed he had been drawing her in closer and closer until her breasts brushed against the hardness of his body. Gasping, she looked up, only to get caught in the mesmerising green of his eyes.

They stared at each other for a few moments, both tense and unsure, before Mordecai cleared his throat. "Are you sure you've never danced before? You're doing a good job."

Dana flushed under his praise, liking more than she should the feeling of happiness kind words from him brought. *Gods, am I really that starved for affection?* she wondered to herself. *Or am I simply starved for him?* "I really have not. I hardly have the time for such things. Besides, who would I dance with?"

Mordecai cocked his head, looking genuinely curious. "There aren't any other people, or gods or whatever, in Otherworld?"

"Of course, there are. It is a world just like this one – only filled with lives who have already lived – or are yet to live," she explained.

"Like the Christian idea of Heaven and Hell?" Mordecai asked.

Dana scrunched up her nose as she thought about the best way to answer. Theology and ideology were complex topics. "Kind of. It is a realm or another plane of existence, I guess you could say. The *same* as Heaven and Hell. Those exist too."

Mordecai stopped moving. "Really?"

"Of course. There are as many places for the dead and the yet to be born as there are the gods that construct them," Dana explained. They had stopped moving but Mordecai seemed to have forgotten that he was still holding onto her. She felt no need to remind him.

"So ... there are other gods?" Mordecai asked. "You're not ... *it*?"

Dana chuckled, "*It*? No, not at all. Seriously, Mordecai, you have been alive for over a millennium. You are a keeper of the element of death. How can you be so ignorant of other gods?"

Mordecai frowned, "It's been a long time since any history was taught to our paladins and wardens. And what was documented over the years was lost when Garret destroyed the Warden Chronicles. I guess …" he paused, considering his words. "I guess I have forgotten as much as I have learned."

Dana did not know why she was so surprised to hear the admission, but she was. Was Mordecai correct? Was she so out of touch with her own creations? How could she not know how ignorant and uneducated they had all become? "Because I was so focused on my own needs and my own desires. I was focused on our daughter," she suddenly understood.

"What are you talking about? Dana?" Mordecai lifted her chin, forcing her eyes to meet his once again.

Dana shook her head, breath shuddering out. "You are right – I am a terrible goddess. I failed my people. All these years, I was so focused on Max – focused on ensuring she lived up to her destiny that I did not realise I was failing at my own."

Mordecai finally let Dana go, spinning away from her and running his hands through his hair. He stood with his hands on his hips and his back to her as he shook his head, cursing nothing and everything at the same time. Finally, he spun back around. "No," he stated, harshly. "No. I was wrong. I'm a fucking self-righteous prick who has no idea what he is talking about. You're right – I know nothing about you; how you live, what rules you follow, what your damn job is. I've just been so fucking angry, Dana. Angry with myself and with you. Angry with the whole fucking world. I was hurt and guilty and lost, and all I could think about was finding Max and hurting you. I thought if I did that, everything would all be better. But it hasn't worked that way."

Dana smiled knowingly. "I know exactly what you mean. As soon as I felt Max spark to life inside of me, nothing else mattered. Literally. Everything became about her. It is what any good mother should feel," she allowed. "But not what a good *god* should feel. This is why we aren't allowed to create life with our own bodies. Why we should not have our own children. The conflict is too great. Priorities change ..." Dana murmured, speaking of her and her deity colleagues. *Tempus, Tanda, I am so sorry,* she prayed. "I must leave now," she informed Mordecai, her mind reeling with her newfound awareness. She needed to talk to her two counterparts immediately.

"Hey, wait a minute. Where are you going? And what do you mean *we*?" Mordecai asked, snagging her arm in a secure grip.

Dana looked down at the grip but did not try to remove it. He was not hurting her, just trying to keep her from poofing away. "You have just helped me see another side of this. Thank you," she told him. Mordecai had a confused look on his face that was adorable as hell and she barely stifled her giggle – and her need to caress his frown lines away.

"I thought we were dancing? How did this turn into some big existential revelation?" Mordecai wondered.

She did laugh out loud this time. "Dancing must be good for the soul. You are a good teacher," she informed him.

"And you are beautiful," he suddenly said, looking at her like he had never seen her before.

Dana felt her eyes round and she took a step back. "What? Oh, I, uh, I really do need to go." She had no idea what caused the sudden shift, but now that he was looking at her with something other than anger and hate, she had no idea what to do about it.

"You're nervous," Mordecai stated, looking amused by the thought.

Dana drew herself up, "I am not nervous. I just really need to go. Thank you for what you said – about not understanding, about being a prick." She grinned at him.

He snorted, "Anytime. But seriously, I know it wasn't an apology for the way I've thought about you these past fifty-odd years. But, if you stick around, you might just get one."

Air caught in Dana's throat and she pressed down hard on her chest with her palm to calm the furious beating. Although she had never held her breath for an apology – she truly felt she did not need nor deserve one – she had been longing for Mordecai to look at her with something other than malice for years. Too bad it was on the heels of her own personal realisation. She truly did need to return to Otherworld and sort her shit out – as Max liked to say.

"I look forward to that. But I really need to go," she said regretfully.

Mordecai's eyes traced her face, narrowing a little before he said, "The 'we' you mentioned?"

"Right," Dana nodded.

"Will you be back?" Mordecai then asked.

Dana quickly calculated times in her head. She had been Earth-side for a few days, which meant she would need to spend double the time back in Otherworld before she could return. She was yet to explain how her visits worked with Max, let alone anyone else. And she did not have the time now either. Instead, she simply replied with an affirmative. "Yes, I will be back. But likely not for a couple of weeks." To her surprise, Mordecai looked annoyed with the news, and within one blink to the next, he was once again cold and aloof, looking down at her with an expressionless, but undeniably, handsome face.

His voice was clipped when he next spoke. "Are you even going to say goodbye to Max?"

Dana reached for her daughter mentally, quickly cringing when she discovered Max and Ryker were otherwise engaged. "Umm, perhaps you could tell her for me? She is, uh, busy. With Ryker."

Mordecai screwed his nose up in disgust. "Oh, by the Goddess! It's the middle of the day!" Dana could not hold back her giggle and Mordecai shot her an irritated look before he thawed a little, shoulders slumping. "I'll tell her," he offered.

"Thank you," Dana said, sincerity ringing in her voice. She was not just thanking him for passing on her message to Max. But also for the dance, for his admissions, for the wake-up call, and also for the easing of antagonism between them. She hoped the two small words were enough to portray all that and when she received a small nod in return, she felt relief and the beginnings of true happiness. Perhaps when she returned, things would be different. Perhaps, they could even be friends.

CHAPTER SEVEN

Mordecai was shaking as he prowled around the outdoor obstacle course of the training lodge. He knew his Order was anxiously waiting for him to allow them to touch him and recharge his vitality. But after using his domain, he often needed space before anything else. He had attended the lodge over ten hours ago, intending to check on some paladins who had lost their liege's in the battle. Many knights were still lost, finding themselves grief-stricken, ashamed and Orderless. He had been somewhat derelict in his duties because he had been so focused on Max's Order after she blew herself up. And then they had the Trials for the new IDC, and then the construction. Well, he'd had a lot on his plate. Still, when Blu had come to him and asked if he would help Glenn, Mordecai had felt a rush of guilt. Glenn was the only surviving paladin from Cinder's Order and he knew the man must be devastated to not only lose his soldier brethren, but also his liege.

After absorbing much of Glenn's darker emotions, Mordecai found himself moving from one paladin to another. Many of the adrift paladins were staying at the lodge, having nowhere else to go. The homes of their wardens reverted back to the property of the IDC – as was tradition. That too was going to change, Mordecai knew. Paladins were going to be compensated for their time and they would also be allowed to own belongings and property. But that didn't help the ones currently grieving and homeless. His skin prickled as dark energy moved around him – and *through* him – using him as an outlet or a filter. Hurt and pain, grief and loss, needed to be absorbed or it wreaked havoc on the whole world – and not just the person it emanated from. That was his job and also where his domain and that of Life overlapped a little. Pain knifed into his chest and he bent over, breathing through the pain.

"Mordecai, let us –" Aiden began, only to have Mordecai shove him back. The prickling, writhing element of death was still too near and he wouldn't risk his paladins. "It's our job," Aiden reminded him, frustration clear in his voice, as he read Mordecai's thoughts. Mordecai ignored him, counting his breaths.

"It is okay. I have this."

Mordecai jerked himself upright and saw Dana placing comforting hands on his paladins as she wove her way through them. They parted like the red sea. *Naturally,* he thought, snidely. Dana had said she would be gone for a couple of weeks. It had been closer to five. After their little interlude in the hallway, he had thought perhaps they could talk out their differences. Maybe even be friends. But the longer she was away, the more his doubts crept back in and the more his anger returned. She couldn't be trusted to keep her word. He needed to remember that.

She stopped only when she was within touching distance of him. When she reached out, Mordecai side-stepped her. "What are you doing here, Dana?"

"I said I would be back," came her calm reply.

Mordecai was shaking so badly now that his teeth were chattering. His vitality was dangerously low, and his temper wasn't helping the situation. "You said you would be away for two weeks. It's been over four." His words sounded like the accusation they were.

"I know. It could not be helped," Dana said, ever calm. She reached out a hand again.

Mordecai snapped, "Don't touch me, Dana. I mean it." He was

feeling raw and vulnerable, and the last thing he wanted was Dana to know it.

"It hurts so bad," Dana murmured, ignoring his snarling words and placing a hand on his chest.

"It's supposed to!" he retorted.

Dana nodded, "Yes. It is. But that doesn't lessen the burden." She moved forward and placed her other hand on his opposite pec, warmth spreading from her palms in an outward motion. "My wardens; nature's warriors. You do me proud. You have ever since you held that frog in your hands and sang to it as it died."

Mordecai barely noticed when the cold stopped invading his body and warmth took its place. He was too intrigued by the gorgeous woman staring up at him like he hung the moon. "Frog?" he questioned.

"You don't remember? A hawk decided it was going to make the little fellow its meal for the evening, but it accidentally dropped it. You found it on the ground and even though you could not do anything to save it, you still held it as it died. You offered it comfort and peace, and it died knowing it was not alone."

Mordecai did recall the incident she was speaking of. He had been perhaps four or five years old. "It was just a frog," he muttered.

Dana's smile was like the sun as she replied, "The shell the soul housed was of no relevance. It was still a soul in need. It was still a soul who was dying. And that is why you felt compelled to take away its pain in its final moments. That is when you and your parents knew for sure you were linked with Death."

"Yes," Mordecai agreed, reaching up and linking his fingers with Dana's. He was warm all over, the feelings of grief and loss that had bombarded his system for the past ten hours were nothing but echoes now. Dana had taken it all away. "You were watching me even then?"

Dana shrugged a negligent shoulder. "I was watching everyone. It is kind of what I do."

Mordecai felt trapped in her gaze and he moved slowly to cup her face in his palms. "Tell me, Great Mother. Do you ever get tired of watching? Do you ever just want to *do*?"

Dana's breath caught in her throat. "Oh, you have no idea how much I want to *do*."

"I think I do," he murmured, before lowering his head to hers and covering her lips with his own.

It was like a galaxy exploded behind his eyelids. Colours and lights filled his vision and his whole body felt like he had been struck by lightning. His body was alive with sensation as the soft mouth beneath his pecked at his lips teasingly a few times before opening and accepting the hungry caress of his tongue. He mapped her mouth, their tongues duelling and stroking, even as his hands gripped her full hips and pulled her forward and up. She gasped when she felt his hardness and he growled, capturing her mouth again and swallowing the sounds of her pleasure. He let his hands roam over the curve of her delicious arse, rubbing it and imagining it red with his handprint.

"Ah, you might want to hold off on the whole sex thing until you're behind closed doors."

Tobias's voice penetrated Mordecai's lust-filled fog, and he pulled back, breathing harshly. Casting a single dirty look at his paladin, he glanced back down at Dana – and nearly came in his pants. Her lips were swollen and shining and deliciously red. Her cheeks were flushed, and her pupils were blown wide. Her breath was coming in short pants, making her breasts push into contact with his chest repetitively. And her glorious hair was in disarray thanks to his hands fisting it. "Oh, yeah," he said. "I want to sex you up so bad."

Dana's eyes widened and she took a hasty step back. She patted at her hair as if that were going to fix the mess it was in, looking everywhere but at Mordecai. "Uh, we can't be doing that."

Mordecai ignored the raging hard-on he had, amusement creeping in when he observed her obvious embarrassment. "Why not? As I recall, we were rather good at it."

Dana coughed, her cream cheeks turning an appealing pink. "It is not that I don't want … I mean, I *want*. But … you do not even like me," she ended, rather lamely.

Mordecai gestured to the hard length of his dick, clearly outlined by his pants. "I like you just fine."

Dana frowned at him. "That is not what I meant. I am not going to sleep with you just because you turn me on. You hate me, Warden."

His amusement fled in a second. "I don't hate you."

"Since when?" Dana challenged.

Mordecai eyed her for a moment before spinning and taking a few deep breaths. It was hard to concentrate when temptation was standing so close to him. And that kiss? It had been explosive. The chemistry he'd told himself had been a lie all those years ago clearly was not. He hadn't remembered anything incorrectly. It had been the best sex of his long life, and he had no doubt another romp between the sheets with Dana would be just as incredible. But that wasn't all he wanted from her. Was it? He didn't actually know, and that meant Dana was right to stop. And to question him. He might not have all the answers, but he did know one thing. He turned back to face her.

"I don't hate you, Dana. If I'm being honest, I believe I really did hate you once. I hated myself as well," he was quick to add. "But I don't hate you anymore. I don't hate myself anymore, either."

"That ..." Dana drew in a deep breath, the beginnings of a smile on her lips. "That is good to know."

"Good. Great. Uh ..." he rubbed the back of his neck, realising they were indeed very exposed where they were. Thankfully, the only other people outside were his four paladins. But that brought no comfort at all. He was never going to hear the end of this.

"Maybe you should talk?" Madigan suggested, using his head to gesture toward Dana – who still looked highly uncomfortable.

"Right. Talking. Good. I can talk. Can you talk?" Mordecai questioned – like a total fucking moron.

Dana's smile was genuine and relaxed this time. "I can talk," she confirmed. "Tomorrow? I have yet to tell Max I am back. I want to see our daughter very much."

"Our daughter ..." Mordecai mumbled, feeling the truth of those words for the very first time. They shared a daughter together and he knew absolutely nothing about her – other than the fact she was a great kisser and a goddess.

"Mordecai?" Dana asked.

He jolted. Hard. "You called me Mordecai."

Dana looked confused. "That is your name."

"Yes. But you never call me that. You always call me Warden," he pointed out.

Dana looked startled for a moment, and then thoughtful. "I suppose I do."

"I like it when you say my name," he said, just for clarification in case it wasn't obvious.

Dana smiled, "Then I shall call you Mordecai from here on in."

His name on her lips had his dick twitching once again, and he wondered if he was going to regret telling her that.

CHAPTER EIGHT

*D*ana blinked a few times, wondering if she had somehow transported herself to the wrong property. The front of Max's home looked nothing like it had just a month ago. When Dana had last left, the house had been surrounded by trees and rather dense bush on every side. The only clear area had been the driveway and the back of the house – and that was because the back was all beach and ocean. Now, huge areas of trees had been cleared and four smaller log cabins appeared to be emerging from the earth. Dana's powers burst forth in a rainbow of light as wind swept them from one structure to the next. Each building was being made from the trees that were cleared from their exact locations. Each tree had been asked and was willing to give up its position so that Max's Order could extend their home front. Dana blew out a relieved breath, finding no pain or anger from the culled landscape, just acceptance and happiness to be useful.

She should have known better. There was no way Max would allow the senseless removal of living things simply for the sake of affording her paladins some privacy. For that is exactly what they were for. She had been privy to a few discussions about creating more room for the Order of Aurora and their extended family. Ryker had built a truly spectacular home by the sea and although it was large, it was now bulging at the seams. The knights, true to their nature, had refused to move away and simply 'work in shifts' as Max had proposed. The building of new homes close by on the same land was a compromise to everyone's satisfaction. Dana had not been expecting so much work to have been done in the time she had been gone. Two of the four structures were nothing more than foundations. But the other two looked largely complete from the outside. It made her wonder just how much progress had been made at Eden.

"This is what happens when I disappear, I suppose," she murmured. She had been gone longer than she initially intended, and she also had not checked in via the veil more than twice. It had been difficult because she was fast becoming attached to the mortal plane. But it had been necessary. Not only had she spoken to the other members of her Triumvirate, but she had also gotten a huge surprise in the form of a strapping young man.

Sensing life – endless life – Dana bent down and helped a small beetle onto the back of her hand. Smiling, she said, "Hello there, Bert. How would you like to hear a story before I go in? I could certainly use some advice." The little slater bug gave no reply but he did continue to sit and watch her expectantly. "Okay, well, I returned to Otherworld in a bit of a tiz …"

"Temp! Tanda!" she yelled into the black void that took up one whole corner of Otherworld. No other occupants of Otherworld ventured anywhere near the endless black. Only Dana, as Mother Nature; Tempus, as Father Time; and Tanda, as Death, could travel the roads of infinity. Which is what the other two must be doing, Dana thought to herself, because they were nowhere to be found in Otherworld. "I had an epiphany. Finally. We need to talk. Come on, give me a break, huh? So I made a boo boo. It is not like you both have not been there and done that yourselves," she yelled. Silence met her ears and she was just ramping herself up to taunt them again when a voice from behind startled her.

"I think they're fucking with you."

Dana yelped, spinning and sending some of her power outward in a defensive motion. The young man in front of her merely smiled and caught the raw elemental magic between his hands. "You ..." Dana *began, finding her mouth too dry to continue.*

"My name is Gaias," the man spoke once more.

"Gaias?" Dana repeated. Feeling a rush of air at her back, she turned to see Tempus and Tanda. The pair looked exactly the same as they had for eons. Tempus had a real silver fox look going for him with silver hair and a short, trimmed matching beard. His eyes were impossibly blue and the few wrinkles he had were on his forehead, around his eyes and near his mouth, attesting to a life lived with many smiles and much laughter. Tanda was almost his polar opposite. Dark skin, smooth and blemish free, with a completely bald, shiny head. His eyes were as black as obsidian, only lighting up with gold and silver when his powers were active. That was not to say they lacked warmth, however. Tanda was a good man, and an affectionate one. But he was very choosy with whom he gave his friendship to.

"What is going on?" Dana demanded, looking askance at Gaias.

Tanda didn't smile with his mouth but Dana could detect warmth and humour in his eyes when he replied, "Don't you recognise him?"

"Of course, I recognise him!" Dana snapped at one of her oldest and dearest friends. She turned to Gaias and held out her arms. To her relief, the young man stepped straight into them and hugged her just as hard as she hugged him. She was not ashamed of the few tears that escaped, and she gave a small laugh as she pulled back, taking in the visage of the fair-haired, green-eyed youth in front of her. "I do not understand."

"Your daughter set him free when she killed Emmanuel. I simply helped him into a body," Tanda offered.

Dana shook her head, unable to comprehend what Tanda was telling her. Once, many, many years ago, Dana had birthed pure souls. The souls were nothing but energy and never destined to reside in a physical body. The souls were like children to her because she created them with her own body. But she did not carry them as she had with Max, nor were they made with the aid of another. Custodians were made by pure power with the purpose of being *pure power. She had intended for there to always be one custodian on Earth at all times.*

Their presence was to be a balancing factor for the rapidly changing nature of the planet. But after a time, when the vulnerable souls kept getting lost or destroyed, Dana had not used her powers to create more. But somehow, Gaias, the flesh and blood man standing before her, was the last custodian she had ever created. The custodian who had been consumed by the infected warden, Emmanuel, and cursed to live on inside of the beast for decades.

"Max set you free?" she asked Gaias directly.

"She did. When she went supernova. She set all of us free. All of the souls Emmanuel had been collecting," Gaias informed her.

"And I, being in charge of where souls go, decided the custodian deserved a body of their own," Tanda explained.

"And I, being in charge of all things time, decided now was the time for him to step up," Tempus added.

Dana shook her head, "Step up? As what?"

Tempus smiled, "As your protégé of course."

"And that is when I had a nervous breakdown," Dana concluded to her audience of one. Bert scuttled around the back of her hand, his tiny legs tickling her skin and making her smile. "It seems I now have choices. Choices I had no idea were even a possibility. Is it not refreshing to know that even I can still be surprised?" Dana began walking down the path to the front door, placing Bert on a plant as she passed and thanking him for listening. Before she could even climb the stairs, the rarely used front door opened.

"Mum! You're back," Max cried from the doorway. A yipping bark followed a second behind.

Dana watched as Max took the stairs carefully, staring in wonder at how much Max's stomach had grown. "Wow," Dana said, reaching out and touching the belly when Max was close. "You have certainly popped."

Max rolled her eyes. "Why does everyone keep saying that? I'm pregnant. My tummy is supposed to get bigger."

At twenty-six weeks along now, Max had a point, Dana thought. But the difference in the bump – as well as the strength of the kicks beneath her palm – had her feeling regret at having missed the moment when the 'pop' had happened. "I am sorry I was gone so long. I had things to take care of."

"Mum, you don't need to explain yourself to me. I know you're busy. I'm just grateful I get to see you at all," Max said, causing Dana to blink rapidly. "Now, come on. We still have time before dinner for you to tell me all about that kiss."

Dana paused in mid-pat of Zombie who had jumped up against her hip. He was likely almost fully grown now even though his demeanour was still very much that of a puppy. "What kiss?"

Max rolled her eyes, dragging Dana along by the arm and into the house. "I know all."

Dana allowed her daughter to lead her through to the kitchen and dining area, which was teeming with boisterous life. Rosa and Penelope were at the stove along with Jasminka, Beyden, and Axel. There appeared to be some kind of cooking lesson going on. "You have a son now, Axel. You need to learn to cook more than two-minute noodles," Rosa was saying. Dana could not help but laugh at Axel's wide-eyed look as he scanned the amount of pots and pans on the stovetop.

Turning to Max, Dana finally replied, "You do not know all. *I* know all." At least, she had certainly thought so before her trip back to Otherworld. Now, she may be just as clueless as the rest of the population – which was a scary thought. "And I know for a fact you cannot read me. So how do you know about the kiss?" Max had never been able to see Dana's soul any more than she could see her own.

"Kiss?" Cali's head shot up like a bloodhound tracking a scent from where she was feeding Maxwell a bottle in the comfy chair in the corner.

"What kiss?" Celeste asked, walking closer.

Max grinned, "The kiss she and dad just had at the Lodge. Apparently, it was x-rated – *triple* x-rated – and the ground almost caught on fire where they were standing."

"What?" Dana sputtered. "That is not true. How?"

"Aiden called me. We have a deal about this kind of stuff," Max admitted. "Come on, 'fess up before dad arrives here for dinner. He's not technically living here anymore, you know."

"What do you mean not living here?" Dana asked, startled.

"The new headquarters is practically complete," Max informed her. "Those chadens don't mess around. It has walls, a roof, and floors. Running water, heat, air con – all working. It has no furnishings and the rooms haven't all been decided yet, but dad is having his suite fitted out as we speak. He has decided to stay in the area permanently and will live at the HQ at Eden with his Order."

"Wow. That is ..." Dana trailed off.

"Good?" Max offered, frowning in confusion from Dana's hesitance. "It's good, right?"

"Yes, of course it is. I am so glad he will be staying on. I guess it just makes me –" *Jealous,* Dana thought. She was jealous of the ease in which Mordecai could make this place his home. Make Max and her family his home. Which was extremely unkind and very unbecoming of a benevolent goddess, she knew. But she could not help her feelings any more than any other person in the room.

"Envious," Jasminka filled in the blank. "You're envious. I get it. I was jealous as hell when I first came here. And more than a little resentful when I thought I had to leave. But you know what solved that?"

"What?" Dana asked, giving the human doctor her full attention.

"I stayed."

Dana sighed, leaning back against the large island. "If only it was that simple."

"But you're like a god. I mean you're *our* god, or goddess, or whatever. Can't you do whatever you want?" Axel inquired.

Looking around, Dana saw the same looks of curiosity and confusion on most faces. Glancing at Max, Dana noted she alone had a look of resignation and understanding. Recalling how little Mordecai had known of their theology, Dana did not blame everyone for their lack of understanding. "It is not so simple. I am a part of the Triumvirate. I am one of the original three entities in the cosmos – in *reality*. I am bound by rules of my own making."

"The Triumvirate? It's real? And you're one of them?" Darius asked, standing up from his seat at the table. "I've read about the Big Three but I thought it was just a myth."

"The Big Three?" Dana's lips twitched, knowing Tempus and Tanda would get a kick out of the name.

Darius flushed, looking at his brother. "That's what Dex used to call them when he read me stories when I was a child."

"It is," Dex admitted. "I'd forgotten. Or rather, I had believed them to be bedtime fables."

"They are not fables," Dana admitted.

"Okay, for those of us who have never heard the word Triumvirate in their lives – what the hell is it?" Ryker piped up.

"Mother Nature. Father Time. And Death," Darius supplied.

"Did you just say Death? And Father Time? They're real?" Ryker asked, eyes wide.

"They are. We three were the first of our kind," Dana said.

"Uncle Tempus and Uncle Tanda are cool," Max offered into the silence of the room. "I didn't always remember them, but I have since I regained my memory this last time."

"Uncle Death?" Ryker wheezed in disbelief.

Dana was amused because they had all come such a long way in treating her more like family than a deity. But apparently learning there was a Grim Reaper and a Father Time was still a lot to take in. "Other planes have other rulers of course – other gods and goddesses – but the Triumvirate are the original. It is a huge responsibility and not one I can simply ignore in favour of just doing whatever I want."

Silence reigned for several moments before Beyden raised his hand. "Uh, you said *other* gods and *other* planes of existence."

Dana smiled and nodded at the gentle beast paladin. Dana found him endlessly endearing. "Yes, there are other Gods and Goddesses, including *the* God," she said in answer to his question.

"Greek gods? Roman gods? Wiccan gods? All real?" Lark peppered her with questions.

Dana shrugged negligently. "Sure. They are not all involved with this world in the here and now, but yes – all real."

"Zeus? Zeus is real?" Lark was getting excited.

Dana rolled her eyes, "That guy? Yes, he is real – a real *prick*. Truly, if you ever want a lesson in arrogance, just ask Zeus."

"I bet this is what a stroke feels like," Darius commented. Diana patted him on the back in a comforting way, but even she looked shocked by the revelations.

"Anyway," Max said, clapping her hands and gaining everyone's attention. "The point is, if mum stays here and crosses the line like she did before she will be subject to the same punishments as she was before."

"Punishment? What the fuck do you mean *punishment?*"

CHAPTER NINE

After cooling his jets for a while, Mordecai and his Order had driven back to Max's home for the evening meal. He and his brothers had officially moved out just two nights prior. The HQ was by no means complete, but his set of rooms on the upper floor was set up enough to house him and his paladins. It wasn't that he didn't love being around Max and her family, but he was a more reserved individual and he valued his space. Something that was in short supply at Max's home. The HQ had been designed with three storeys, the top level being reserved for a series of suites for the IDC as they travelled in and out of the country. Mordecai's wing of five bedrooms, a living room, a kitchen, and three bathrooms was going to be a permanent home for him and his Order. For the first time in memory, Aiden, Bastien, Tobias, and Madigan would have their own bedrooms. Everyone was very excited, even though the rooms only consisted of beds for now.

After an aggravating drive where he was forced to endure teasing from his Order about the kiss he shared with Dana, they had arrived and been greeted by Zombie. The dog was always excited to see him and they had all delivered pats and tummy rubs before the happy dog had run off, leading the way to the kitchen. It was no surprise most of the house was congregated there. It was the heart of the house. But what was a surprise was hearing Dana talk about a Triumvirate. Such a word had been tossed about when he was a child, but as Dex said, Mordecai had believed them to be naught but tales. The only true goddess of their people was Mother Nature. His mind was reeling with the new information, wondering exactly what it meant for Dana when his ears pinged on the word *punishment*. That's when he saw red and his protective instincts went into overdrive.

"Punishment? What the fuck do you mean *punishment?*" He practically shouted as he stalked into the room.

Dana's hand flew to her chest and she gasped. "Mordecai."

He ignored the way his name sounded on her lips, instead focusing on what Max had just revealed. "What is Max talking about, Dana?"

Dana sighed, looking suddenly exhausted. Still, she answered, "What I did that night with you – it broke all manner of rules. Rules I helped create. Rules I help maintain. And rules I help enforce."

"Are you saying you were punished for sleeping with me?" Mordecai's voice was incredulous.

"I ..." Dana looked around at all the curious faces, snapping her mouth shut.

Growling, Mordecai strode forward and grabbed her hand. Tugging her along with him, he pulled her from the room. He mentally told his Order to stay as he walked with Dana outside, not stopping until they were standing alone on the beach. "Talk," he commanded.

"I do not know where to start," Dana admitted, looking a little lost and unsure.

Mordecai told himself to calm down, willing his heartrate to return to normal as he reached for patience. He hadn't meant to go all caveman, but the thought of Dana being hurt felt like a punch to the gut. It made him feel nauseated and made him want to strip her down and look for injuries. Which was utter madness. He had only just resolved not to hate the woman. Still, there was no denying his visceral reaction to the thought of her being punished. Tugging on the hand he still had a death grip on, he urged her to sit on the sand. He winced a little as the cold sand permeated his slacks. The sun was setting and the sand, as well as the air, was very cool. Looking over at Dana, he noted she was wearing a blue loose shirt over a pair of skin-tight white pants. Although the shirt had long sleeves it wasn't very thick, and he cursed himself for not thinking of her comfort. "Come here," he said, gesturing her forward.

"What?" Dana squeaked as Mordecai simply plucked her up and placed her between his legs where he was sitting on the sand.

"I can't do much about the temperature of the sand, but at least I can keep your top-half warm," he explained as he wrapped his arms around her shoulders, pulling her close so her back rested against his chest. He pulled his knees up so she was effectively cocooned, and he rested his chin on top of her head. Inhaling deeply, he felt a little lightheaded from how good she smelled. Not to mention how unbelievably soft her hair was. And then there was the softness of her breasts as they pressed against his forearms ... "Maybe this was a bad idea," he muttered, more to himself than to Dana.

"No," Dana was quick to reply. "It is very cold. I am much warmer now. Thank you."

Mordecai tightened his arms a fraction before urging Dana to explain once more. "Start at the beginning."

Dana blew out a breath, her head falling back and resting on his shoulder. Her pretty eyes peered up at him as she began to talk. "The curtain you speak so forcefully about –"

"I'm sorry about that. You were right; I had no idea what I was talking about. I was an arse," he interrupted, still feeling fear from the word *punishment* and wanting so badly to make things right. For years, he had allowed his anger to lead him instead of his head. No more.

Dana squeezed his forearm, silently acknowledging his words. "Well, the veil can act as a window, it is true. But from the time I conceived Max until the time she went supernova, it was nothing like a curtain for me. It was more like prison bars."

Mordecai stiffened, "You were locked up?"

"Locked *out* is more accurate," Dana admitted.

Mordecai allowed the words to roll through his mind for a moment before they finally clicked. "You couldn't cross the veil?"

"No. Not at all."

"So, when you said you couldn't do anything all those years Max was lost here – you meant it literally." It was a statement rather than a question.

"Very literally," Dana confirmed. "I could see and I could hear, but I could not pass."

Mordecai felt his anger returning. "Why didn't you say anything before?" he ground out.

Dana peered back at him once again, her face close to his. "And why would I?"

Mordecai opened his mouth only to snap it closed before he finally got the words out on his third attempt. "Why? Because I was horrible to you! You let me think you didn't give a damn about Max and her wellbeing. You let your people think you were ignoring them – ignoring their prayers in their greatest time of need."

Dana faced the ocean once more, her eyes lingering on the sun setting in the distance. "The truth does not change anything, Mordecai. Besides, you were – *are* – more than entitled to your anger. My paladins and wardens are more than entitled to their pain and grief and bitterness. The why of how I was absent for so many years is irrelevant. It only matters that I *was* absent."

"But not of your own choosing," he pointed out.

"No. Not of my own choosing," Dana's voice was sure and firm. "Although, you need to understand that I did understand and accept my punishment. I had earned it. I hate the consequences of my actions and I wish more than anything I could have helped our daughter and my guardians of nature. But I broke the rules. Important rules."

"You're not allowed to have sex? No, that can't be right. It's not like you were a virgin that night," he quickly added. Silence met his statement and he felt his insides start to knot up and sweat form on his forehead. "Dana? You weren't a virgin, right?"

Dana stared resolutely ahead, saying, "It wasn't the sex. Do not worry. Sex is allowed. I was punished for creating a new thread."

Mordecai blew out a breath of relief. He wasn't sure his ego could handle it if he found out he was Dana's first. There was no finesse and no consideration that went into his lovemaking that night. He was too raw, too angry, and too drunk to do much more than ensure Dana had orgasmed with him. Putting those thoughts to the side, he latched onto what she had revealed. "A thread?"

Dana nodded, relaxing back against him once more. "Every life force has a thread – an origin and a destination. Now, that thread, it can take many detours on the way, get tangled up, turned around, burn out, get cut. That is free will, you see. It is free will that allows these deviations from the original path. It allows people – and all living things – to end at a different place or a different time than they were originally destined to when the thread was first created."

"Wait, are these the threads Max often talks about? What she can see with her weird custodian-hybrid vision? The threads of light connecting souls, people, places …?" Mordecai guessed.

Dana nodded. "Yes. Exactly. They represent a lifetime of choices as well as our fate."

"Okay," Mordecai allowed, trying to follow Dana's information. "So, destiny is fluid?"

"In a very literal sense; yes. But as much as our life threads can be altered, there is one rule that is universally infinite; we all get just one thread. One thread to do with as we will in that one lifetime. I can see the threads, the same way Max can. But I cannot create them. The Sisters are responsible for that. My thread had no biological children. In any time, in any place. Custodians are entirely different – made of energy and formed from power – they have no physical bodies, even though I refer to them as my offspring." Dana paused, stroking Mordecai's arm in an absent way. "Somehow, when we slept together, we created a whole new thread."

"We created Max," he stated.

"Yes," Dana smiled back at him. "We created Max. A child unforeseen by the Fates themselves. It caused a conundrum amongst the deities. Luckily, I was not the first. A precedence had been set millennia ago. I was one of the gods to bestow the punishment at the time. It was only fitting that I received the same. Balance. The scales must always be balanced."

"Virtual imprisonment? You weren't hurt?" Mordecai pushed for clarification, his mind reeling.

"For every year I harboured the new life force, I would serve double that time in isolation behind the veil. No more interference in the world I helped create. No more answering the prayers of the beings I was charged with protecting and maintaining nature. Nor those of the ones born with the birthright to guard them. I could watch, and I could listen, but I could not act. It was a prison with no walls – yet with surround sound." She shuddered, gripping his arms tighter. "But I did hurt, Mordecai. More than you can imagine."

Mordecai tightened his arms and legs, practically squishing her but she didn't protest. Instead they sat in silence and watched as the last orange glow of the sun disappeared from the sky and was replaced with a blanket of dark blue. Soon the sky would be black and millions of stars would be visible to the naked eye. He rocked the woman in his arms and held her as she cried, and he wondered how he could have ever thought her cold or unfeeling. She felt so much – too much. She was like Max, a sponge for energy everywhere, but unlike Max, who now had her large Order to share her burden with, Dana had no one. She'd had no one for several eternities. Mordecai vowed then and there to do better by her and just like that, he let go of his final feelings of resentment and angst.

Gently tilting her face up, he wiped her wet cheeks tenderly. "We should head in. What little warmth the sun provided is gone now that it is set," he whispered.

Dana maintained eye contact, her mouth quirking a little. "Oh, I can fix that," she promised.

Heat wafted off Dana like she was a damn heater, filling the small space between them and infusing him with warmth. He huffed out a breath, telling himself he should have known better. The woman was a goddess of nature. She controlled all the elements just like Max. "If you could do that, why didn't you do it before?"

Dana pulled out of his arms, turning to face him fully even as she remained seated between his upraised knees. "And why would I deny myself the pleasure of your arms?"

His amusement fled, sexual tension taking its place. He watched her lick her lips as her eyes darted to his mouth and knew she was thinking of the kiss they had shared earlier that evening. He wanted nothing more than to lay her back against the sand and ravish her. But he knew that wouldn't be wise given the circumstances. He may have let go of his negative feelings toward her, but his mind was still reeling with all the new information and the revelations it brought. Dana had been a virtual prisoner for years. She had been trapped and helpless to watch as her daughter struggled to find her destiny. And all the while Mordecai – and hundreds of other wardens and paladins – had cursed her name. It was true, Max had sacrificed herself for their people. But so had Dana. The one-eighty of his feelings needed time to process.

Dana, clearly sensing his reticence, pulled back. "I apologise. I didn't mean to take liberties where they were not welcome."

Mordecai stopped her with a hand over her mouth. "Dana, let's be clear; I'm fine with you taking all manner of liberties, okay? I just think we shouldn't indulge in them right now. On the beach. With over a dozen pairs of eyes watching us," he finished dryly.

Dana's eyes darted to the house and she giggled when she saw numerous faces pressed to the windows. The sound was innocent and carefree and had Mordecai hardening in his pants faster than he could blink. Groaning, he reached down to adjust himself, Dana's eyes tracking the movement. "You're not helping," he informed her.

"If you really want my help …" she licked her lips once more.

"Dana," he said, warningly.

Dana shrugged and smiled impishly at him. "You cannot blame a girl for trying."

CHAPTER TEN

"Father Time is responsible for the fabric of reality. Tempus not only constructed this reality, but he also maintains it. Tanda, on the other hand, is responsible for the transport of souls. Whether it be coming or going," Dana lectured to her enraptured audience.

It had been a week since her revelations with Mordecai and she was pleased to say their relationship had well and truly mellowed. The friendship she had been hoping for with the father of her child now felt solid. She had spent the past week explaining everything she was able to about Otherworld, the deities, the veil and how it all worked with the occupants of Max's home. The Order of Aurora now had a sound grasp on what was real and what was legend. Unfortunately, for their tiny human brains, much of what they believed to be legend was in fact reality and Dana had thought some of their heads might implode from the information. After seeing her immediate family educated, she had resolved to enlighten her other guardians and warriors as well. As such, she was now at Eden, talking to a large crowd of wardens, chadens, and paladins. Including the entire IDC.

"Coming or going? Death is responsible for life?" Dawn asked, clearly intrigued by the notion.

Dana nodded. "Life and death are two sides of the one coin. All souls are created equal. Well, almost all souls," Dana amended, smiling at her daughter in the crowd. "It is what people choose to do with them that decides their fates when Tanda comes to collect. Besides, Tanda is only the 'Death' god in this realm. There are many others just like him. As well as those who work with him. But they are not as powerful," Dana added as an afterthought.

"Because he's one of the Triumvirate, like you," Knox stated.

Dana nodded and smiled. She felt great satisfaction in teaching her people. She also loved the simplicity of just talking with them as well. Although she had acquaintances and even a select few individuals she considered friends, she had never given much thought to how isolated she was over the eons. Once, she and her colleagues had walked the earth freely and were worshipped as the Gods they rightfully were. But over time, she – along with Tempus and Tanda – had withdrawn. Their legacies becoming more lore than anything else. She was lucky, the warden society largely still viewed her as a real Goddess. But Tempus and Tanda were more forgotten. Thinking on it now, she realised the exact moment they had retreated semi-permanently behind the veil. It was after that precedence had been set and they felt the need to make an example of it. Dana sighed regretfully, *oh, boys, we really screwed up, did we not?* Dana thought, not expecting a response. She therefore jolted harshly when Tanda responded.

'We are not immune to human infallibilities. Although, you and Tempus do appear to be more susceptible than I.'

Tanda's internal presence was gone as abruptly as he arrived, leaving him with the last word. As usual. Still, it was telling that he was monitoring her on this side of the veil in the first place. She allowed the discussion to ebb and flow around her, her gaze searching and touching on her daughter. Her dark red hair shone in the winter sun and she absently stroked her unborn babe as she talked with Blu and Hyde. To think Max was a one in a billion oddity of accidental fate. And now she was carrying a whole new deity herself. It made Dana wonder just how much of an 'accident' Max's new life thread was. Yes, she had thought to create a weapon – a cure – for the chades, but she truly had not expected a genuine, new life thread to sprout. She could have sworn she heard Tanda chuckle in her ear. Spinning quickly, she ran straight into a solid wall instead. At least, that is what it felt like. But her spiking pulse and hardening nipples told a different story.

"Mordecai," she breathed.

"You okay? You seem to be on a mission," he said, releasing her upper arms where he had reached out to steady her.

Dana simply nodded, struck – as always – by the raw, masculine beauty in front of her. His jet-black hair shined like a raven's wing and his eyes were as green and as clear as a pure cut emerald. The hint of Scotland in his voice was the icing on a very delicious, very sexy cake, and she longed to hear him whisper filthy things in her ear as he stripped her naked. Shaking herself out of her lust-filled thoughts, she took a full step back and congratulated herself on her steady voice as she replied, "I am fine. I thought I heard – never mind."

Mordecai's eyes searched her face for a moment, a frown pinching his brow as he looked around him. "Are you sure everything is okay? I could have sworn my domain went haywire for a second there. If there is any chance of danger, I need to know."

Dana winced and silently chided Tanda. Of course an old and powerful Death Warden would be aware of the presence of a Death God. "There is no danger here. I promise."

Mordecai scrutinised her face for a few more seconds before relaxing, his four paladins following his lead behind him. "I see your talk went well." He gestured to the crowd who were talking excitedly amongst themselves.

"Yes," she said, excitedly. "It is a positive step, do you not think? Education, facts, history."

"Indeed. We are destined to repeat the worst of our histories if they are forgotten." Mordecai snorted in derision, "I've seen it happen enough in my lifetime."

"As have I," she agreed.

They stood together in silence for a few moments before it began to get awkward. Dana peered up at Mordecai, wondering if she should say something about the weather. Or perhaps Max, she thought. The one thing they could always talk about these days was their daughter. Thankfully, Aiden stepped forward, offering her a small bow and a quick grin.

"My lady, perhaps you would like to see Mordecai's suite in HQ? We've been here over a week now and he has done nothing further than put sheets on his bed."

Mordecai scowled at his Captain. "And? You don't expect me to sit around picking paint colours, do you?"

Aiden shook his head, "No. In fact, as someone who is going to be living in those rooms too, I sincerely urge you not to. You have no taste whatsoever. But Dana on the other hand ..." he turned his rakish grin on her once more. "You created nature itself. You're like the original interior designer."

Dana laughed. "I would love to take credit for all the beauty that exists in the world, but I merely created the seeds. Evolution has wrought many miracles – thanks to the aid of my wardens and paladins."

"Pfft, you're too humble. I bet you've got a great eye for colour. Mordecai, take Dana to your room," Tobias picked up Dana's hand with care and grabbed Mordecai's more forcefully. He then smooshed their hands together and spun them bodily around. He went so far as to give his liege a shove, though he didn't attempt the same with her.

Mordecai snarled, shooting daggers at his Order and Dana had no doubt he was giving them a mental tongue lashing through their link. He finally swallowed down a curse and turned to her. "Would you like to see my place?"

Dana pursed her lips, holding back her amusement with effort. "I would love to."

Mordecai grunted and began leading her across the green expanse of Eden in the direction of the huge, three storey building that was now very much completed – on the outside at least. Nobody but Mordecai had moved in and no meetings had yet to be held there either. "You wouldn't find them so amusing if your soul was intertwined with theirs."

"I would say there are worse souls to be bound to," Dana offered.

"I am grateful to be shown around. I cannot believe the progress. And just in time too. I will be returning to Otherworld tomorrow."

Mordecai stumbled, whipping his head down to look at her. "Tomorrow? For how long?"

"For at least two weeks." Mordecai's silence was telling. He disapproved of her actions. Placing a hand on his arm, she brought him to a stop. "It is not that I don't want to be here. I have –"

"Responsibilities. I know," Mordecai cut in. His smile was sardonic as he looked down at her. "I'm not trying to be an arse. You're an important person with a really fucking important job. I like having you around is all," he ended with a shrug.

His words gave her such happiness – and such hope for the future. But was that hope fruitless? Her time spent with Gaias had been brief and filled with more questions than answers. She really had no idea what it meant that her last custodian had been given a body. Just because Tempus said he was her protégé did not mean she could suddenly give up her life in Otherworld and live fulltime on Earth. Did it? She had no clue, and Tanda and Tempus had been unusually enigmatic when asked. It was something she planned to gain clarification on. Regardless of whether she and Mordecai turned their friendship into anything romantic, she wanted to see and hear and touch her daughter every day.

"I am very glad to hear you say that," Dana finally said, shaking off her introspection. "But I was not going to say responsibilities. I was going to say I have rules I must abide by – scales that must be balanced."

Mordecai frowned down at her. "What do you mean?"

Dana ran her hands through her loose hair as she explained. "For every day I spend here on the mortal plane, I must spend two in Otherworld."

"Say what, now?" Mordecai's confusion was clear.

"'Tis true. It is not against the rules for me to visit here. However, it does come with consequences. Double the time must be spent over there." Dana had only explained the situation to Max earlier in the week. Max had been surprised but had taken the information well, suggesting Dana visit for one day and then spend the next two days in Otherworld. Rather than staying for big chunks of time and then losing even longer chunks when she returned. It was a good idea – a logical one. Too bad Dana did not want to spend a mere single day in Mordecai's presence at a time.

"So, the longer you spend here, the longer you are gone? Sounds like a crock of shit to me," Mordecai informed her, before opening the double frosted glass doors of the IDC headquarters.

They did not say much as Mordecai walked her across the cavernous entryway and over to a set of stairs. They walked up six flights – two flights for each level – before reaching the top storey. Here, the hallways were just as empty and bland as the rest of the building was. Reaching out with her senses, Dana found it to be almost completely devoid of all life. But she knew that would not be the case for long. The structure had spirit and it was just waiting for people to give it purpose. Mordecai led her all the way to the end on the north-facing side. Opening the door, he ushered her in, and Dana paused just inside the threshold.

"Wow, Aiden was not exaggerating," Dana muttered, more to herself than Mordecai. The living room was spacious but completely empty. She could see that the kitchen was yet to be fitted out, and there was no paint on the walls nor was there any flooring.

"Yeah, well. Compared to some of the places I've crashed over the years, this place is a palace," Mordecai said.

She wandered around, opening doors and discovering which rooms were those of the paladins. Their spaces were already infused with their energies. She was happy for them. They were already making it their home. It was not until she was standing next to Mordecai's bed that she realised she was alone in a bedroom with the only man she had ever had sex with. The Valhalla Order had not followed them. Dana's heart began to pound. Turning quickly, she came to an abrupt stop when she saw Mordecai casually leaning against the doorjamb. He had his ankles crossed and his hands in his pockets of his dark slacks.

His hands are in his pockets. Why is that so sexy? even her thoughts were breathless.

"Make yourself at home," his voice rumbled out, amused and lightly accented.

"Oh, I am being impolite, am I not?" Dana asked, feeling sheepish. Of course she was being impolite. She had just wandered into the man's sleeping chambers, she scolded herself.

Mordecai pushed himself off the wall, hands still in his pockets as he walked toward her. The dark grey knitted jumper he wore stretched across his chest, moulding his physique to perfection. "You are welcome in my bedroom anytime," he told her, eyes shining down at her. "And in my bed."

Dana could not help the tiny moan that escaped her throat. *Am I really going to do this again with him?* she questioned herself. Running her eyes over his hard frame – and taking note of his already hard member between his legs – Dana decided, *yes*, she was most definitely going to do it. And then, with a single thought, she stood naked before him.

CHAPTER ELEVEN

"Holy shit!" Mordecai exclaimed, jumping back. "You're naked!" he pointed out stupidly.

Dana raised her eyebrows and looked down at herself. "Indeed I am. Is it not better to be naked for such things?"

Mordecai's breath wheezed from his lungs as he took in the image before him; creamy, unblemished skin, full, heavy breasts with the palest of pink nipples – nipples that were already hard. Her waist flared appealingly and the neat thatch of hair between her toned legs was a mere single shade darker than the riotous red hair on her head. He wondered how drunk he must have been on that night all those years ago. Because he couldn't remember seeing anything as beautiful in his whole life as Dana standing proud and unselfconsciously naked before him right then.

"How –" his voice broke. "How did you get naked so fast?"

"I am a goddess. I can pretty much do anything. I simply thought it," Dana explained, shrugging negligently, and causing her breasts to move.

"You simply thought it." Mordecai swallowed. He spent so much time thinking of Dana as the woman who had deprived him of time with his daughter, then the woman who wilfully ignored him, and finally simply as the woman he desired, that he had all but forgotten she was one of the most powerful beings in the universe.

"You seem perplexed," Dana noted. "Should I … should I not be naked?" she then asked, looking a little unsure now.

"Naked is good!" he immediately shouted. "Especially on you. But I didn't bring you here to have sex."

Dana's cheeks pinked. "Oh. I seem to have misread the situation."

"I'm not complaining – don't get me wrong," Mordecai rushed on to say, unable to keep his eyes from the temptation standing in front of him. "But I don't want you to think I was going to take advantage of you."

Dana huffed, crossing her arms over her chest and plumping her tantalising breasts. "Perhaps I am long overdue to be taken advantage of."

"It's been a long time?" Mordecai asked, endlessly pleased with the thought.

"Only about fifty years or so," came her dry response.

Mordecai stilled. "You haven't slept with anyone since me?"

Dana looked away as she replied, "I haven't been with anyone but you – *ever*."

Mordecai literally felt his jaw drop, he was so stunned. "You were a virgin that night?"

Dana nodded once, still not looking at him.

"Oh, dear gods. I defiled Mother Nature!" he shouted, yanking on his hair as he began to pace.

Dana laughed, "It was a good defiling, never fear."

Mordecai shook his head, "I sincerely doubt that. I was drunk off my arse, raw with the pain of death soaking into my very pores. Not to mention, I thought you had escaped from a mental asylum."

"It was the best night of my life," Dana assured him, voice soft. "Other than the night our daughter was born."

The best night of her life? he thought, incredulous. He barely recalled anything other than having the most intense orgasm of his existence.

'Well, don't you think you need to make it up to her then?' Aiden's voice came through the Order link loud and clear.

Mordecai cursed his nosey knights, but he didn't blame them for their interference. It was so natural to have the bond wide open, especially when he was out of their sight. He had entirely forgotten about how much he was sharing. He hastily turned away from a still very naked goddess so they could no longer see her with his eyes.

'As if that will help. The image is permanently seared into my brain,' Tobias informed him.

"I'm going to kill them all," Mordecai vowed darkly. Dana's chuckle washed over him like a physical caress, causing goosebumps to pop up everywhere and he slammed the door closed on the mental link that had been open for close to sixteen hundred years. Because as much as he hated to admit it, Aiden was correct. He had a lot to make up for. Mordecai slapped himself across the face mentally. Hard. Then he turned to the naked woman standing next to his bed.

"I can do better."

Dana's frown was one of puzzlement. "Do what better?"

He walked toward her, lifting his top off in the process. Her quick gasp had him smiling smugly as he tossed the material in the corner of the room. "The sex," he clarified. "I can do the sex better."

Dana licked her lips, eyes traversing the naked expanse of his chest. "Better? I am not sure that is possible. The first time around we created a new life thread. An apparently impossible cosmic phenomenon."

He came to a stop in front of her and hooked an arm around her bare waist, pulling her in tight to his body. The feel of her skin against his own was like getting electrocuted. His whole body came alive with sensation and his vision narrowed to the woman in his arms. "Let's give it our best shot then, shall we?" he replied to her earlier comment.

Mordecai lowered his head, capturing Dana's mouth in a kiss filled with passion and promise. Dana met his tongue with her own, giving as good as she got. He let his hands roam, mapping the smooth skin of her back before cupping the arse that taunted him in all those tight jeans and the leggings she insisted on wearing daily. He couldn't fault her for the fashion style she adopted, but he did wish he was the only one privy to such enticing views. *At least he was the only one to see her like this,* he thought. Then he recalled what she had said about being a virgin the night they had met and he pulled back, staring down at her. He knew she had slept with him for a purpose, but he was still humbled she had chosen him out of literally anyone else in the world. What's more, she was choosing him again, *only* him. *Yes, I need to do better,* he silently vowed.

"Get on the bed," his voice rasped out.

Dana showed no hesitation whatsoever as she took two steps back, all the while keeping her eyes on him. She then sat on the bed and scooted back on her butt before laying down and spreading her legs a little. Mordecai could make out moisture teasing the curls between her legs and he felt his knees go weak. Deciding he needed to move while he was still capable, he quickly toed off his shoes and unbuttoned his pants. He carefully lowered his zipper and shoved his slacks and briefs off in one motion. He moved somewhat gingerly toward the bed, rather than lunging for it like he wanted to, because he feared his legs could stop working at any moment and he didn't want to fall down and snap his dick off.

Dana smiled and welcomed him with open arms, and he immediately zeroed in on the breasts that moved freely with her every movement. Palming them, he rubbed and squeezed the fleshy mounds as if they were his own personal stress balls. Dana didn't seem to mind if her moans for more were any indication. Her nipples were stiff and looked hard enough to cut glass. Leaning down, he pulled one into his mouth, rolling it around his tongue and revelling in the strong, almost painful grip, Dana had on his hair. After suckling for several seconds, he kissed his way to her other breast and paid it equal homage. By the time he was willing to release his new favourite treat, Dana was gasping and writhing on the bed, her hips swivelling and her neck arching back. Unable to resist the temptation, he placed his lips against the graceful curve of her neck and began sucking. Hard. Dana moaned, her hands rising to grip his hair once more and lock his mouth to her body. After several long seconds, Mordecai pulled back – and felt an almost animal satisfaction when he saw the dark red welt on her pale skin. He wasn't sure how long a hickey would last on an immortal goddess but seeing his mark on her made him supremely satisfied. It also made him unbearably hard.

Shifting so her hips cradled his, he nudged his erection through her slick folds, teasing them both and testing her readiness. When she mewled and arched her back, letting out a breathless, "*Mordecai ...*" he knew he had reached his limit. He said her name and waited with bated breath for her to look at him. The question he was going to ask died on his lips when he saw the raging lust in her eyes – as well as the unspoken permission. So, instead, he simply nodded his head and grabbed his shaft, lining himself up for a trip to paradise.

Even though his body was on fire, he still took his time entering her, pushing forward an inch at a time before stopping and allowing her body to adjust. He ignored the demands of his own body, telling him to thrust all the way in one go and piston until his waiting orgasm burst forth. But he was determined Dana know no pain and discover all the pleasures the body could give. It was a divinely torturous five minutes before his hips were finally nestled tightly against her pelvis with no room to spare. Dana's body rippled around his in the most intimate of caresses and he grit his teeth, already feeling sweat rolling down his face. Dana wasn't helping his 'go slow and show Dana the stars' cause. She had locked her legs around his waist and was urging him to move by digging her heels into his arse. All the while muttering and moaning filthy things that he had no idea she knew. Her nails scored his back before her hands came to rest on his waist and she opened her eyes, startling him with the wild desire he saw in the blue-green depths.

"Warden! Move!" she demanded, squeezing her thighs.

The order made him grin and he rotated his hips just once in a circular motion before stopping. "You mean like this?"

Dana growled, slapping his back with her palm. "Mordecai ..."

And just like that, his teasing amusement fled. The sound of his name on her lips really was the biggest aphrodisiac to him. She said it in a light accent he had heard nowhere else in all his travels, and her eyes became all dewy as well. He was sure she didn't know about the last part and he wasn't ready to investigate the reasons why yet, but he knew he loved it. Kissing her until she was breathless once more, he lifted his head up, "Say it again."

Dana's eyes went soft and they began to shine with an unearthly light before she tugged his head down. Nipping his earlobe, she soothed it with her tongue, whispering; "Mordecai."

Mordecai shivered in ecstasy from head to toe – and then he allowed his threadbare control to snap. Withdrawing from the gripping heat of Dana's body, he pulled back so just the tip of his dick was left inside her body before getting a solid grip on her hips with his hands, settling his weight on his knees and heels. Dana gasped, her back curving in an erotic arch, forced that way by his new position and the fact she kept her legs locked around his waist. Eyes locked on her body, he slammed back into her in one stroke, groaning when the action caused her full breasts to jiggle. The sight was so unbelievably sexy that he did it again and again and again, until sweat began to blind his eyes. Shifting positions, he came down on top of a panting and flushed Dana and took her mouth in a fierce kiss. Dana's legs fell to the sides and she planted her feet flat on the mattress, using it as leverage to meet his frantic movements with equal fervour.

With every thrust, his body – and he feared, his heart – were taken to new heights. Until finally, he felt his balls draw up tightly in their sac, warning of an imminent release. Going by the breathless moans and the way Dana kept yanking on his hair, Mordecai figured she was close to the precipice too. Still, just in case, he reached a hand down, finding her clit swollen and slippery with juices, and pressed down on it. Hard. Dana screamed, her nails scoring his back as her body tightened around him almost to the point of pain. Barking out a harsh gasp, he rammed into her as much as her rippling sheath allowed, coming with a furious yell as the most intense pleasure ripped through his body – and into hers. Pressure built in the room as they continued to grapple with their orgasms that seemed never ending, until a loud boom followed by what sounded like hail falling met his ears. If he didn't know any better, he would say they were in the midst of a storm.

Finally coming to an exhausted stop, he looked down at Dana, watching as his sweat dripped off his face, landing on Dana's flushed skin. He swore he saw the salty drops evaporate in tiny puffs of steam. It wouldn't surprise him. The woman underneath him was scorching hot. Clearing his throat, he tried to still his panting breaths enough to speak. "What ... what was that?"

"I believe it is called an orgasm," came Dana's self-satisfied reply as she stroked her hands up and down his flanks.

Mordecai groaned, rolling off Dana to land on the mattress beside her. It had been one hell of an orgasm but that wasn't what he was referring to. He looked over to the left and sure enough, the glass from the window was shattered. The sky outside was edging toward total darkness. It had been late afternoon when Dana had finished up her little tutorial but apparently, they had lost another couple of hours to their passion. The boom and the 'hail' he heard must have been the window blowing out and the sound of the glass falling to the floor. "The window is broken."

"What?" Dana asked, peering over his shoulder at the mess of glass on the floor. "Oh dear. I think that was me," Dana admitted, looking contrite and proud at the same time.

Mordecai couldn't resist and kissed her once more, taking his time to pour his feelings into the gesture. He felt incredible, and he was smart enough to know that the woman he currently held in his arms was incredible as well. Pulling back, he grinned at her, "Your orgasm shattered the window."

Dana cocked her head to the side, and she looked straight ahead in an absent way before she winced, her cheeks flushing with further colour. "Not just this window. Every window."

Mordecai's eyebrows shot up. "What do you mean every window?"

Dana chewed on her lower lip, admitting, "Every window in the building is broken."

"Holy shit!" Mordecai exclaimed. "There's got to be hundreds of windows in this place." He paused, thinking about it for a moment, before deciding; "I am the man!"

Dana rolled her eyes and gave him a shove, "Yes, yes. You are very manly and virile."

He couldn't keep the smug look off his face even if he wanted to. Still, he cringed a little when he realised how much work it was going to take to get fixed. Not to mention what people were going to say about it. "I am never going to hear the end of this," he shook his head.

"Fear not. You are with a goddess," Dana winked at him before rising from the bed.

Her long, wavy red hair was a mess and she shook it back, exposing her full nakedness to his eyes once more. Raising her arms, she tilted her head back and closed her eyes. Mordecai felt the atmosphere change immediately. The air felt alive with energy, causing the hair on his arms to stand up. Looking around, he saw a rainbow mist swirl around the room almost playfully for a moment before it rushed to the pieces of broken glass, swooping them up and piecing them back together within the window frame. Similar mist rushed under the crack in the door and Mordecai watched in awe as the window was knitted back together in seconds.

"There. All fixed," Dana dusted off her hands before she strolled over to the attached bathroom.

"All fixed?" Mordecai repeated stupidly.

Dana smiled. "All the windows are fixed. Perhaps nobody noticed, hmmm? Now, are you going to join me in the shower?"

Mordecai closed his mouth long enough to scramble from the bed and follow Dana into the bathroom. The powerfully magical display going to the back of his mind in favour of showering with a wet, naked goddess.

CHAPTER TWELVE

The following morning, Dana lay where she was, content to watch Mordecai dress. He truly was a fine example of the male species. His body was well muscled and in complete proportion. She felt herself throb between the legs, remembering just how well-made he was in a certain department. Forgoing underwear and tucking himself into his dark slacks, he paused with his hand still on his dick. Dana raised her eyebrows, "Problem?"

"I really do tuck to the left. Just like you said," he replied, eyes narrowing on her.

Dana felt her pulse kick up from the intensity in his gaze. He really was very predatory, she thought, shivering a little. "What? Why are you looking at me like that?"

"Just how closely have you watched me over the years?" he asked, stalking forward with his pants half zipped and chest still bare. "You've clearly watched me dress. Have you watched me shower?"

Dana pulled the covers up higher over her breasts to hide the effect his silky words were having on her nipples. She cleared her throat, "I might have … once or twice."

"Hmmm," Mordecai mumbled, placing a knee on the bed and looking down at her. "And have you watched me do this?" He reached into his slacks and pulled out his half-hard dick. He stroked it a couple of times and had it fully hard and long within seconds. "Well? Have you?"

"I ..." Dana's throat was so dry there was no way she could possibly talk.

"Oh, I think you have. You dirty, dirty little goddess. Using your powers for perving has to be a breach of protocol or something," he said, still casually stroking his dick. "I think you owe me."

Dana's eyes flew to his. "Owe you how?"

"Fair is fair. You need to return the favour. Touch yourself," Mordecai demanded.

Dana moaned a little, the mere tone of his voice causing a rush of moisture between her thighs. She was as turned on as she had ever been in her life, but she couldn't possibly do what Mordecai was asking ... could she? Mordecai had backed up and was now standing with his arms crossed over his impressive chest. His cock, still thick and long, was hanging out of his pants and pointing straight at her like a tuning fork. Dana licked her lips, delighted and intrigued when his cock bobbed in the air in direct reaction to her. Making eye contact with him, she slowly lowered the blanket and pushed it down past her navel, baring her breasts to his hungry gaze.

"Touch yourself," Mordecai urged. "Pinch your nipples."

Dana had never felt so exposed in her life – and never so desired. Keeping her eyes on his, she reached down and rubbed circles around both her nipples. Teasing him and teasing herself, she licked her finger and then rubbed it over a stiff peak. Mordecai's filthy curse was music to her ears, making her feel more powerful than all the mystical powers of the universe did. Finally obeying him, she pinched her nipples in tandem, pulling and tugging on them until her hips were writhing beneath the blankets.

"The blankets. Move them," Mordecai ordered, breath coming in harsh gasps as he gripped his cock in an iron hold.

Feeling bold and sexy, Dana used her toes to pull the blankets down. She gripped the fluffy material with her big toe and slowly tugged it down, releasing it only to get another grip and drag the blanket down another few centimetres. When her hot sex met the cooler air of the room, Dana arched her back, stifling her own curse. Reaching down, she rubbed her sensitive clit with the pads of two fingers, spreading the juices there. She was wet and slippery and so turned on, she wasn't sure how much longer she could tease her man before she caved and brought herself off.

"Fuck yourself with your fingers."

"Mordecai!" Dana gasped out, her eyes reeling wildly in his direction.

His eyes were blazing like jewels as they watched her fingers move over herself, and his hand was now moving roughly over his shaft. Moaning, Dana obeyed and went for gold, pressing two fingers inside of herself at the same time. She used her other hand to tug on her nipples over and over again. Mordecai growled and swore, stalking closer to the bed. Standing above her, he jacked his flushed cock furiously and Dana knew what his intentions were. Caught in the headiness of lust, she kept plunging her own fingers into herself, using her palm to press down hard on her clit at the same time. The effect was so pleasurable it boarded on painful and she locked eyes with Mordecai, daring him to finish how she knew he wanted.

Mordecai's grunts and groans grew in intensity and she heard him swear colourfully a second before she felt warmth splash against her breasts. Moaning herself, she increased her own movements, gasping in relief when she felt her own orgasm crash over. Mordecai groaned, collapsing on the bed and giving her an exhausted, sloppy kiss. Dana returned it then spent the next few minutes trying to regain her breath – and her wits. Looking down at herself, she saw she was covered in the evidence of Mordecai's release as well as sweat. She looked well and truly fucked out, not at all like the nature goddess she had been for millennia. She was damn proud of herself.

"Stop looking so smug," Mordecai mumbled.

"I think I've earned some smug," she replied, primly.

Mordecai sat up, his eyes taking in her body – and everything on it. "Maybe you have," he allowed. Then he grinned and swept down to capture her lips for a decadent kiss.

Pulling back and kissing her nose, he got up and went to the bathroom. Dana heard water running before Mordecai stepped out with a wet washcloth. He wiped her down – her breasts, stomach, and between her legs. The last made her blush furiously and had him laughing. "You are too cute," he said, bopping her on the nose. He then threw the towel on the floor and crawled back into bed with her.

"I'm not cute," she retorted. "I'm a goddess."

"You'll get no complaints from me about that," Mordecai said, drawing her against his chest.

Dana laughed. "I feel good," she then admitted.

"I would certainly hope so," Mordecai said, running his hands over her back and settling them on her butt.

"I mean it. No wonder all the loved-up couples walk around on cloud nine all the time. Love feels good," Dana admitted, snuggling further into Mordecai's strong embrace. Too bad he chose that moment to move.

"Hold up," he pushed away a little, levering himself up on an elbow so he could look down at her. "Did you say love?"

Dana stilled, everything in her locking up when she realised what she had just said. Yes, she loved Mordecai. She had loved him for years. And it wasn't just because they had created a child together or because he was her first and only sexual experience. It was because of everything she had seen and everything she had felt from him over the years. But she had an unfair advantage. She had those years of watching and feeling. She had minutes and hours of him laughing and smiling and joking. Of him crying and erupting with violence. Of him healing and making friends and making enemies. She may not have had a lot of time to physically talk with Mordecai until recently, but she knew him. She knew what kind of man he was – knew his heart and his soul. So, yes, she loved him. Very much. Looking into the emerald depths of his eyes, she refused to withhold anything from him ever again. So she took a deep breath and told him everything she had just thought.

She ended her little speech with; "I don't expect you to feel the same way, Mordecai. I know I have an unfair advantage. There's no pressure."

Mordecai was sitting up with his back to the headboard and staring straight ahead. When he continued to do so for the next few minutes, Dana deflated, knowing she had messed up her chance of a relationship with Mordecai before it had ever really begun. Peeling back the covers, she went to leave when she felt his hand on her arm.

"Where are you going?"

"I thought I'd give you some space," she said, not turning around. She didn't want to see dismissal in his eyes.

Mordecai grunted and tugged on her arm, pulling her back onto the bed. He quickly rolled on top of her and pinned her arms above her head. "Did I say I wanted space?" Dana shook her head. "That's right. I didn't. Dana …" he released his hold on her wrists and cupped her face instead. "I may not love you yet. But I want the chance to. I want to love you, Dana. Give me time. Let me make up that advantage you have."

Dana chewed furiously on her lip, anything to divert attention from her brain to her eyes – which were starting to leak. "You want to love me?"

Mordecai smiled, keeping his eyes on hers as he took small sips of her lips. "Very much."

Tears of happiness and tears of gratitude began to run down her cheeks. Mordecai bent down and kissed them away and Dana wrapped her arms around his shoulders, holding on extra tight. "Okay," she mumbled against the bare skin of his shoulder.

Mordecai lifted his head. "Okay?"

"You have yourself a deal," she grinned, laughing when Mordecai whooped loudly.

Now all she had to do was figure out how to tell Tempus and Tanda she was leaving the Triumvirate. And hoped like hell her unexpected and mysterious protégé was up to the job.

CHAPTER THIRTEEN

Mordecai came to a dead stop just outside his bedroom door. There were four morons grinning like adolescent schoolboys standing directly in front of him. "Get out of my way," he pushed past them, making his way to the only appliance in the still unfitted kitchen: the coffee machine. "You look like a bunch of idiots," he told them, listening to the magical sounds of coffee beans grinding.

"And you look like you've been ridden hard and put away wet," Bastien pointed out.

Mordecai ran his hands through his still wet hair before scratching at the whiskers on his face. He had made no effort to shave that morning, having better things to do with his time. But he probably should have made the effort to pull on a shirt, given how he was covered in scratches from a certain goddess's fingernails.

"Or is it Dana who was put away wet?" Tobias taunted cheekily, playing chicken with his life.

Mordecai scowled at them all. "I suggest you keep your comments about Dana to yourself. Otherwise I'll have her rip out your tongues."

"You don't want to do it yourself?" Madigan asked, sidling up next to Mordecai so he could get his own cup of coffee.

Mordecai grunted. "That woman can handle herself. Trust me."

Silence met his statement for a few seconds before he heard their laughter – and he shared in it. He felt damn good. Better than he had in more years than he could count.

Aiden walked over and gripped his shoulder. "We're happy for you, Mordecai. I cannot think of a more fitting woman for you, my liege, than a goddess. You deserve her."

Mordecai resolutely swallowed down the lump in his throat, croaking out a, "Thank you," before drinking his scolding coffee in one huge gulp.

"And where is our goddess this morning?" Aiden asked, looking in the direction of Mordecai's room.

"She poofed herself away a few minutes ago," Mordecai replied.

Madigan looked concerned, "Back to Otherworld?"

Mordecai shook his head. "No. Not yet anyway. She said she was going to talk to Max."

Madigan looked relieved, along with the others. "That's good. So … what now?"

"Now we have to do a bunch of mental health checks on a bunch of chadens. I also promised Dawn I would take a look at those two paladins who are infected," Mordecai replied, voicing what was on their agenda today. The chadens had been reacclimatising very well, but the IDC were under no illusions about how hard such a transition must be. As such, Mordecai and Dawn were doing routine checks with their elements to ensure the chadens were okay – both physically and mentally. There had been only one more new case of a paladin showing signs of infection since Celeste was accosted on the beach. Dawn and Jasminka had been working diligently to identify the mechanism as well as treatment and a cure. But they were hitting roadblocks – even with Max's help. Dawn thought Mordecai's death domain might be able to shine some light, so he was going to meet her at her new clinic at the Lodge. The clinic would soon be moving to the new building where he now lived, with the infirmary staying as it was at the training lodge for the new recruits. Such a thing had never been done before. Paladins who were injured were simply forced to suck it up. Even wardens who were hurt or drained had been left to the care of their paladins in their own homes. Mordecai was warmed to see a shift of inclusion and caring for their people.

Tobias made a rude noise, drawing Mordecai back from his thoughts. "That's not what Madi meant and you know it. What now with Dana? Are you two a couple?"

"Are you going to get married and have more magic babies?" Bastien quickly followed up.

Mordecai sent them all a droll look, ignoring them and walking into his room to finish getting dressed. Of course, he couldn't escape them so easily and they followed close on his heels. They didn't say anything but he could feel their laser eyes on him as he turned around, no doubt taking in every scratch and bite on his back and shoulders. "We're working on it, okay?" he said, finally snapping.

"Which part? The couple part or the baby part?" Aiden teased.

Mordecai shook his head. "No babies." He paused, gulping. "I don't think. Do you think?" he then asked, a little panicky. After all, their last encounter had made Max and he hadn't taken any precautions last night. Was there such a thing as goddess contraception? he wondered.

Tobias rolled his eyes, "Relax. Dana warned you last time she was going to use your DNA to try to create an omnipotent being, didn't she?" Mordecai nodded his head furiously. "Then I'd say your swimmers are safe," Tobias clapped him on the back. "Now, about the windows …"

Mordecai's steps faltered on the way to the door and he heard raucous laughter behind him. He closed his eyes and counted to ten before moving again, not acknowledging his sworn knights. He knew it. He was never going to hear the end of it.

∼

When Dana had magicked herself out of Mordecai's embrace that morning, she did not have to travel far. As it turned out, it was close to mid-morning and Max and her Order were once again at Eden, ready to work, after retiring for the night to their home by the sea. Dana had paused when she saw all the knowing grins and teasing looks as she walked over to the group, but she held her head up high and continued on. *So, I had sex*, she thought. *It is not like the lot of them are not always going at it like rabbits.*

'Hardly like rabbits, mother. Just because you and father have that type of stamina, doesn't mean we all do.' Max teased her mentally. *'Which is really ick by the way.'*

"Titania ..." Dana scolded, falling into old habits and calling Max by the name she had bestowed upon her at birth. It was not often she made the mistake. Although she still believed the name fit her daughter, Dana really did see her as Max now.

"What's a Titania?" Axel asked, looking confused.

Max smirked at her fire paladin. "It's not a what. It's a *who*. Me. I'm Titania."

Axel's wide eyes met those of his counterparts. "Your real name is Titania?"

"My real name is Max," Max quickly corrected. "But ..." she smiled at Dana, reaching out to hold her hand in an affectionate grip. "I'll always be Titania too."

Dana returned her daughter's smile, relieved she had not caused offence.

"So, uh, your nickname would be ... *tit?* Or maybe *titties?*" Axel asked, trying to hold back his laughter. He quickly yelped however, when Ryker grabbed him in a none-too-gentle headlock.

"I dare you to call her that," Ryker urged, squeezing for good measure.

Axel choked, tapping out on Ryker's arm because he couldn't talk. Ryker released him and Axel stepped back rubbing his throat. "Dude, chill. I won't call her that – out loud." He then took off running when Ryker pulled his duel sickles from their sheaths.

Dana chuckled, hugging Max close to her side. "I am so happy for you, sweetheart. Everything is working out – just like you said."

"Hmmm," Max agreed. "Who would have thought?"

"Okay, okay. Enough cheek from you," Dana kissed Max's forehead and let her go.

"Now, all we need is for you to get your own happy ending," Max offered.

Feeling a tingle of awareness shoot down her spine, Dana turned her head to find Mordecai's eyes on her as he strode with purpose across the clearing. "I am working on it," Dana murmured.

She was more than a little surprised when Mordecai did not slow his movements, instead running right into her and pulling her hard against his chest. His head swooped down and his mouth landed on hers, promising all sorts of pleasures. And, she hoped, a future. It was certainly telling that he kissed her so openly and in front of so many of their kind. Not just Max's Order. There were dozens of chadens, wardens and paladins around, all eager to help create the new hub of their society.

Dana pulled her mouth from his, her hands resting on what she knew were perfectly hairy, perfectly muscled pecs. "Hello," she said, ducking her head under his chin.

Mordecai's laugh rumbled through his chest, causing pleasant vibrations against her cheek. "You are the most intriguing mix of innocence and worldly. How could you possibly still have the ability to blush after last night?"

"Oh. Gag!" Max said, scrunching up her nose.

Mordecai's green eyes widened and he looked around, as if only just noticing they had an audience. And then he blushed. Hard. Dana thought it was adorable.

"Aww, are you blushing?" Ryker taunted, smirking at Mordecai.

"I can make Max leave you," was Mordecai's immediate retort.

"No, you can't," Ryker snarked back.

"No, he can't," Max agreed, grinning.

"Whatever," Mordecai said, looking around at their audience. "What the fuck are you all looking at?" he practically yelled, causing everyone to scatter. He then gave Dana his full attention once more. "I will be busy here for a few hours. Then I am heading to the training lodge. Will I see you later?"

Dana bit her lip, her eyes greedily seeking out the truth in his. "Do you want to see me later?"

"Yes."

The reply was perfect in its simplicity and Dana found herself smiling widely. "Then you shall," she promised.

"What about Otherworld? I thought you were returning? Are we really going to have to wait at least two weeks to see each other again?" he asked, looking annoyed at the prospect.

Dana's happiness wilted a little. *Is this how it was going to be?* She wondered. Were they doomed to spend a little time together only to be punished with double the time apart? Something that had been a mere annoyance to her suddenly became terrible and she vowed to talk with Tempus and Tanda that day.

'Never fear, my dear. We are already here,' Tempus's voice invaded her mind.

CHAPTER FOURTEEN

*D*ana whipped her head around to the cliff's edge, her gaze immediately landing on the other two gods who had been with her since the beginning of time itself. Tempus was dressed as always in a smart suit; this one was charcoal with a pale blue dress shirt. He wore no tie and had the first couple of buttons undone on his shirt, revealing a hint of his tattoo. Tanda, on the other hand, looked like some kind of skater-boy in ripped jeans, black and white Doc Martin shoes, and a faded Metallica t-shirt. The row of silver hoops in his left ear went from the lobe to the tip and shined in the winter sun.

"Dana?" Mordecai questioned. He was squinting in the same direction as her, but he clearly could not see what she was seeing. Still, he was tense and appeared ready for battle as his Order quickly flanked him. "What is it?"

Before Dana could reply and assure him everything was fine, Max squealed and took off running. Well, as fast as she was able to considering she was almost seven months pregnant. Max ignored the yells and warnings from her Order and she flung herself at Tanda, crying, "Uncle Tanda!" Dana transported herself next to the gods before over a dozen heavily armed paladins arrived seconds later. There was lots of cursing and questions as Max moved on to Tempus, giving him the same treatment and a happy, "Uncle Tempus!".

"What the fuck is going on?" Ryker yelled, clearly unhappy.

Dana held up a staying hand. "These are my colleagues – and my friends. Tempus and Tanda." That shut everyone up.

"As in, Father Time and Death?" Darius asked, eyes wide, even as his grip on his sickle remained tight.

"That would be us. At your service," Tempus bowed, smiling at everyone over the top of Max's head.

What followed was thirty minutes of hectic conversation, laughter, and awkward silences. Thankfully, the tension in the air no longer felt fraught with danger. Although Max's entire Order were yet to sheath their blades. Mordecai, for his part, was staring avidly at Tanda. When the usually stoic God of Death winked at him, Mordecai literally jumped, before scowling and telling his paladins to "fuck off" for laughing.

Finding herself next to Tempus and a small distance away from the crowd, she asked, "Is it time?"

"You're asking me?" came the amused reply.

Dana slid her eyes to the left, a smile quirking her lips. "And who should I ask about matters of time if not Father Time himself?"

"Bah," the silver fox waved a dismissive hand. "As if you need our permission to do anything."

"The laws of nature might not deem it so, but I would like it nonetheless," Dana revealed. She looked to Mordecai who was watching her exchange with sharp eyes. She smiled reassuringly at him. "He wants to love me, Temp."

Tempus sighed and turned to face her fully. "I know. And so he shall."

Dana felt her heartbeat skip out of rhythm. "He shall?"

"He shall," a voice said from behind her.

Dana spun around, finding Gaias grinning at her. "Gaias? What are you doing here?"

"Now, what would a retirement party be if your replacement wasn't here?" he replied.

"What?" she was breathless.

Tempus patted her on the back. "You asked if it was time. It is."

Dana cast her eyes to Tanda, then to Max – or more specifically her bump – before looking at Tempus once more. "Only my time?"

"For now," Tempus said.

Dana bit her lip and nodded her head. She knew Tanda's time in the Triumvirate was coming to an end at some point but was yet to be informed of the same for Tempus. It was strange, when one set of gods stepped down, there was always a replacement waiting in the wings. It was true, she had not known her own time was upon her until Gaias popped up in Otherworld. She had believed Tanda would be the first to descend. But, looking around her now, she was beyond grateful it was to be her.

"What about you?" she asked Tempus, presently.

"Ah, you and Tanda are set. No such luck for me yet."

His voice held no censure, but the response made Dana sad nonetheless. She was about to get everything she never even knew she wanted but her friend was not yet done with his service. It seemed unfair. "Are you at least going to talk to him while you are here?"

"Who?" Tempus feigned ignorance.

"Your son," Dana spoke bluntly. "Your punishment – your lockout from the veil – ended several lifetimes ago. Do you not think it is time to say hello?"

Tempus was saved from replying by Max, who suddenly appeared next to them. Her swirling eyes were locked onto Gaias. "I know you," she whispered, taking a slow step forward. Gaias smiled and reached out a hand to her. Ryker immediately pulled Max back and Darius, Lark, and Beyden quickly formed a solid wall of muscle between them both. "Guys," Max said, exasperated. "He won't harm me. Besides, you know we are surrounded by the three entities who pretty much shaped the universe, right?"

"I don't care. I don't know him," Ryker stated, not letting go of Max for a second. "Where the hell did you come from? How many more of you can we expect to just pop up?" Ryker turned his disapproving eyes on Dana.

"But I do know him," Max said, peering around everyone to look at Gaias once more. "Don't I? You're the Custodian. The one Emmanuel consumed and imprisoned."

Mouths dropped open in shock and a pin could have been heard falling to the soft grass from all the shock resonating through the minds and bodies of everyone congregated on the cliff's edge.

Gaias smiled at Max but made no move to reach for her again. "I am. I owe you a debt I can never repay. I did not think I would ever be free. Nor all those hundreds of other poor souls. I had no idea supernova was a thing," he added, winking.

Max laughed, pushing her way through her stupefied paladins. "Just between you and me? I didn't either." Then, in typical Max fashion, she threw herself at him and wrapped him up in a big hug. Ryker – and the rest of her paladins – cursed and groaned but didn't immediately yank her back this time. "How the hell did you get a body?" Max questioned, releasing the young man.

Gaias pointed to Tanda. "Death caught me, threw me into this meatsuit." He looked down at himself. "It's strange. As a pure soul, I never thought to have a body. Is it a good one?" he asked, looking curious.

Surprisingly, it was Ivy who answered, "Oh, yes. It's a good one," she practically purred.

Beyden's eyes widened and his whole face turned red, "Ivy!"

"What?" Ivy shrugged. "You don't agree?"

All eyes turned to the undeniably handsome young man, who simply grinned. Lark was the one to break the silence by agreeing with his lover. "I totally agree. But wait a minute, Custodians are like your offspring, right? Max is your daughter. Basically, a Custodian in flesh and blood. Does that mean Gaias is Max's brother?"

Dana thought about it for a moment. It was a question she had asked herself many times since finding out what Tanda had done. "Custodians are born of my magic; pure souls, pure energy, pure power. It is true I thought of them as offspring. They were the closest I ever thought I was going to get to having a child. I knew I was not going to birth one from my body. That turned out to be wrong of course. Max is my flesh and blood child, made the old-fashioned way. Her magic and powers are her birthright – her inheritance. Gaias has a soul I created but a body I did not. I do not share blood with him. But I do share magic."

Dana looked at Gaias, knowing he was there to take her place so she could step aside and live a life full of love and happiness in the mortal world. How could she not love him? she thought. How could she not appreciate him and feel the same affection for him as she did for Max? She could not, she decided. Smiling, she finally answered Lark, "Yes, Gaias is Max's brother. I claim him as my son – if he would have me," she added, looking at Gaias.

Gaias smiled and nodded his head, words apparently lost to him. But that was okay. Dana did not need the words. She understood. Gaias was a soul burdened with overseeing nature and its wardens millennia ago. At the time, he was an *it,* with no comprehension of what living a real life was like. Then he had been trapped for what must have felt like an eternity inside a very literal hell. On top of that, Tanda had thrust him into a physical body. He was no doubt floundering to compute all the changes. But one thing she was sure of – he now had a family. And she knew they would all band together to help him work it out.

Leaving her new son to the tender mercies of Max's crew, Dana sought out Mordecai. She pulled him aside, and he came willingly. Likely because he was too overwhelmed to protest, but Dana did not mind. "Are you okay with me having a son?" she asked him.

Mordecai opened and closed his mouth a few times before throwing his arms up in the air. "Sure. Why not? The more the merrier. Besides, look at our daughter. She's already claimed the poor lad. Another stray for her collection," he added softly.

Dana could not help but laugh when she looked over and saw Max chattering away at a very bewildered Gaias. Gaias cast a 'help me' look over Max's shoulder and Diana and Beyden quickly stepped up, diverting Max's attention. Dana smiled, *yes,* she thought, *he will be just fine.* Looking behind Gaias, she made eye contact with Tanda and Tempus. The pair simply nodded at her and her breath rushed out. The permission to pass on the title – to step down – was there. She could see it in their eyes, but more importantly, she could feel it in their hearts.

'This is right,' they said. *'This is meant to be.'*

Dana blinked back her tears and turned to Mordecai. "Do you still want the chance to love me?" she asked, bluntly.

Mordecai blinked and pulled himself up straight. But his face softened after a heartbeat and he nodded his head. "I do. Very much."

"What if I told you I was retiring and I am able to travel between the veil at will, with no need to balance the scales? What if I told you I can stay on this side permanently with no risk or repercussions?" She stepped in closer, her body brushing against his and creating fire everywhere it touched. "And what if I told you I wanted to stay with you?"

Mordecai searched her face for an endless moment, raising her hands to cup her cheeks, "I'd say …" he lowered his mouth to brush hers. "Thank the Great Mother."

EPILOGUE

Mordecai wrapped his arms around Dana, bending a little so he could kiss her cheek and rest his chin on her shoulder. It had been three weeks since Dana had dropped her little bombshell about Gaias and about her essentially becoming the Crone. He dared not call her that out loud, nor did his paladins, but it was an accurate moniker. She was now the Wise Woman, the predecessor, making way for a new generation of gods. Mordecai was yet to talk to Gaias – other than the brief meeting with him and the Triumvirate that day on the cliff – but he and Dana had spent many nights discussing the new Keeper of Nature. Usually after a marathon of lovemaking, Mordecai thought – more than a little smug. Their relationship was going strong and although Dana hadn't officially moved in with him at the new HQ, she spent more nights there than she did in his old guest room at Max's place. Dana had, however, helpfully made several suggestions for decorating his suite. And to his astonishment, painted and furnished it all with the blink of an eye. Giving up her position in the Triumvirate had not lessened her powers at all.

Dana snuggled back against his chest, a happy sigh falling from her mouth as she watched the IDC argue over paint colours for the council chambers. "I do not know why they are arguing. They are going to decide on pale grey – just like the rest of the walls."

Mordecai chuckled. "This is the council we're talking about. They may be new and have good hearts, but they are still politicians. They will always argue about everything."

"Discuss. I believe discuss is a better word," Dana said.

"Whatever you say," he agreed, kissing the top of her red head, and taking in her heady fresh scent. He stepped back but kept his arm around her waist as they watched on. Not ten minutes later it was decided the walls would be painted grey. Just like the rest of the public areas in the building. Mordecai barely stifled his laugh when Dana peered up at him with her eyebrows raised. "I know, I know. You told me so."

"That I did," came her self-satisfied reply.

Her gaze shifted and Mordecai noted the shift in her expression. He immediately felt his stomach drop. "What's with the look?"

"What look?" Dana blinked up at him, the picture of innocence.

He snorted, "You don't fool me. That is the exact same look Max gets when she is up to one of her machinations. What have you done?"

Dana smiled, her eyes sparkling with amusement as well as untold knowledge. "I have not done anything. I simply suggested to Knox that he might be of benefit to Dawn. She has a lot on her plate, what with overseeing the orphanage construction and fit-out with Celeste, and her clinic that she is trying to get up and running. Not to mention the training she is starting for life paladins and life chadens. It makes sense for her to have a helper. A personal assistant if you will."

"Right. A personal assistant. As if her own four paladins of eons aren't help enough?" Mordecai asked, cocking his head in the direction of Dawn's excellent Order.

Dana hummed, watching Knox approach Dawn with keen eyes. "An extra pair of hands never goes astray."

Mordecai spun Dana around, making her gasp as she fell against him clumsily. He wrapped both arms around her securely before saying, "These better be the only pair of hands you ever need." He then squeezed her rump for good measure.

Dana's eyes softened with what he now recognised as love. Dana said the words often to him – usually in the throes of their lovemaking – and he revelled in them. He was yet to say the words back, wanting more time to get to know the real Dana and shed the perception he had of her. Fifty years of hard feelings could not be erased overnight, but he was well on the way to that love he had told her he wanted so badly.

"Yours are the only hands ever to hold my butt, Sir Mordecai," Dana informed him. She stood on her toes, pecking his lips. "And the only ones I will ever want. I love you."

Mordecai groaned, swooping down and kissing them both breathless. "Thank the Gods," he murmured.

"And the Goddesses," Dana added.

Mordecai pulled back and grinned; "Those too."

BOOK TWO

KNOX

PROLOGUE

It roamed the earth aimlessly for more years than it could keep count of. Monitoring time was pointless, anyway; the black pit of nothingness was timeless. Still, one day, it stumbled across a small hollow of trees located next to a busy, noisy road. It should not have been appealing, nor should it have been safe. But the place had called to something inside of the creature, long believed lost. So, it had taken up residence in the trees, watching as people came and went. They were unappealing to the creature, sparking neither raging hunger nor curiosity, and it merely hovered nearby, insubstantial as the wind. Others of its kind would come and go, bringing an echo of comfort and a shared awareness for a brief time. But, like everything else, those feelings were fleeting.

Until one day, a being with power so bright it hurt the creature's black eyes, walked into its hideaway. Like a moth to a flame, it was drawn to her. Its body starving, and its mind nothing but madness, it stalked forward in shadow form, unconcerned others of its kind were doing the same. They were of no consequence to the creature, just as the other beings surrounding the power were not. Taking on a more tangible form was necessary to feed, and it did so a bit reluctantly. It hated looking down and seeing its long, pale, spindly fingers, because, even in the void of its mind, it knew they were not always like that. It watched impassively as three other pits of despair attacked and were cut down by the warriors protecting the food source. The creature's fingers twitched with the need to act but it could barely recall what it was supposed to do. Air caressed its face, moving the greasy hair off its forehead, but leaving the creature feeling hollow because it could not feel it. It knew it should be able to. Knew the air should bring aid. Instead, it taunted. Just like everything else.

Especially, it thought, *the female with all the delicious energy.*

Moving forward, it opened its mouth wide, focused only on getting to the source. A female raised her weapon and a male rushed toward him with hate and the promise of murder in his eyes. The creature welcomed death and hoped the warriors were successful. Otherwise, there would be no stopping it from taking everything the small female had. It would drain her until her body was nothing more than a dried-out husk. To its shock, the male was propelled backwards by an unseen force.

"No!" the shiny, bright female yelled. "Not that one!"

Confused, hurt, and starving to the point of pain, the thing that was once a man paused, snarling all the while. The urge to inhale was strong. She shined like the sun and he wanted to feel the sun. He wanted to feel warmth and comfort and something *good* for once in its miserable, never-ending existence. But it stayed where it was, waiting for what, it did not know.

"Go," the female said, looking directly at them. Followed by, "Go now."

The creature snapped its mouth closed, the look of pity and understanding in the female's eyes its undoing. It made it feel shame, and it made it feel hope for the first time in recent memory. And so, instead of consuming her life force as the horrific voices in its head pushed it to do, the creature commanded its body to fold in on itself and prayed the wind would answer just this once and take it far away from temptation.

It could have been mere minutes or years later, for all the creature knew. But one of the same warriors returned, this time with a new female and a male that made the creature's skin tingle and the voices riot inside its head. Once fully manifested, it sniffed the air, trying to determine what was so different about the male. The creature had never felt anything like it before and it was even further disgruntled to learn there was no bright spark among them. That angered the creature enough that it moved quickly toward them, intent on causing harm. It received a jolt however, when the strange male lifted off the ground and his eyes turned a familiar black. The hesitation cost it dearly and it soon found itself trapped by small shackles of air. That pissed the creature off, having its own element used against them, but no matter what it tried it could not free itself. The creature was then forced to listen as its worst, most shameful characteristics were talked about.

"He's a complete unknown. What's more, his degeneration is far worse than yours ever was. Look at him," the young male demanded. "He's so white he looks like an albino, his hair is like limp black straw, and his mouth does that creepy unhinging thing."

The creature hissed, taking exception to the words. It knew it was a lost cause, its mind had debilitated to the point of madness, but not quite to the point where it had lost all cognitive awareness. Life was incredibly cruel. After a while, the young one dared approach and the creature took a swipe, barely missing flesh and bone. Trying to advance again, it stilled when it heard something it thought never to hear again. Its name.

"Knox. That's your name, isn't it? Knox? You were once an Air Warden."

The voices inside the creature's head grew louder and the abyss grew colder and darker, causing the pain to writhe and wriggle once more. Giving in, the creature ignored the temptation of its old name and opened its mouth, prepared to kill the male even though its meagre energy would not sustain the creature for long. It was still better than nothing. Besides, they were taunting it. The male continued with its useless words for a time, and the creature continued to ignore them. It couldn't afford the hope they wrought. That was, until the female spoke.

"Hey! Quit it! This guy here is your best bet. Either let him try or I'll put you down right now. It would save us time and put you out of your misery. Choose," she demanded.

The creature stilled once more, pushing aside the black pit of hunger and despair, and actually processed her words. They truly wanted to help? It wasn't ignorant of who and what she was. She was an executioner. She would take its head if it gave her half a chance. But perhaps they were offering the same to him? A chance? Unable to reply, the creature stood still and hoped they understood it was as compliant as it was going to get. Unfortunately for the young man, he began to glow and emanate a familiar and very powerful energy. Knox was unable to stop himself from rushing to meet the energy and trying to inhale it as quickly as it could.

It would be much later, when it realised it had referred to itself by name for the first time in decades. And exactly what had been given back to it that day.

A name.

An identity.

A life.

CHAPTER ONE

"My lady," Knox bowed low, showing respect and deference for Dawn's position. Not only was she a member of the IDC, but she was one of only two female life wardens on the planet. She was really freaking important. "I am at your service."

Dawn didn't respond right away, her bright, hazel eyes narrowing on Knox for several seconds, before she sighed, the sound filled with disappointment and causing Knox to study her more closely. He hadn't had much to do with Dawn since his return to the land of the living and had never been lucky enough to run into her in his previous life either. To his knowledge, they had always been stationed on different continents, with him being largely in South America and Dawn in Europe. As a life warden, Dawn had no doubt travelled regularly and had probably been in Australia many times over the years. But Knox had lived permanently in South America, moving only within that region with his Order and his sons and had never set foot in Australia until he had been recalled just before the Great Massacre. And from that moment on, his life had irrevocably changed. His transition into a chade had not been a slow degeneration, but a swift decline into madness and pain. After his hopeless existence for decades, he had been cured, reunited with his sons, given a purpose with Dave's Dive, and then a leadership role with the chadens. So, he hadn't had much time to get to know many other wardens or paladins, let alone the new members of the IDC. He was more than happy to get to know the beauty standing before him though, but Dawn seemed less than pleased with the prospect.

Dawn's voice, when she finally spoke, was dry. "Thank you. But I assure you, I can service myself."

Knox felt his eyes widen and he very deliberately did not look at any of his sons. They were notorious pranksters as well as flirts and Dawn had made that way too easy. Knox cleared his throat, "I'm happy for you. I happen to have made a career out of servicing myself too. But I think we might be talking about two different things here. The Great Mother seems to think I may be of some assistance to you. Regarding the orphanage and the clinic, and perhaps even the ill paladins."

Dawn's hazel eyes were wide, and she covered her mouth with her hand, shaking her head furiously. "Gods! I did not mean it like –" she snapped her mouth shut, glaring at her four paladins, who were lined up behind her. She then schooled her features and turned back to Knox. "I simply meant that I am capable of handling all the tasks I was given. But thank you."

'Hmm, that thank you sounds remarkably like fuck off,' Kai noted, speaking to Knox directly through their very new Order link.

'Yeah, no shit,' Knox agreed. He didn't bother turning to his three paladins who had ventured closer upon hearing the conversation. Blu, Max, and Mordecai had given Knox permission to form an official Order with his sons a couple of months before the new IDC was formed. He may not be a warden anymore, but he required vitality just the same. At first, he had been reluctant to accept the offer from his sons. He feared hurting them in any way and he wasn't sure he could trust his newfound healing. But, after much open communication, he had learned that his reluctance to form an Order with them was hurting them anyway. After being separated from him for so long and thinking him dead or lost forever to

madness, they craved closeness. Knox could safely say it was the best decision of his life, and his boys were right. Their relationship had grown by leaps and bounds, and they were all managing to straddle the line between father/son and liege/knight well within their Order of Domus.

Refocusing on the matter at hand, Knox tried again. "I have no doubt about that, my lady. As a female life warden, you are more than qualified to handle whatever life throws at you."

For some reason, his compliment fell flat once more, with Dawn's face shutting down. He looked over Dawn's shoulder to find one of her male paladins gesturing quickly with his hand in a slashing motion near his neck. Knox wasn't the smartest man in the room, but he knew that meant to shut the hell up. He snapped his mouth closed but couldn't deny he was starting to feel a little frustrated. He was usually much better received by women.

"Yes. Well. This life warden is not in need of your aid," Dawn's voice was clipped and cool and she spun around to leave.

Knox reached out and grabbed her arm in a gentle loose grip. They both immediately gasped, and Knox dropped his hand with a swift apology. He had no idea why Dawn was gasping but Knox had felt something like electricity jump from her arm to his. It wasn't altogether unpleasant, but he didn't think it was normal either. Still, not only had his orders come from Mother Nature herself, he was also a stubborn son of a bitch, so he tried one more time to figure out what was going on with the complicated woman in front of him. "Don't go. I apologise. I seem to have offended you in some way."

Dawn rubbed her arm, frown lines coming to life on her forehead as she looked down at the limb. Then she looked up and met Knox's gaze directly. She stared at him for a moment before her shoulders slumped and she sighed, shaking her long hair back over her shoulders with the motion of her head. "No. *I* am the one who should be sorry. You've caught me at the wrong time – I'm in a poor mood. I was just the wrong audience for your word choice."

"My word choice?" Knox quickly replayed the conversation in his head. Sure, there had been a misunderstanding and an innuendo in the beginning of their conversation, but even then, he had been nothing but polite.

"When you repeatedly referred to me as a life warden," Dawn said, obviously thinking she was clarifying things, but it only served to confuse Knox more.

"But you *are* a warden of the life element," Knox pointed out, talking slowly.

"I am," Dawn allowed. "But that is not *all* I am."

Knox reared back, a lightbulb turning on in his head. It appeared Dawn had taken exception to him mentioning her status. Knox couldn't say he fully understood her reasons why, but clearly it was a sensitive issue for her. He, of all people, understood what it was like to be judged on *what* you were, rather than *who* you were. First, as a chade and then as a chaden. So it was no hardship to say, "Of course not. You are also a woman and a friend – and all manner of other things I haven't yet had the privilege to discover. But I sure would like to."

Dawn looked surprised. "You would?" she asked.

He wanted to jump up and down and say *hell yeah!* But he remained the mature adult he was, instead replying calmly, "I would."

"Huh. Okay, well. That's good … I guess." Dawn looked at him like a puzzle she was trying to solve. "Please accept my apologies for my behaviour. Not the best first impression, huh?"

Knox appreciated the self-deprecating humour, and he chuckled. "Trust me, I've certainly had worse. And yes, I accept your apology. Although, it's hardly necessary. If this is you in a bad mood, I think you're doing okay."

Dawn shook her head, "As I said, you've been unlucky enough to catch me at a bad time. Thank you for accepting my apology – and for being so understanding." She paused, cocking her head to the side in thought, before barking out an appealing laugh. "I can't believe I said I service myself."

Knox smiled and then felt his grin widen as he watched Dawn giggle and shake her head. Her cheeks flushed a lovely shade of pink and her thick, chestnut hair swished around her shoulders with every move of her head. It seemed she wasn't as uptight as he had been starting to believe. In fact, her sense of humour was alive and kicking and she wasn't afraid to laugh at herself. Knox appreciated that in a person. "Should we start again? I am Knox, an air chaden. These are my sons as well as my Order," he gestured to his three boys over his shoulder without turning. "And Dana thought I might be of some assistance to you."

"Assistance ... would be nice," Dawn allowed, speaking slowly as if not fully on board with the words yet.

But Knox didn't care. He was taking them as acceptance and running with them. Dawn had intrigued him, made him laugh, and shown she was independent. She was also astoundingly beautiful, with a statuesque body of an Amazon warrior of old. He was eager to spend more time with her any way he could. Helping her out at Dana's request was the perfect excuse. "Excellent. Just tell me where you need me and when and I'll be there."

"That ... would also be nice," Dawn said, just as slowly.

Knox grinned. It seemed the woman didn't quite know what to make of him. He could definitely work with that. Still, one thing was troubling him. "If I may ask, what had you in such a mood?"

Dawn's mouth firmed and her eyes narrowed in the direction of a male warden in the corner of the room. "I admit, I'm a little sensitive about the whole 'female life warden' thing as it stands. I was placed on a pedestal as a child and treated like royalty. I'm sure a lot of wardens would have loved it, but I always found it to be ..." she trailed off.

"Fucking annoying?" Knox filled in the blank.

Dawn was startled into a laugh, her eyes lighting up happily. "Yes. Fucking annoying. Anyway, that douche nozzle over there," she gestured to the man she had been staring at. "He is a life warden. He seemed to think I would welcome his advances to make little life warden babies. It is our duty, after all," Dawn added, mockingly.

Knox felt his whole body tense up and he clenched his fists. His feet began to lift off the ground and air swirled around him in a menacing fashion. Kai, Kane, and Kellan were quick to move next to him, each reaching out and placing a hand on him to soothe and calm him. Knox took a few deep breaths, feeling his feet hit the floor again.

He knew his anger was over the top – he hardly knew Dawn. But the thought of some prick soliciting her for sex and/or babies made him see red.

"I'm going to go punch him in the nutsack," he stated. Before he could move, Dawn's warm laugh gave him pause. And he looked over to find her smiling and happy.

"I think we're going to get along just fine, Knox," she said, absolutely delighting him. "And I think you and my potentate will also become good friends. He had the same idea, though it included nose-breaking instead. I'm going to tell you what I told Micah; I can take care of myself. Percival isn't the first to solicit me in such a way and he won't be the last. Still, it clearly affected me more than I realised, considering I practically jumped down your throat when we first met. But Percival had just gotten through giving me a lecture about how special I am – being a female life warden and how it was my responsibility to continue on the legacy."

"I understand," Knox said. And he did. He didn't blame Dawn one bit. He looked over at Percival one last time, assuring himself he wouldn't forget the other man's features and hoping they would cross paths at some point in the future. He then looked at Micah, Dawn's Captain and potentate. The other man gave him a knowing look, as well as a small nod, and Knox knew they were on the same page.

"Well, thank you. Umm, tomorrow I will be at the orphanage with Celeste. Although the headquarters here are almost complete, there is still a lot to do and a lot to organise for the children's home," Dawn informed him.

Knox nodded his head. There was still a lot of physical construction to be done, as well as the entire interior and the landscaping. His chadens had started on the HQ building first and now that they were down to the finer details, like paint colours as the IDC had just been discussing an hour before, they were now focusing their attention on the new orphanage. Knox was so proud of his fellow chadens and all they had accomplished at Eden. To say they were proving themselves to be useful as well as valued members of society was an understatement. That was not to say Knox was under any illusions. He knew how hard it was going to be for paladins and wardens to accept chadens back into their exclusive world. As chades, many of them had done terrible things. And on the flip side to that, rangers, wardens and paladins had committed atrocities to chades as well. The chade infection had a lot to answer for and it caused numerous physical as well as mental and emotional injuries. But the one thing it didn't do was erase the memory of the time they all spent as chades. It was going to be a long road. *But at least we have a road now,* Knox reminded himself.

Getting himself back on track, he nodded to Dawn and her Order. "We will meet you there. Mid-morning okay? I have some things to see to myself with the chadens in the early hours."

"Yes. Of course. That would be fine," Dawn replied.

Knox began to walk off, his boys in tow, but he paused when Dawn called his name. "Yes?"

"Thank you," she said simply, smiling at him.

Knox felt like her smile hit him straight in the gut. "It's my pleasure," he said, immediately praying their relationship was going to be just that. A pleasure.

CHAPTER TWO

"I'm nervous. Why am I nervous?" Dawn queried, pacing back and forth along the cliff's edge of Eden.

"Because you're waiting for a smoking hot man to turn up and help you hammer in some nails." All eyes turned to Piper. Dawn's second in command shrugged, "What? That wasn't a euphemism. You're literally building a door today."

Dawn groaned, ignoring Piper as well as her other three paladins as she looked out over the cliff and at the vast ocean below. She liked to think she was in a better mood than she had been yesterday when poor Knox had first introduced himself, but the truth was she was tired. She had spent the better part of the night tossing and turning in bed, replaying her initial conversation with Knox over and over. The whole thing made her cringe and she had her doubts that the chaden would even show up. If she were him, she would boycott the meeting – no matter what the Great Mother said.

"Oh, he'll show up. Don't worry," Reid said, looking smugly male.

"How do you know?" Dawn asked.

Reid looked pained for a moment before glancing at his three counterparts. "You explain it," he said to Willow, giving her a little shove in Dawn's direction.

Willow, not one for taking crap on any level whatsoever, shoved Reid back. "She hasn't understood for the past five hundred years. What makes you think she will now? I'm not explaining crap. I'm just going to sit back and watch the show."

Dawn frowned at her Order, completely clueless as to what they were talking about. It was true, she didn't have the best track record when it came to men. And she was absolutely terrible at picking up on signals. Did her Order know something about Knox she did not? The thought caused her belly to jitter, though she did not understand why. She had never spoken to Knox before yesterday, although, she had talked with his sons on a few occasions. They were very handsome young men, as well as charismatic and too charming for their own good. She had no trouble deciphering their flirtatious behaviour at all. Besides, she happened to know their bark was worse than their bite, so to speak. Sure, they were ladies' men, but they weren't as prolific as their reputations suggested.

"So, you think he will come? Even though I embarrassed myself yesterday?" she asked her Order. She had no idea why it was so important to her that Knox come. Nor why the thought of him thinking ill of her bothered her so much.

"Dawn, you did not embarrass yourself. Nothing about you is embarrassing, and I guarantee Knox feels the same way. It was just bad timing and poor word choice on his part. Although, it is normal and expected to be shown respect, Dawn," Micah pointed out.

Dawn sighed, turning from her paladins once more. She knew it was expected. She knew it was normal. But that didn't change her feelings. By the time she had reached one-hundred and had already gone through two council mandated Orders, she had been sick of the title of 'Life Warden'. At the time, her local council in London had taken it upon themselves to place the strongest life paladins with her – no matter that she didn't like any of the men chosen. But after breaking two Orders within eighty years, the local council had thrown their hands up in the air and finally called in the IDC. Garret, Mordecai and Blu had attended her personally and did what they could to diffuse the situation. Even back then, she had been one of only a handful of female wardens attuned to life. Nobody had wanted to upset her further. In the end, it was Mordecai and Blu who had thankfully given her permission to create an Order of her choosing.

It had taken her less than a week to choose her childhood friend, Micah, as her Captain. He was a life paladin as well as a potentate. Piper, a paladin affiliated with death came next, followed by Willow and Reid. She caused a bit of a stir with those two because they were neither life nor death paladins – the typical balancing factors for life and death wardens. But Dawn had felt a natural and instinctive draw to the siblings and had asked them personally to join her Order. Willow as an earth paladin, and Reid as a water paladin, had been suitably shocked at the offer, but after a mere day they had agreed, both feeling the connection as well. It had been smooth sailing since then, and even though they respected her and her position, they did not fawn over her or smother her. Still, they were rather strict in making sure others showed her due respect. The way Knox had introduced himself had no doubt gone a long way with her Order.

"Look, here he comes. No need to worry yourself sick over something so silly," Micah pointed out from behind her.

Turning, Dawn was struck by the loose-limbed gait of the chaden. He moved as if the air itself parted for him – which, it could very well do. Chadens were still very much enigmas. His dark hair was kind of long, waving behind him like a soft flag, and his grey eyes were lit up with merriment at something one of his sons said. Dawn took her time to study him some more as the four men made their way to them. Knox had a square jaw and a straight nose. He had more lines on his face than most wardens, but Dawn could not fault him for those. The last few decades of his life had been pure hell. Comparing his face to that of his identical sons, Dawn could easily see the resemblance, although his sons had none of the harshness in their visage nor countenance. Their lives had known grief but not the physical hardship of their father. They still looked young and baby-faced, gorgeous enough to be on a cover of a magazine. But, to her, their father was far more alluring.

Aiming for casual but in charge, Dawn stood up straight and plastered a smile on her face. "Good morning."

Knox's face froze for a moment, his eyes travelling over her features before he grinned, offering a wave to everyone assembled on the cliff. "Morning."

Dawn stood in silence for a moment, wondering what the hell she was supposed to do with him. She knew Dana had thought he may be useful, but Dawn was yet to speak with the woman and question her. It was true, Dawn had a long list of things to see to. But she revelled in finally being useful to her people in a hands-on way. The idea of requiring aid for her responsibilities stung a little, but as she peeked at Knox's aura, she saw a man who desperately wanted the same thing. He yearned for purpose and the chance to prove himself. Dawn felt he had already achieved both of those things, but as a perfectionist and an overachiever herself, she couldn't fault him. So, it was with much greater enthusiasm that she welcomed him and formally introduced her paladins.

"Thank you for coming. I'm not sure if you have officially met my Order? This is Micah, my potentate, Piper, my second in command, Willow, and her brother Reid. We are the Order of Adalla."

Knox's smile was genuine as he said hello to everyone before introducing his own paladins. "Kai, Kane, and Kellan – my sons and paladins. Kai is a potentate and we don't really have a second in command. We don't really have a first in command either," Knox added, rolling his eyes before whispering to Dawn in a conspiratorial way, "I'm not allowed to play favourites."

"Please, everyone knows I'm the favourite. The baby is always the favourite," Kellan pointed out.

"You wish. The oldest is the best and favourite," Kane quipped.

Kai rolled his eyes, "As if. We all know *I'm* the favourite. I'm the only potentate, clearly I'm the superior model."

"You're the middle model. You're simply a carbon copy of both of us. We bookended you and you got all the potentate abilities by osmosis," Kane said, nudging his brother with his shoulder.

All three men grinned at each other and Dawn could see the very deep, very unique connection they all shared. She wasn't surprised. Triplets were incredibly rare in their society, especially identical triplets. Had they been born wardens, they would likely have held a higher position than her, even though they were affiliated with air. "Well, today we are constructing the front door," Dawn finally offered, gesturing to the now complete building behind her.

It was a truly lovely piece of architecture, and now that the windows were going in, it was time to fit the exterior doors. There were still many chadens working on the project, but as one of the people put in charge of the running of the orphanage, Dawn had wanted to help with the entryway. It was symbolic. The problem was, she had no idea how to do that. There was a pile of materials and tools waiting to be put to use, as Celeste had promised. Speaking of Celeste, Dawn's best friend was supposed to be there helping with the symbolic door raising.

Knox walked over to the gaping hole in the entranceway before looking at the piles of lumber. "Is this for the door?" he asked.

Dawn nodded, "Yes. Do you know how to build a door?"

Knox grinned, "As a matter of fact I do. Dave's motel as well as the bar required extensive renovations. It was a steep learning curve, but it gave all of us chadens something tangible to do."

Dawn jolted a little over the reminder of his chaden status. It was so easy to forget he was anything but whole and well. Looking between him and his sons, she felt a whole bunch of pity as well as admiration well up for them all. "Will you help me?" she asked, figuring Celeste would either show up or she wouldn't. She knew her friend was also very busy, and Dawn didn't begrudge her time with her son or lover either.

"I would love to," Knox replied. He gestured at his sons, who happily moved forward to lay the wood and tools out neatly.

What followed was a quick yet detailed rundown of how a door was made, hinged, and hung. Dawn found the whole thing very enjoyable. Or perhaps it was the company that was so pleasant. *The view sure was*, she thought. She was so busy checking out Knox's very fine arse, that she missed the nail she was attempting to hammer and hit her thumb instead. "Ow!" she cried, jumping up and shaking her hand. "Ow, ow, ow, ow!"

"What happened? Let me see," Knox demanded, looking concerned. He grabbed her hand in a firm yet gentle grip and winced when he saw how red the top of her thumb looked. "Ouch."

Dawn glared at him, "That's what I said."

Knox chuckled, the laugh lines surrounding his mouth and eyes crinkling in an appealing manner. "I heard you. I think all of Eden heard you."

Dawn snatched her hand back. *So much for him being appealing*, she thought. *He was a complete jerk.*

Knox held up his hands, "I'm sorry. I don't mean to laugh. I know how much that hurts. Here, let me help before all the blood rushes to your nail and it turns black."

Dawn was about to tell him not to bother. Life was hers to command and it had healing properties to a certain extent. Besides, a few hits of vitality from her paladins and her poor thumb would be good as new. But she became entranced as his dark grey eyes became even darker until they were almost black. The wind picked up around them and a small whirlwind of cool air brushed over her thumbnail. It tickled as much as it soothed, and Dawn smiled at the small but mighty tornado. It dissipated after a few minutes and Dawn was left staring at her now painless thumb. It still looked like it was going to bruise, but it no longer hurt.

Looking up, she was about to thank Knox when she blurted out instead, "Your eyes."

Knox froze, immediately ducking his head. "Ah, sorry about that. A remnant from being a chade. I, ah, just remembered I needed to do something. I'll see you later, Dawn. You've done a great job here this morning."

Knox fled before Dawn could so much as utter a goodbye. "Um, thank you!" she called after Knox's retreating back. She then looked back at his sons, who seemed to share a commiserating look with her own paladins before they hurried after Knox.

"And that had been going so well," Willow shook her head.

"What had? The door? Yes, I think I've done a great job," Dawn agreed, looking down at the completed door. All they had to do was put the hinges on and hang it. It was a shame Knox had to leave.

"Yes, Dawn. The door," Willow rolled her eyes at her.

Dawn narrowed her own eyes, "Why do I hear sarcasm in your voice?" she demanded.

"Sarcasm? I'm sure I have no idea what you're talking about," Willow said, eyes wide and innocent.

"See," Dawn pointed at her paladin. "That right there. Sarcasm."

Micah patted Dawn on the shoulder, "Ignore her. Come on. Let's get this fabulous door you built hung up."

"Let's," Dawn agreed. But she spent the next hour with one eye focused on the door and one eye searching for Knox.

CHAPTER THREE

Knox ignored the knowing looks of his sons as he flitted around Eden, talking with chadens and answering their questions. Yes, he had basically been assigned to Dawn for the foreseeable future, but he still had responsibilities with his fellow chadens. He, along with Dex, were their constants in this new and complex situation they found themselves in. Knox knew they were all grateful to have been made whole again, the affliction that was the chade disease was in their pasts now. But it was still a recent past and being a chade was traumatising. He'd been lucky. He had his sons to ground him, to make his new life worth living. But a lot of the chadens had no family, and no friends. They were also so new in society that not many wardens or paladins went out of their way to make friends either. Knox couldn't really blame them. The changes wrought in their society in such a short timeframe were huge. Still, Knox knew the chadens needed something to live for, and something to ground them. Thankfully, the IDC was giving them the former by delegating them work and showing trust. And Knox was happy to be the latter for as long as it took.

Seeing Dex talking with Celeste as well as Slate in what would be the backyard of the orphanage, Knox headed their way. "Hey. Everything okay?" he asked.

"Knox," Dex looked surprised to see him. "Hey. I thought you were playing personal assistant to Dawn."

Knox shrugged, avoiding eye contact with his good friend and fellow chaden. "I am. Just taking a break, checking on other things, you know?"

Dex squinted at him, but it was Celeste who called bullshit. "What did she say?" Celeste asked, looking amused but sounding resigned.

Knox looked up, "What do you mean?"

"Dawn is my best friend, so I'm not going to talk behind her back. However, I want to give you fair warning; she is a little clueless sometimes. I know, I know, it seems crazy, right? I mean, she is mature and confident, and her domain is life. She can literally read you like an open book. Not to the same extent as Max, of course, but she can still see your aura. But, trust me when I say, Dawn can be a little oblivious. I think it's because she's trained her brain never to pry into people's privacy. It kind of puts some blinders on her under certain circumstances."

Knox listened to Celeste keenly. He had noted Dawn's less than stellar observational skills in some areas. But then she was more adept than Sherlock Holmes in others. Add in those astounding looks, and Knox was more than a little intrigued on a purely male level. "What kind of circumstances?"

"The kind of circumstances that involve her accepting compliments for anything other than her duties. Or judging when someone likes her for more than just her status," Celeste divulged.

Knox thought about that for a moment, before saying, "So, basically any time it has to do with Dawn just being Dawn?"

"Precisely." Celeste leaned in close and whispered in his ear. "As well as around sexy men – such as yourself."

Knox grinned, more than a little relieved and happy to hear it. He shook a mocking finger at Celeste, "Now, don't go flirting. You had your chance. I offered you pizza and you declined it."

"Pizza? Did someone say pizza?" Max's voice reached them a

moment before the short woman herself. She looked around the small group, her face falling comically. "There's no pizza."

Knox bowed low, "I am so sorry to disappoint you, my lady. But we were talking about metaphorical pizza."

Max's brows knit as she thought about it for a moment, before deciding, "It's hard to choose what is better at this stage. I'm so hungry. But then, Ryker cut me off two days ago," she revealed.

"Cut you off from what? Pizza?" Dex asked, confused.

Celeste giggled, "Dex, pizza is a euphemism for sex."

Dex's eyes popped wide. "It is? Since when?"

Knox laughed, enjoying the easy banter as well as the camaraderie. He watched as Ryker, Lark, and Beyden moved swiftly toward them, he and his three sons making room for Max's three paladins in their little circle.

"Max." Ryker's voice was exasperated. "Please do not disappear like that."

"Although, how she can be so stealthy with that stomach of hers is anyone's guess," Lark chimed in, softening the words with a quick smile.

Knox looked at Max's pregnant belly and took note of how far it extended from her body now. It was also very, very round looking. To his inexperienced eyes, she looked about ready to pop, but he knew she still had a couple of months to go. But then, she was very short and the only place for her belly to go was straight out. When Evangeline had gotten pregnant with the triplets, she had also been huge, but she had been over six-feet tall, creating the illusion of a smaller bump for the better part of the pregnancy. But then, she had done her best to hide all signs of the impending birth for the longest time as well. Shaking his head to rid it of thoughts he had not dwelled on since his return, he refocused on the ongoing conversation.

"I was just telling everyone how you won't have sex with me anymore," Max stated.

"You what? Max!" Ryker bellowed.

"What? It's true," Max fired back.

Ryker looked pained but also resigned as he took Max's hand in his own. "Babe, we've talked about this. No sharing details of our sex life with the world."

Max shrugged, "It's just Dex ... and Celeste ... and Knox ... and the triplets ... oh, and Slate. Hi Slate," she added, waving to the man.

Knox winced, having entirely forgotten the earth warden was even there. He had stepped away when Celeste began talking about Dawn, and although he wasn't exactly within the gossiping ring, he was still close enough to hear all that was being said.

Slate smiled small, nodding at Max. "Hello, my lady."

Knox found it interesting that Max didn't correct Slate. Usually, Max hated being referred to by any formal title.

'It's because he needs to. It would make him uncomfortable to call me Max. He feels the need to make amends.'

Max's voice rang clear and true in his mind. It wasn't the first time she had spoken to him directly, so it no longer surprised him. Max was powerful and full of unique abilities. He simply nodded back to show he had heard and made a mental note not to tease the other man about it. If Max felt it was important, then it was important to Knox as well. Still, he addressed him, drawing him into the conversation. "I'm sorry I interrupted earlier."

"It's fine. We were just discussing the landscaping for the back area here," Slate divulged.

"Cool," Max chirped, "What did you decide?"

"Slate thought that instead of getting a bunch of earth wardens and chadens to stimulate everything with their powers, that it would be good to put out a call for everyone to come and join in a planting day," Celeste replied, smiling widely at Slate.

Slate looked slightly uncomfortable under everyone's scrutiny. "It was just a thought."

"It's a wonderful thought. Thank you, Slate. Let's do it. Start spreading the word. We can have kind of like a community day where everyone can have a look through the new HQ and the orphanage – even though the latter isn't ready yet. HQ is coming along nicely now and almost completely decorated. It will be officially opening soon."

They talked for a few more minutes, deciding on a date one week from now and also dividing up who would inform who.

"Dad will tell Dawn," Kai volunteered out of the blue.

Max turned to Kai, eyebrows raised. "He will?"

Kai grinned, "Yep. He needs something to break the ice. He's hiding over here because he took something she said the wrong way and it hurt his feelings."

"Kai!" This time it was Knox's turn to bellow.

"What? It's true," Kane supported his brother.

Everyone was staring at him. "I am not hiding from Dawn. And my feelings aren't hurt," he told them all. They all continued to stare at him until he snarled at them all and stalked off – straight in Dawn's direction, just to prove a point.

The closer he got to the tall beauty, the more anxious he became. Because, yes, he had been hurt. He tried very hard to forget that his body and his powers were permanently altered thanks to his chade status. But using his powers was second nature to him and he hadn't thought twice about using them to help poor Dawn's thumb. Which was why he practically ran away when she had mentioned his eyes. It had been a stark reminder that he was a changed man. That he was a lesser man. And for some reason, he did not want Dawn to see him that way. Which was why he took the cowards way out, relaying the information about the gardening and community day to the first of Dawn's paladins he reached. Willow. She listened politely, but the look she gave him was full of hidden meaning. Knox nodded slightly, promising himself he would get his head back together before their next meeting. He was due to meet up with Dawn at the Training Lodge the following day and he hoped one night was enough to think on what Celeste had told him.

CHAPTER FOUR

Knox showed up at the Training Lodge bright and early, his sons dutifully in tow. Dawn released the breath she hadn't been aware she had been holding. She had spent the night fretting over Knox and wondering if she should just tell him she didn't require his aid. Just because she enjoyed his company didn't mean he felt the same way about her. He was no doubt just doing his duty as the Great Mother had commanded him to do. Dawn was sure it had nothing to do with actually wanting to help her at all. She was opening her mouth to let Knox off the hook when he spoke first.

"I'm sorry about leaving so abruptly yesterday. I thought you had an issue with my eyes. You know, the whole black pits of despair thing," he stated bluntly.

Knox's grin was self-deprecating, but no less appealing to her as he made his statement without so much as a good morning. And then she processed what he said. She was suitably horrified and rushed to say, "Oh, no. I didn't mean it like that, honest. They just surprised me is all – kind of mesmerised me. That's why I commented on them."

"Mesmerised?" Knox looked sceptical. "They don't bother you? *I* don't bother you?"

Dawn was genuinely perplexed. "Why would you bother me?"

Other than for the fact that he was causing her to have sex dreams for the first time in her entire life, that was. Her Order, having heard her inner monologue, snickered in her head. She shushed them, not bothering to be embarrassed. Some boundaries had been torn down centuries ago.

Knox smiled at her, looking more at ease. "Because I was a chade. Because I still have some of the traits of a chade."

"The fact that you were once unwell does not bother me in the slightest. Other than feeling sorry you had to go through that of course. And you no longer have any traits of a chade. The chade was an infection. You now have extra abilities, sure, but that is a side effect of the infection."

Ever since the truth had been revealed about the chades, Dawn had come to hate the term. She didn't believe it was an accurate descriptor because it made it sound like the wardens were whole new people – *less* people – rather than merely sick people. If she had her way, she would call it the Chade Virus and chadens would be called wardens. That wasn't to say Dawn didn't approve of Max giving them a new title. She actually did. And she thought it was a clever way to give them back some of their power, as well as satisfying the wider community. Still, Dawn couldn't change her other feelings either. She explained as much to Knox, only realising she had been lecturing him on her personal doctrine for a solid twenty minutes.

"I'm sorry," she chuckled uneasily. "I'm sure I've bored you half to death by now."

Knox was looking at her with shining eyes and a small smile. He shook his head, "Not at all. In fact, I could listen to you all day."

"You like politics?" she questioned, unsure why her Order shook their heads at her and groaned as if they were in pain.

Knox looked at them and grinned, before turning back to Dawn. "Celeste was right. No. Idea," he said slowly and succinctly.

"You've been talking to Celeste? And what do you mean?" Dawn asked, hoping beyond hope her best friend hadn't said anything to humiliate her.

"When I said I could listen to you all day, it was because I love the sound of your voice. And I heartily approve of what you were saying. You are very intelligent and very eloquent," Knox informed her.

Dawn felt her pulse accelerate, loving what Knox was saying but not sure whether to believe him or not. She was also not sure how to respond. So she simply said, "Uh, thanks?" before moving on to a new subject. "I am shifting a large amount of things from the infirmary here to the new clinic at HQ. Mainly the computers, as well as all the paper records. Most of the equipment is staying because we are getting all new equipment there. Jasminka is still making her lists of things she says we will need."

Dawn had become good friends with the human doctor shortly after she arrived. Jasminka shared a lot of the same traits as Dawn herself did, and they had simply clicked. Jazz had made it her life's work to help and heal people, offer them support and counselling, as well as hope. In essence, that is what Dawn's purpose was as well. She had been so excited to learn all about human healing methods from Jasminka, having been barred from such knowledge before. She was responsible for a human domain – a bodily domain – and yet, they were not taught how the body worked. Dawn thought it was absolutely ridiculous and had been pushing for a basic health care system for years. Now that she was on the IDC, she was able to ensure such things happened. And the new clinic at Eden was an exciting start.

"Heavy lifting then?" Knox smiled happily. "You've come to the right place."

"Because you are very strong and muscular?" Dawn asked, before she could stop herself. Knox was wearing a simple t-shirt and well-worn jeans. Both were rather tight, accentuating his leanly muscled frame.

"I was thinking more in terms of my element," Knox corrected her, a blast of warm wind rushing past her face. "But, hey, I like your version better."

Knox's bright grey and yellow aura shined around him like a halo, Dawn's special sight catching her by surprise. She had not intended to peek. But Knox was so happy and relaxed, that his aura was simply sparkling. It was lovely, full of warmth and humour, love and respect, as well as telling her Knox was a born leader. She knew nothing about him as a warden before, and nothing about his previous Order, but she could see the great well of power he carried so effortlessly. The man before her was whole and unbroken. "She really did do a wonderful job," Dawn murmured.

Knox tilted his head to one side, giving Dawn his full attention once more. "Who?"

"Max. There is no taint within you at all. I wonder if this is how your aura looked before …" she trailed off, catching herself before she touched him with her hands. She also abruptly realised what she had been saying. Dawn felt herself flush. "And I'm being rude. I apologise."

"No," Knox was quick to say. "It's totally fine."

"I'm just so curious," Dawn tried to explain. "As a life warden, I find it hard to believe I was ignorant of the infection all this time. How could I have missed the signs? Surely their auras should have warned me."

"You can see my aura right now?" Knox asked. "What's it like?"

"Shiny," Dawn promptly replied. "Happy. Healthy."

Knox wiped his brow in a teasing manner, "Phew. That's good to know."

Dawn returned his smile, feeling very comfortable in his presence. Peeking at his aura had confirmed something she had already suspected; Knox was a good man. And good men were worth getting to know, she told herself. Piper and Willow chimed in agreeing wholeheartedly with her through the bond.

"How did chades look to you?" Knox asked presently.

Dawn frowned a little but answered honestly. "Like blackholes."

Knox's smile was sad, "That is how it felt."

"I'm sorry," Dawn repeated.

"It was hardly your fault," Knox pointed out.

"I'm not to blame, no. But in a way I was still responsible. As were the rest of the wardens. But I feel especially responsible because of my domain. Life – with all it entails – is mine to read and mine to feel. I can manipulate it to a certain degree. But when I looked at a chade I saw nothing but an abyss – a lost cause. I failed to see a sick man. And that fault is most certainly mine."

"Dawn, *nobody* saw a sick man," Knox said.

"That doesn't take away the pain." Dawn's voice was resolute. "And thus, doesn't take away the blame."

∽

As the day wore on and Knox worked side by side with Dawn as she sorted what needed to be moved and what needed to stay, he contemplated what he knew of Dawn so far. He hadn't bothered to argue with her earlier in the day, knowing there was no chance of changing her mind. She clearly held herself to a high set of standards and when she failed to reach them, she beat herself up over it. Society probably had a lot to answer for there. No doubt she had been told from a young age that she was special and nothing less than perfect was acceptable. That she was a life warden first and *Dawn* second. But he knew it was her personality as well. She was kind and compassionate with a strong moral compass. She was a woman to be admired for sure. *And admire her I do,* Knox thought to himself. *And not just for her amazing body or that spectacular face of hers.* No, his feelings for Dawn were much deeper than that. It bothered him a little – being so enamoured of a woman so quickly and he wasn't sure what to call it.

'It's called a crush, dad,' Kellan's voice could be heard through the Order link loud and clear.

Knox smiled, mentally agreeing with his son, feeling true joy that they were connected on such a level. Once, he had thought never to see them again. And yet, here they were, bound on a level that surpassed that of parent and offspring. Knox had never been so proud.

"You're all aglow. What are you thinking about?"

Knox returned his attention to Dawn, his eyebrows raised in silent query. He was more than a little smitten when she blushed, ducking her head and releasing a self-deprecative chuckle.

"And I'm doing it again, aren't I? Being invasive. I apologise. I am not usually so nosey, I promise you. You're just ..." she trailed off.

"Easy to read?" Knox volunteered.

"More like *nice* to read," Dawn corrected.

Knox couldn't deny how good it felt for Dawn to associate him and nice. But he was curious as to what she meant. "What do you mean?"

"Oh," Dawn reached up and began twirling a thin strand of her hair around her finger. "It's nothing – silly really."

"Dawn, nothing you could say would ever be silly to me," he assured her.

Dawn searched his face for a moment, as if gauging the truth of his words before turning and looking at her paladins who were hanging out with the triplets. Willow and Piper nodded their heads and waved enthusiastically, causing Dawn to face Knox again. "I'm sorry. I've had poor judgement in the past with who I share things with. I sometimes trust my paladins more than I trust myself."

"I can understand that. I still doubt myself at times. But my sons are my anchor – I have the utmost respect and faith in them," Knox revealed.

Dawn smiled, "Your anchor. I like that." Then she explained herself; "Every person has a feel to them. Thanks to my element, I can sense that. And because of my empathy, I can feel it too. Some people are hard, some are raw, some people sting, some are easy, some are soft. And some, well, some just make you smile and want to curl up next to them like a cat beside a fireplace."

"And I'm like a fireplace?" Knox was loving this.

Dawn's smile was shy as she nodded. "Yes. Cosy. Nice. It is so refreshing to meet a nice guy."

"Not into the bad boys, huh?" Knox teased, pleased with her estimation of him. Although, he felt a little bad boy wouldn't go astray either.

"Bad boys have their merits," Dawn replied, ever serious and thoughtful with her answers. Then some frown lines appeared, and she cocked her head to the side. "Wait, are you flirting with me?"

Knox felt Dawn recognising flirty behaviours was a step in the right direction. Although, looking at her smirking paladins, he had to wonder just who had thought of it. "Do you want me to be?" he retorted – totally flirting.

"I ... don't know," Dawn answered slowly.

Knox climbed to his feet, commanding the wind to pick up and carry several loaded boxes. He looked back down at Dawn, "Why don't you think about it and let me know, huh?" He then sauntered out of the room with as much confidence as he could muster. He pointedly ignored the jeers from his sons inside his head telling him to add some sway to his junk-trunk, or flex his arse cheeks for Dawn's benefit.

CHAPTER FIVE

One week later, Knox was elbow-deep in dirt and loving it. He hadn't really thought of himself as having a green thumb in the past, but there was something to be said for digging around in the dirt and planting. Or perhaps it was simply the company he was keeping these days, he mused. A quick glance to his left showed Dawn chatting happily with Celeste as the pair arranged some coloured flowers into a small flower bed. Knox had been spending every other day with Dawn as she continued to oversee the interior construction for the orphanage and the new clinic in HQ. They had successfully set everything up with the end result being a medical infirmary complete with a laboratory and five beds for ill or hurt paladins, chadens or wardens. Knox had heard grumblings from particular wardens believing such a thing was not necessary but Dawn, as well as the rest of the IDC, shrugged it off and continued to educate the naysayers patiently. Well, some of them anyway, Knox allowed. He chuckled when he recalled Max's words to a group of visiting wardens.

"Get your heads out of your arses. Wardens may heal quickly with the help of vitality from their paladins, but paladins don't have that luxury. Besides, don't you think it will be nice to be able to have some-

where to go and talk about all your repressed emotions and daddy issues? I know a bunch of you bastards have those," Max scoffed.

"Something funny?" Dawn asked, smiling at him.

Knox was struck by her beauty once more, the smudge of dirt on her chin making her even more endearing to him. He wanted to reach out and wipe it away, but he wasn't sure where he stood with taking such liberties. Instead he smiled, admitting, "Max."

Dawn looked over to where Max was kneeling on the ground, somehow covered from head to toe in dirt and arguing with Ryker about lifting a tiny pot. "She is funny, I'll give you that."

The way Dawn said *funny* had Knox laughing out loud. It was clear she was using the word more in the *insane* context than the humorous one. "She is. But thank the Goddess for her."

"Indeed," Dawn agreed. "And that is something we can now do as well."

Knox followed Dawn's line of sight, watching as Dana stood with Mordecai, both arms wrapped around the warden's waist and a serene smile on her face as she watched the proceedings. When Dana's eyes came to rest on him, she nodded her head at him. Or, to be more accurate, gestured with her head. In Dawn's direction. Knox scowled at her, shaking his head. Dana widened her eyes and nodded her head back, pointing at Dawn this time. Knox knew of the trickery Dana had used to get Celeste and Axel back together. Apparently, she had the same agenda when it came to him and Dawn. Whilst it was nice to know he had a goddess rooting for him, he thought Dana might just be wrong this time. In the week following his attempt to overtly flirt with Dawn, he had received no definitive signs back. Dawn was her usual happy, chatty, oblivious self and Knox had resigned himself to the friend zone. Something he didn't oppose at all. The only thing was, he already had lots of female friends, and he wanted more than that with Dawn.

'Then do something about it,' Dana urged, startling him by speaking in his mind.

Knox pursed his lips, informing Dana, *'I already did.'*

'Oh, please, you call that trying? Even Ryker did better than that.

He said some crap about butterflies and dying – it was really romantic,' Max chimed in.

Knox looked at Max only to find her watching him along with Dana. *'Dead butterflies are romantic?'* he queried.

'You're missing the point, dad.'

Kane then joined the conversation, because why not? Knox thought. He was beginning to get a headache. *'And what is the point?'*

'The point is, Dawn may be a little slow on the uptake. But you aren't. Get flirty with it,' Kellan urged.

Knox grumbled to all the voices in his head, doing his best to ignore the suggestions that ranged from dead butterflies to tequila to basketball. *'Basketball?'* He raised his eyebrows at Kai, who was working in another section of the garden.

'I like basketball,' came the mild response.

Before he could respond to that random comment, Dawn reached over and grabbed his wrist. The warm touch startled him, and had sparks shooting through his hand. He looked up only to get caught in Dawn's hazel eyes.

"You're doing it wrong," Dawn informed him after clearing her throat and releasing him.

Knox raised his eyebrows, looking down at the hole he had just dug with his small spade. "Wrong? How the hell do you dig a hole wrong?"

Dawn laughed, "Before I met you, I would have wondered the same. But you've just demonstrated it."

Knox mock-scowled at her, delighted she was bantering with him. Perhaps he had been premature with his friend zone assessment. He was doing just fine on his own without all the asinine pointers from well-meaning friends and family, he assured himself. "Fine," he said. "What's wrong with my mighty hole?" To his dismay, several people around them paused what they were doing and looked at him.

'Mighty hole?' Max's question bounced around in his head and he could see her laughing her butt off across the garden. Her paladins asked her if she was okay, clearly not privy to their conversation and thankfully not hearing his comment. Max waved them away.

"Mighty hole?" Dawn repeated, humour in her eyes. She was

clearly holding back laughter as she pointed to it. "Well, that is precisely the problem. It is too *mighty*. You're planting pansies, not an oak tree."

Knox looked down, realising he had been so distracted by the ingrates in his head that he had dug a hole nearly a full metre deep and almost half as wide as that. Not wanting to look like more of a moron, he hastily said, "Actually, I was thinking we could put a pond in here."

"A pond?" Dawn's face lit up and she smiled wide. "I love that idea! Maybe Blu or Caspian could help with that. What do you think?"

Knox cleared his throat, begging his dick not to get hard when they were surrounded by all these people. But it was a battle of wills when he had Dawn's amazing cleavage to contend with. "For sure. That's exactly what I was thinking. Great minds think alike."

'Nice save,' Max said, giving him a thumbs-up.

"I know we are trying to be inclusive and do things largely without our powers, but I think in this instance, enlisting a water warden would be helpful," Dawn was saying.

Knox agreed. He knew less about ponds than he did about gardening. It was true that the earth wardens could have simply coaxed the seeds within the soil to grow, but Knox felt Slate had a good idea when he suggested they involve everyone and do it by hand. There were still a few earth wardens there overseeing the planting – and doing some coaxing – Slate included. But overall, wardens, paladins, and chadens were all getting their hands dirty equally. Knox was beyond content as he looked around the growing garden. Just then, he saw Ryker frown at something on the ground and then pick it up. To Knox's surprise, he called Slate over, moving away from Max and his Order, and the two bent their heads in what looked to be an intense discussion. "What do you think that is all about?" he nudged Dawn. "I thought Ryker didn't like Slate."

Dawn looked over and squinted at the pair, a smile gracing her face. "Ooohhh," she said.

"What? What does that mean? What did you see with your life hoodoo?" he questioned, seriously tempted to use the wind to eavesdrop for him.

"None of your business. And don't go enlisting the wind to help you either, Knox," she reprimanded him.

Knox tried to look innocent. "How did you know that was what I was thinking?"

"Please," she said, returning to her digging. "You're an open book."

If I'm such an open book, how come you can't see how much I want you? Knox silently asked. He was gearing up to talk to Dawn again when a familiar cold swept through his body. Jumping to his feet he saw Dex do the same, as well as several other chadens.

"What is it?" Dawn asked, looking concerned. She was immediately surrounded by her four paladins.

"I feel something ..." Knox answered absently, searching the garden for signs of danger.

"Dad?" Kai questioned, his sickle out, moving swiftly to his side with his brothers.

Knox couldn't see anything but there was no denying his feeling of unease – and recognition. Something was there. Something insidious. Something dangerous. *Something sick,* Knox thought. "Clear everybody out," he yelled to anyone and everyone who would listen.

Ryker was already on the case, hustling Max away with the rest of her paladins. Mordecai tugged a protesting Dana away, and other wardens were swooped up by their paladins. Soon, the only people left in the pretty half-finished garden were Dex, Knox, and the triplets. At least he thought they were – until Dawn spoke.

"Is it a sick paladin?"

Knox spun around, "What the hell are you still doing here?" He glared at her knights, "Get her out of here."

Dawn crossed her arms over her chest, her paladins not even twitching. "They obey my orders, not yours. And if there is a sick paladin, I will deal with him."

Knox scoffed in disbelief. "You will deal with him? You're a Life Warden, Dawn. Your powers are passive. What are you going to do? Sing him a song? Leave. Now." Knox wasn't trying to be a prick; he was simply worried about her. Especially when the feeling of darkness spread across the fresh lawn, a shadow building from the tree line.

Dawn pursed her lips, looking pissed, but there was also a flash of hurt in her eyes. "Good to know what you really think of me," she said. "Do I need to remind you that I outrank you? And have you forgotten I have been working with the sick paladins ever since the first case? *I* am the expert here. Not *you*."

"Oh really? Pretty sure being a walking stick man filled with hunger and hopelessness for fifty years as I tried to consume my brethren and defiled my element gives me an advantage," Knox snarked.

"Will you two cut it out?" Dex demanded. "Sheesh, I had no idea the sexual tension was so bad between you."

Knox was about to refute the comment – vehemently – when not one but two paladins staggered out of the trees, causing Knox's inner radar to go haywire. Like Dex, and all the other chadens he assumed, he had a connection with the infection. Like recognised like, he supposed, and the two men were definitely infected. They were thin and dirty and their clothes were torn. They weren't wearing any shoes and their eyes were hollow and listless. They were by far the worst infected paladins Knox had seen since all the wardens had been cured of the chade virus. There had only been a handful of paladins showing signs of the degenerative disease since the big battle, and Nikolai and Max had dealt with those swiftly. Although, Knox acknowledged, Dawn had been learning and doing all she could for them as well. But these paladins must have been lost somehow, they obviously had been living outdoors – perhaps even since the fight all those months ago.

'No wonder they look so far gone,' Kai's voice could be heard loud and clear through the bond.

"What's the plan?" Kellan asked, sickle at the ready.

"Incapacitate," Knox was quick to say, pity filling him as he looked at the two listless men. He knew they were only driven by their infinite hunger now, but he stepped forward and tried to talk them down, nonetheless. It was the least he could do.

"We are going to help you, okay? But you need to stay still." No response, and no indication they comprehended his words. Knox looked at Dex, receiving a small nod of encouragement. "Can you understand me?"

"They are too far gone," Dawn murmured softly from behind him. "Their auras are almost completely gone. The void is close."

Those four words caused a chill to skitter down Knox's spine and he swore when he saw the two paladins move swiftly toward them. "Stay back," he ordered Dawn.

"I can fucking help!" Dawn yelled.

Knox had heard Dawn swear only once throughout their entire acquaintance. Unfortunately, he didn't have time to wonder why the sounds of Dawn cursing caused him to become aroused. He would have to analyse it later because as one paladin charged toward Dex, the other headed straight for Knox. It advanced in a lumbering gait, very different from the graceful floating the other chades used to do. His eyes were vacant and hollow – and black. So black and shiny Knox could see his reflection in them. And instead of seeing himself as he was now, whole and healthy, he saw the creature he had become all those years ago. And so, instead of fighting the paladin, instead of calling upon his own connection to his element, Knox froze. He simply froze.

Memories that had been dulled since his return and being reunited with his sons rose to the surface. Feelings of hunger and pain and that deep, deep abyss were like knives piercing his psyche. He therefore didn't see the swift, outstretched hand of the paladin before it was too late. The air left his lungs with a painful whoosh, Kane falling on top of him after having tackled him. The infected paladin's sharp claws passed harmlessly through the air. Knox shook his son off and attempted to get to his feet, but what he saw next froze him to the spot. Dawn was moving up behind the paladin and Knox had not felt such fear in years.

She was going to get hurt. She was going to get herself killed, he thought frantically. But before he could muster the wind, Dawn calmly placed her hands on the back of the paladin's head. The paladin dropped like a stone, clearly unconscious. She didn't spare Knox a glance as she walked over to where Dex was holding a snarling, spitting paladin with his powers. She placed her forefinger and middle finger to the centre of the paladin's forehead, rendering the man unconscious as well from some kind of Vulcan mind meld or something. As she calmly walked away, not saying a word, Knox was frozen for a whole new reason.

Dawn was a total badass.

And he had royally fucked up.

CHAPTER SIX

*D*awn was both nervous and excited to attend the formal IDC meeting that day. The brand-new Headquarters had officially opened the day before and she and her counterparts had broken in their new council chambers with the appointment of the Local Council. Caspian had been beyond thrilled to take on the position of the chief, and Darius had been given the role of the local paladin member. One other paladin, one chaden and three other wardens – each from a different domain – completed the local council, and Dawn was satisfied they would do an excellent job. Even though the IDC was now going to be based out of the area, there were still many things the local council would be in charge of. The new IDC were about inclusion and delegation. They were wasting no time now that the HQ was open, and Eden was officially the hub of their society. It was basically their parliament. And that day, they were going to be formalising Orders.

Dawn couldn't wait to place paladins with wardens they felt a natural bond with. With her own experiences of two failed Orders before finally finding the right paladins, she was a big advocate for the rights of wardens and paladins alike to choose their own Order. Of course, it wasn't as simple as a warden choosing a paladin they liked, but the days of forcing strong paladins onto powerful wardens was over. The same went for the seemingly meeker paladins and wardens.

"Are you excited?" she asked Dex, who was standing next to her, searching the room. There were three wardens and five chadens that were hopeful to find their paladins that day. And then there was Dex. He had decided it was time to enlist some paladins to provide him with vitality on a permanent basis. Dawn wasn't privy to the deal Dex and Ivy had with each other regarding recharging, but Dex felt the time was right to take on paladins once more. He also wanted to set an example for other chadens, as he would be only the second chaden to create an Order. Knox was the first.

Dawn had not seen Knox since the incident with the sick paladins four days earlier. To say she was disappointed in his reaction to her initially staying was an understatement. She had thought Knox respected her more than that. Although, she supposed it was her own fault. She had made such a big deal over being seen as a woman, as Dawn, and not as her title, that it made sense he would disregard her abilities. *I can't have it both ways, I guess,* she thought to herself.

Willow snorted rudely and loudly in Dawn's head. *'You most certainly can have it both ways. And you should. Do not accept anything less.'*

'I haven't. Ever,' Dawn reminded her. *'It's why I'm still single at over six hundred years old.'*

'To be fair, I think Knox was just trying to protect you. I mean, he certainly looks very sorry. Look at him, he looks like a sad puppy,' Piper said.

Dawn looked over to the corner where Knox was talking with Simon, Patrick, and Vance. The three paladins had once been a part of the Magne Order when Dex had been known as Charlemagne. Today, they would be re-forming that bond as the Order of Absolution – and Dex would once more be their liege. Dawn was so happy for all of them, and clearly, Knox was too as he looked to be encouraging the three men and offering support. But Piper was right, there was a shroud of sadness and regret around Knox. Dawn hated seeing his usually pretty aura so dim and she resolved to speak with him before the day was over.

"Dawn?" Dex prompted, looking down at her with an indulgent look on his face.

"I'm sorry," she said, realising Dex had probably been trying to answer her question for the past five minutes. "I was speaking with my Order." It was half true, she told herself.

"That's what I figured. It's all right. But in answer to your question; yes, I'm excited. Scared too. I failed those men once before. I don't want to do it again," Dex revealed.

Dawn turned to him, giving him her full attention. "Dex, you didn't fail them. You got sick."

Dex shook his head, "I abandoned them. The circumstances don't matter. I let them down."

The words were remarkably similar to the ones Dawn had used when discussing the chades with Knox. It struck her then, as it had when she saw Knox with the ill paladin, just how hard it was to come back from such a dark place. Knox and Dex and all the other chadens were heroes in her eyes.

'I'm sure Knox would like to hear that,' Micah, of all people, pointed out.

'Perhaps,' Dawn allowed, setting aside such thoughts for the moment as Blu called the meeting to order.

Dawn seated herself at the horseshoe shaped table in the front of the room. It was a good set-up and ensured all members could see everyone clearly. It was also on the same level as the rest of the room – unlike the last table which had been set high above the citizens. Dawn looked around, noting that there were more female paladins than male paladins in the room – a testament to days gone by when male wardens believed women were the weaker sex. It meant there was a skew in the ratio of female vs male paladins needing to find an Order. Trying to get a gauge on potential bonds, Dawn took a look at some auras. Searching the room, she was angry and saddened to find so many unhappy paladins. The vast majority of them being women.

Pursing her lips, she looked at her fellow IDC members. "Looks like we won't be forming as many Orders as we initially believed."

Hyde raised his eyebrows, looking confused. "What do you mean?"

"Half of these paladins don't want to be here," she revealed. The other seven members of the IDC looked at her then, giving her their full attention. "Truly," Dawn added.

Max squinted into the crowd, her eyes doing that swirly thing Dawn thought was really cool before she sighed and shook her head. "Dawn's right. A lot of these paladins are still recovering from the losses of their former lieges or have a great distrust for the whole process. And some of them are even here against their will."

"Against their will?" Mordecai asked, looking pissed by the notion.

"Yes," Dawn confirmed. "Perhaps we should have held private meetings first rather than arranging this one big day. We could have picked up on these issues before now."

Blu shook his head, "We are trying to do better than the old IDC, but we still have a lot to learn. Do not be so hard on us," he smiled kindly at Dawn. "We will get it right."

She knew Blu was correct. Still, there was one thing she could do to help right then and there; talk to her people. "Do you mind?" she asked her colleagues, gesturing to the crowd.

Blu smiled, "Not at all."

Dawn stood up, noting the way Knox's eyes tracked her every movement. She commanded her racing heart to calm down, reminding herself she would deal with the Knox dilemma later. Right now, she had facts to straighten out. "Who is here because they want to be here? Raise your hands," she called out, figuring being direct was the best approach. When nobody moved, Dawn frowned in frustration. "It is not a trick question. Who wants to form an Order today, receive their coat of arms, and begin serving a liege?"

Finally, there was some movement. Simon, Patrick, and Vance stepped forward. "Uh, we sure do," Simon said, raising his hand high.

Dawn smiled at them in thanks. That was a no-brainer, but it was enough to encourage other paladins to speak up too. After much shuffling and much mumbling, three of the chadens and only one of the wardens would be forming an Order that day. There simply wasn't enough paladins who wanted to join. "What is your real fear?" Dawn asked a group of four female paladins who had stood in stony silence, glaring at the earth warden who had petitioned to have them in his Order. He was one of the wardens going home Orderless that day.

"He wants us to have sex with him," one of the women finally admitted.

Hemp, the earth warden in question, raised his chin, "So? It's a perfectly effective way to recharge."

Dawn felt her anger spike, knowing exactly how these women felt. No, it was not the same for her because she could more easily decline all the inappropriate advances she had been met with over the years. Her status allowed her that. But the female paladins of their society had not been afforded the same rights. Dawn ignored Hemp, as well as his idiotic, sexist, misogynistic remark. Instead focusing on the women.

"Ladies, listen up. Your vagina is not a sheath for a cock." Startled gasps met her statement and she wasn't sure if it was because of her word usage or because of the meaning behind them. "You are in charge of your own bodies – including your vitality and what is between your legs. Your vagina is not a placeholder for a warden's erect penis. You are not responsible for your liege's sex life – unless you want to be of course. Do you understand?"

There was nothing but silence for several heartbeats before one person clapping their hands could be heard. Dawn's head popped up, her eyes meeting those of Knox's, to see great pride in his eyes. Knox was proud of her – and it made her feel like a Queen. Others quickly joined in with the applause and Dawn was left feeling well satisfied with her little pep-talk. She only hoped the message sank in, not only to the women, but also to men like Hemp. She saw Knox moving through the crowd and she walked to meet him. She was on a roll and her confidence was at an all-time high right then. Talking out their differences seemed like a good idea. Before she could so much as open her mouth, Knox was apologising.

"I wanted to apologise for the other day. For what I said and the way I acted. I was scared and defensive and I took it out on you. I just didn't want to see you get hurt," Knox apologised, looking contrite.

She wanted to accept his apology, could even understand where he had been coming from, but she needed to make sure he understood her first. "I am not without my own power. I am not an empty figurehead," Dawn told him.

"I know. You were amazing. You *are* amazing," Knox vowed. His words, spoken with such brutal honesty and awe, had Dawn blushing. "And that vagina speech? Awesome." Dawn's mouth dropped open and she whacked Knox on the arm. "What? I'm being serious. No truer words have ever been said. I swear, the Vagina Speech will be whispered about for years to come."

Dawn groaned, shaking her head. "Don't do that. Don't capitalise it."

Knox grinned, looking boyish and carefree once more. "Too late."

"You are incorrigible," she said.

"I know. It's a part of my charm. Does this mean I'm forgiven?"

Dawn nodded, "It does." She then moved in close, lowering her voice for his ears only. "And I am sorry too. Sorry you had to come face to face with a paladin suffering the way you suffered. I know it was confronting. If you ever want to talk about it, I'm here."

"Thank you, Dawn," Knox said gratefully. "Does this mean I can have my old job back?"

"What do you mean?"

"As your personal assistant," Knox clarified. "We've been avoiding each other these last few days."

"I don't really need an assistant, Knox," Dawn told him. And it was true. She was busy but she liked it that way. She was used to being busy.

"Dawn, I'm going to let you in on a little secret; I don't need to *be* an assistant." His grey eyes snagged hers as he admitted, "But I want to be."

Dawn drew in a deep breath, feeling the silent encouragement from her entire Order. She licked her lips nervously and tugged on her hair until she could twirl her fingers around it. "I still have a few tasks I could use an assistant for." Knox's relieved grin made her breath catch in her throat. Now all she had to do was figure out why.

CHAPTER SEVEN

Knox waited anxiously behind his bar, checking the door every time he heard it open. Dawn had said she would come for a drink that night and Knox was nervous as though it were a date. *Which it is not,* he sternly told himself. It had been just over a month since he had introduced himself to the pretty life warden, and although they had spent lots of time together, it had all revolved around work – or pseudo work anyway. With Knox's duties as PA fulfilled – that is, Dawn having no more jobs she could make up for him to do – they were having recreational drinks.

"Recreational? Then why are you so dressed up?" Kane asked from his position behind the bar. He was unstacking the dishwasher and passing the still wet glasses to Kellan.

Both of them looked at Knox with identical knowing expressions. If Kai were there, Knox was sure he would have had the same expression on his face too. The only problem with having identical triplet sons, Knox thought, was seeing identical looks of 'you're a moron, dad' on their faces. "I'm not dressed up," Knox finally retorted.

Kellan looked Knox up and down. "You're wearing a shirt with buttons and a collar. I haven't seen you in anything but a t-shirt and jeans since you came back."

"I'm wearing jeans," Knox hastily pointed out.

Kane snorted, his grey eyes twinkling in amusement. "You're wearing *new* jeans. Besides, aren't those the ones Cali said make your butt look good?"

Knox grumbled at his laughing offspring, choosing not to answer them. So what if he had only worn the dark denim jeans once before? And so what if that one time, his good friend Cali had informed him his butt was extremely edible in them? It didn't mean he was trying to impress Dawn or anything, Knox assured himself.

"Dad, it's cool," Kai said, startling Knox. He had somehow snuck up on him. "Dawn is fantastic." He grinned mischievously, "We'd be happy to have her as our new stepmother."

"You —" Knox reached for Kai, but he was too quick, darting away and cackling like a hyena. "What are you doing here, anyway? I thought you were having a night in upstairs?" Knox was very much of the same mindset as Max. He believed paladins should get downtime. Not only did it ensure they were rested and therefore sharper on the job, but it was also just fucking manners. Last he heard, Kai was planning to eat dry cereal in his underwear as he binge watched *Lucifer*.

Kellan laughed loudly, looking pointedly at his older brother. "That was before he knew Dawn and her Order were coming. He wouldn't want to miss an opportunity to make moon eyes at Willow."

"Willow?" Knox turned to Kai, who was, much to Knox's shock, blushing. "You have a thing for Willow?"

Kai glared at his snickering brothers before replying, "No more than you have a thing for Dawn."

"Oh, well then," Knox said walking over to his middle son and patting him on the shoulder. "You're doomed."

"So you admit you have a thing for Dawn?" Kane asked. "And not just a 'want to get in her pants' kind of a thing either."

Knox sighed, stalling by looking around his near-empty bar. It was still early, barely five in the afternoon, so he knew the real crowd wouldn't come for another couple of hours at least. It was a Friday night, and more and more people from their society were venturing in for drinks, food, and more importantly, companionship. Knox loved getting a front row seat to seeing wardens, paladins, and chadens coming together as friends. He was beyond grateful the IDC had seen fit to bestow the bar and motel onto him and he only wished he could have known Dave, the previous owner, better.

"Dad?" Kane prompted, shaking Knox from his thoughts.

"Yes. I definitely like her more than that. Although, I wouldn't be adverse to the pants thing either," he added, smiling along with his sons. Knox then turned to Kai, "So, Willow, huh? She's a wonderful paladin. I approve."

Kellan shoved Kai in a teasing way, laughing. "Your approval doesn't matter much, dad. She turned him down."

"What?" Knox asked. It wasn't every day one of his sons got turned down. But seeing the disgruntled look on Kai's face was enough for Knox to grin. It was about time they got knocked down a peg or two. Knox was liking Willow more and more.

"Yep," Kellan crowed. "Told him she wasn't interested in being another notch on his belt. And followed up by making sure we all knew she wasn't into orgies or gangbangs."

"She did not!" Knox sputtered, imagining the look on Kai's face when he heard that.

"Oh, she did," Kai replied darkly. "The woman is as prickly as a cactus."

"I prefer to think of myself as discerning in my tastes."

Willow's sugary sweet voice had all four of them going still before they turned as one only to find Willow standing there with her arms crossed over her chest, a mutinous look on her face. Dawn, Piper, Reid, and Micah were also there, although their faces looked more amused than anything else.

"Willow!" Kai practically yelled. "I didn't know you were there."

Willow sniffed, "Clearly."

Knox watched as his son blushed for the second time in as many minutes, before stepping forward and smiled in welcome to the Adalla Order. "Hi, all. Good to see you. Can I get you all a drink?"

Knox managed to shuffle everyone to a couple of tables he hastily shoved together to give them all some more room. He then took drink orders, unsurprised when all four of Dawn's paladins chose something non-alcoholic. They might be in a bar with friends during their downtime, but they were always on duty. Knox couldn't fault them for that, so he made sure to keep jugs of soft drinks, as well as water on the table at all times, and supplied them with a bunch of snacks as well. After a while, he eventually ran out of things to do and he joined Dawn at her table. His sons went to work behind the bar and Knox enjoyed his time getting to know Dawn and her Order more. He couldn't keep his eyes from flicking to Dawn every minute or so. She would smile and he would look; she would talk and he would look; she would take a drink of her wine – and he would look. Micah caught his eye once, giving Knox a look that was nothing like the one Knox had been giving Dawn. Still, it wasn't as guard dog-like as Knox had been expecting either. It was more of a 'if you do the right thing, I won't have to kill you' kind of a look.

Chadens, wardens, and paladins came and went as the night progressed, and Knox was startled to realise he was now alone with Dawn at their table. Her Order was over at the pool tables, taking bets with his sons about who was better at pool. Knox couldn't help but notice the way Kai stared at Willow. Nor the way the female knight purposely ignored him. "Looks like Kai has his work cut out for him," he said, breaking the comfortable silence that had developed between himself and Dawn.

Dawn followed his gaze, "You sound amused."

"Oh, I am," Knox assured her. "It will do him good to have to prove himself. Nothing worthwhile ever comes easy, after all."

Dawn gave his words some thought, before nodding. "I guess you're right about that. Still, I hope she has more luck than I do when it comes to men. I have the absolute worst luck ever," Dawn informed him.

Before getting to know her this past month, he would have said that was impossible. Dawn was amazing in every way. She was educated and intelligent, kind and compassionate, charming and funny, as well as physically beautiful. But he had learned that she was completely oblivious to her own appeal. She was also awkwardly adorable with her interactions with people. She was such a contradiction, and Knox, for one, found it irresistible.

"In what way? Come on, tell me a story," Knox cajoled. "Otherwise I won't believe you."

Dawn narrowed her eyes, clearly thinking it over, before her shoulders relaxed and she said, "Okay. The last guy I attempted to have a relationship with didn't want to have sex with me."

Knox blinked slowly, sure he had heard wrong. "I'm sorry, what? Who wouldn't want to have sex with you?"

Dawn huffed, "Someone with a very acute sense of smell, that's who."

Knox reared back, more than a little confused. "An acute sense of smell? What are you talking about? You smell amazing!"

"You think I smell good? You know what, don't answer that. It hardly matters. This guy sure didn't seem to think so," Dawn muttered.

Knox leaned forward and took an experimental whiff. Dawn swatted at him but not before he caught her honey scent. He loved honey. "Just as I suspected. Honey."

Dawn raised her eyebrows in surprise, "You think I smell like honey?"

Knox nodded enthusiastically, "Yes. And your personality is sweet like honey too. So, it matches," he winked at her. Knox could tell Dawn thought he was joking, but he had never been more serious.

"Well, maybe I smell like honey ham," Dawn allowed, making no sense whatsoever.

"Honey ham?" Knox asked. "It's tasty to be sure, but I don't see what it has to do with you."

"Because!" Dawn suddenly yelled. "He told me my vagina smelled like ham!"

Knox stilled, absolutely positive he must have heard wrong. "Excuse me?"

Dawn glowered at him, "You heard me – my last lover told me vagina smelled like deli meat."

Knox eyed the breathtaking beauty in front of him for a moment, before opening his mouth – only to be cut off before he could finish his sentence; "Can I –"

"No!" Dawn yelled.

"But –" Knox tried again.

"No! You cannot smell my vagina!" Dawn practically growled.

Knox grinned, "Why not? I happen to love ham."

Dawn let out a thin scream, tugging on her chestnut locks in frustration. "This is a ridiculous conversation. Besides, it doesn't smell like ham anyway. The guy was a moron."

Knox smirked, "And how would you know?"

"Because I've spent a good many days contorted like a pretzel smelling my cooch like any self-respecting woman would do when her pussy was compared to a cut of meat from a pig!"

Knox and Dawn stared at each other for several moments before they both erupted into laughter. They laughed so hard that they leaned into one another for support, and Knox took full advantage, basking in Dawn's non-ham-like scent and warm body. Completely breathless and with watery eyes, Knox pulled back. "Did he really say that?"

Dawn shook her head ruefully. "Unfortunately, yes. Like I said, I have the absolute worst luck with men."

Knox tsked at her, "I'd say you're hanging out with the wrong type of guys."

Dawn snorted, "Oh? And who would be the right type?"

Knox looked Dawn dead in the eye, and said very clearly, "Me, of course."

Dawn's only response was to blink many times in quick succession.

"Dawn? Did you hear me?" he queried, feeling nerves pool in his stomach.

"I clearly heard you wrong," Dawn finally replied.

"No, you didn't. Me. I'm the right guy," he repeated. At Dawn's blank look, he rubbed his forehead in exasperation. "Come on, Dawn. Do you really not know?"

"Not know what?" Dawn was looking more and more confused.

Knox took a chance and reached out a hand, placing it on her knee. "Do you really not know how much I like you?"

Dawn looked from his hand to his face, opening and closing her mouth a couple of times before she said, "You like me? As in …?"

Knox moved in a little closer, so he was speaking intimately. "I like you as a woman, Dawn. I like the way you talk to everyone as if they are equal. I like the way your hair shines with so many colours in the sun. I like the way you say my name. I like the way you laugh. I like the way you twirl your hair around your finger when you're thinking or stressed. I like the way you look, and the way you smell, and the way you sound. I like *you*, Dawn. I like everything about you. How could you not know that?"

Dawn looked so genuinely astonished that Knox simply could not resist kissing the stupefied look right off her face. He leaned in quickly, capturing her lips, and immediately tracing them with his tongue. They parted for him and he slipped inside, her tongue duelling hesitantly with his. Knox groaned, placing his hands on Dawn's rounded hips in order to ground himself. The kiss was so phenomenal he was concerned he was going to float right off the floor. He was gratified to feel Dawn take over the kiss, her moans and gasps guiding him to what she liked.

"I am going to break this over your head!"

Willow's voice reached them loud and clear and Knox pulled back, instinctively ducking, thinking the paladin was talking about him. When no blow came, he slowly turned around, only to find it was Kai whom she was threatening with bodily harm. Standing up reluctantly, he gestured toward the pool table. "I'd better go save my son from your paladin. Pool sticks are expensive to replace," he joked.

Dawn's mouth was red and puffy and still in a perfect 'O'. She was clearly still in shock, Knox surmised. Still, he couldn't resist bending down and gently pushing her chin up. Once her mouth was closed, he placed a chaste kiss there, murmuring, "Think about what I said, okay?" before he went and saved his idiotic son.

If only so I can kick his arse myself, Knox thought. Kai's antics had interrupted the best damned kiss of Knox's life.

CHAPTER EIGHT

The following day, Dawn was curled up on the padded bench on the patio out the back of her rental. It was mid-afternoon and she had spent a restless night obsessing over the kiss she had shared with Knox. Her lips tingled just thinking about it and she licked her lips, swearing she could still taste him there. Dawn looked at the ocean as she thought about what Knox had revealed. If she was so damned irresistible why had she been single for the last couple of hundred years? Other than Andre – aka the ham guy – not a single warden or paladin had approached her because they liked her. Sure, she had the offers and requests from life wardens for the continuation of their domain. But those offers had been for nothing more than breeding purposes. She studied Micah, who was casually leaning against the house beside her, sharpening his sickle. He was undeniably handsome with his dark hair, light blue eyes and boyish dimples. He was six-foot-two inches of naturally brown, extremely toned skin, and his abdominal muscles were an easy half-dozen.

"Why haven't we ever had sex?" Dawn suddenly blurted out.

Micah looked around in every direction, even going so far as to look under the lounger she was sitting on before he answered her. "Are you talking to me?"

Dawn huffed out a breath. "Yes, I'm talking to you." Micah started to laugh, and Dawn smacked his arm. "I'm serious!"

Micah stopped laughing abruptly. "Oh. I can see that. Dawn ..." he looked confused as well as concerned as he sat down beside her. "Do you want to have sex with me?"

The look of sheer disbelief on his face was enough for Dawn to feel downright humiliated. "You know what – forget I said anything." Before she could stand and make her escape though, Micah reached out and grabbed her by the shoulders, effectively caging her in.

"Talk to me," he urged.

The genuine worry in his kind eyes, had her feeling even worse. She didn't need the Order bond to know he was wondering if she was having some kind of breakdown. Dropping her head into her hands, Dawn groaned. "I'm just so confused."

"If you're confused, then why don't we clear it up?"

Dawn had no idea what Micah meant until he grabbed her face and fused his mouth to hers. Her eyes opened wide for a moment, before she allowed him to kiss her, even going so far as to open her lips and touching her tongue to his for a brief moment. When she finally pulled back, she had just one word to say, "Oh."

Micah's smile was patient and sweet. "Yeah, 'oh'. That, my dear liege, is why we have never had sex."

Dawn slouched back against the lounger, chewing her bottom lip. She could still taste Micah there – a not altogether unpleasant flavour. But it also didn't make her want to jump his bones either. All in all, the kiss had been a pale imitation of the one she had shared with Knox. She had absolutely no spark with Micah. Whatsoever.

"Now, care to tell me what this is all about?" Micah sat back, crossing his arms over his chest.

"Knox said something to me, and it came as a total shock. I mean, it was good news, welcome news even. But it came out of nowhere," Dawn explained, waving her arms around for emphasis. "It made me think that maybe I'm bad at reading signs. Like, from guys. Guy signs."

Micah appeared to choke a little, eyes going wide. "You? Bad at reading guy signs? He said that?"

"See!" Dawn pointed at her Captain. "That right there is sarcasm. Again. Which leads me to believe that I am, in fact, awfully bad at identifying signals from men. And I blame my sleep deprived brain for that then leading me to believe maybe I was bad at seeing signals from you."

"Ah, hence the sex questions," Micah nodded his head in understanding.

"Exactly," Dawn said.

"You have not missed any signals from me, my liege," he patted her hand, and Dawn felt herself relax. "You have, however missed signals from pretty much every other interested male – and female – since the day I met you."

Dawn smacked his arm, "I have not!" she wailed.

"Oh, you have," Reid agreed, coming to sit on the other side of her, apparently from thin air. "You missed my signals. Big time. It was hell on the ego."

Dawn's jaw dropped open in shock. "You?"

Reid grinned at her. "Of course, me. Dawn, you are an incredibly beautiful woman as well as being one of the kindest and smartest. I crushed on you hard for the first few years I was in the Order," he revealed.

"You did?" Dawn was positively shocked.

Reid nodded, "I sure did. But don't worry, I got over it centuries ago."

Dawn thought about it for a moment, before leaning in and kissing a very surprised paladin for the second time that night. The kiss was brief, a mere peck, but it told Dawn everything she needed to know. She was no more sexually attracted to Reid than she was to Micah. "Huh. Perhaps I don't pick up on attraction unless *I'm* the one who is feeling it?" she wondered out loud.

"Umm, what was that?" Reid asked, touching his lips with his fingers.

"That was another test. One you failed." She patted his cheek, "Sorry, sweetie."

Reid stared at her for a moment, before a smile lit up his handsome face. "Yeah? Well you failed too. No spark at all. But I still love you."

Dawn grinned, "I love you too."

She was just about to delve into this newfound information about herself so she could hopefully come across as suave and knowledgeable to Knox the next time they met when she heard a growling sound. Looking up she saw Knox standing a few metres away. The first thing she noticed about him was that his eyes were completely black. Hurriedly looking down she saw that his feet were not touching the sand and she knew something was very wrong. She was about to ask him what it was when she saw the way his eyes moved between herself, Reid, and Micah. Those obsidian eyes then narrowed in on Dawn's lips and he sneered at her in a disgusted way before his body collapsed in on itself and he was whisked away on the wind. Dawn felt her stomach drop and a lump form in her throat. She knew, just knew what had caused Knox's distress.

Willow and Piper hurried over, reaching for her with their hands, Piper offering, "Oh, no. Dawn, I think he saw you kiss the guys."

"And very likely heard you tell Reid you love him," Willow added.

Dawn swallowed loudly, looking around at her Order. "What am I going to do?"

"What do you want to do?" Micah asked. "Do you like him, Dawn?"

Dawn didn't even need to think about it. He was the whole reason she was so confused and tied up in knots. She had been trying to clarify things for him, but instead, had made things worse. "Yes. I like him."

"Do you like his brain or his body?" Piper asked further.

Dawn looked to where Knox had been standing, noting the perfect angle it had of her and the lounger and her position sandwiched between two men. "I like both," she then answered, "A lot. The last month has been one of the happiest of my life, and I think it's because I was with Knox."

"Then go after him," Reid urged.

Dawn began twirling her hair around her finger in an agitated motion. "I don't think he'll listen. I mean, I made him go all *other*."

"Then you make him listen," Reid said. Watching her closely as he added, "That is, if you think he is worth it."

Dawn didn't even need to think about that. Casting her insecurities aside, she jumped up and headed for the door.

CHAPTER NINE

Knox didn't stop until he reached the back of the bar. His mind was a whirlwind of thoughts, so it was only fitting his body was too. He had gone to visit Dawn alone, after convincing his paladins he was a big boy and could take care of himself while he dropped in to see his crush. He had been so excited, wondering if Dawn had thought about their shared kiss as much as he had. Only, his dreams had been crushed when he found her kissing another man. He had been too far away to hear what was being said, but there was no denying Dawn had voluntarily kissed Micah. He had been too stunned to move for a few minutes and then even more disbelieving when Reid came along, sat himself down, and Dawn had kissed him too. Knox had moved of his own accord – what he was intending to say he had no idea. But he was rendered speechless when he heard Dawn tell Reid very clearly that she loved him. His darker emotions had rushed to the surface and he had fled before he did anything stupid, like kill Micah and Reid.

"Whoa, what's with the tornado?" Kane asked, looking concerned when Knox finally ceased the torrent of air around him.

Knox pushed past his son, storming up the stairs to his apartment. The bar had fully equipped living quarters above it, featuring three bedrooms, a living room, a dining room and just one bathroom. It was tight quarters for him and his three boys, but they had managed to build a temporary wall in the dining room, effectively turning it into an extra bedroom. It meant everyone got their own space. Knox was happy there, grateful to have a roof over his head and a bed to sleep in every night. He had spent far too many nights on the unforgiving ground, surrounded by nothing but air. Which was why he damned well deserved better than a woman who cheated, he told himself. He swore when he felt his eyes turning black once more, and had to consciously rein in his temper.

"Dad? What's the deal?" Kai rushed over to him.

"Do you need vitality?" Kellan then asked.

All three of them were now surrounding him, looking worried and trying in vain to access the Order link Knox had purposefully shut down. He didn't need anyone else to see his humiliation. "I'm fine. I don't need vitality," he finally managed to respond.

"You are not fine. And you're blocking us out. You promised you would never do that. You swore you would never let us think you left us again," Kai's voice was filled with hurt.

Knox cursed out loud, hating the anxiety he was causing. He knew his sons had real issues with abandonment. What Evangeline had planted the seeds for, his disappearance had sown. He cracked the link open a little before apologising. "I'm sorry. I'm just pissed off."

"Did things not go well with Dawn?" Kane hazarded a guess.

Knox barked out a bitter laugh. "Not exactly. She's sleeping with her Order."

The triplets reared back as one. "What? Who?" Kane asked.

"Dawn," Knox snarled. "She's sleeping with Micah and Reid!" They all looked shocked and Knox couldn't blame them. He was shocked too. But the hurt was quickly catching up.

"What?" Kellan yelled. "Where are you getting this? Dad, there's no way."

"I saw her," Knox said, wearily now.

"You saw her having sex with Micah and Reid?" Kai was incredulous.

Knox huffed out a breath and began to pace. "No, I saw them kissing. She kissed them both. They were all smiling and laughing, all sitting together on the one chair."

"Maybe you misinterpreted –" Kai began.

"I didn't misinterpret anything," Knox interrupted. "By the Great Mother, what a fool I've been. I thought she was just shy or awkward. That she truly didn't see herself the way everyone else does. It was cute and endearing. Turns out, she's just plain not interested. She has all the men she needs on tap already. And after pouring out my heart to her yesterday. Fucking humiliating," he cursed himself.

A knock on the door interrupted the next round of questions and Kane hurried to answer it. He winced when he saw who it was. "This really isn't a good time."

Dawn held her head high as she pushed her way into the room, followed closely by all four of her paladins. "I insist." Her gaze immediately sought out Knox. "Knox, I want to explain –"

"You don't owe me any explanations, my lady," he informed her, voice brittle with formality.

"But –" Dawn attempted to speak again, only to be cut off by Knox once more.

"You're free to do whatever you want. Or *whoever* – as the case may be. Now, if you'll excuse me, I need to get the bar open." Knox gave Dawn a wide berth as he rushed out his front door, leaving his sons to deal with his mess. It wasn't his proudest moment, to be sure, but it was the best way to keep himself from getting hurt further.

He grabbed a broom and began sweeping the already clean floor, when the door to the bar burst open. Knox pointedly ignored the intruder, knowing it wasn't a customer. They didn't open for another two hours.

"Are you proud of yourself for hurting her that way? Do you feel even now?" Micah demanded, charging forward.

"*I* hurt *her*?" Knox scoffed, tossing the broom to the side in a fit of temper. "She was the one who led *me* on."

Micah scoffed, "Dawn couldn't lead you on even if she tried. She is completely clueless about all that stuff and you know it. You're just pissed because you saw her kissing someone else."

Knox got right up in Micah's face, shouting, "Of course I'm pissed! I thought –" he abruptly broke off, spinning away.

"You thought she liked you as much as you like her," Micah supplied for him. "She does," Micah said, voice strong and sure.

Knox shook his head. "Look, I know some wardens and paladins have no issue sleeping around or recharging through intercourse. But I'm not one of them. I also don't share. That is a deal breaker for me."

"Dawn is not one of them either. She abhors the practice. Unless it is consensual of course. I don't think Ryker has a problem with it for example," Micah added.

Knox would not be humoured. "Don't bullshit me, Micah. I saw her. And you. And Reid."

Micah frowned fiercely. "That wasn't what it looked like."

Knox scoffed, "Of course it wasn't. And I suppose I misheard her declaration of love too?"

Micah moved suddenly and with the speed of a soldier. He grabbed Knox by the shirt and slammed him against the wall. "Listen, you prick! You are the first man Dawn has been interested in for centuries! And the first man who has been interested in her for the right reasons. You see the real Dawn. I know you do."

Knox peeled Micah's fingers off one by one. "Correction: I *thought* I saw the real Dawn. Turns out I was wrong." He pushed Micah away, giving the other man his back.

"I wouldn't have pegged you as a quitter."

Knox closed his eyes, drawing in a deep breath and not moving a muscle. He was afraid he would seriously harm the paladin if he didn't calm himself. "I am not a quitter," he ground out through clenched teeth. Spinning to face Micah, he pointed a finger in warning at him. "I know more about survival than you ever will. Don't you dare presume to know anything about my strength of will."

Micah stared at him for a few tense moments before he relented, "Fine. You're a survivor. Good for you." He shook his head, "Was it that you were just looking for an excuse to run then?"

"I'm not a runner either. Watch your mouth, kid," Knox warned.

Micah smirked at him, looking all superior. "Then why are you acting like a brat who got his favourite toy taken away? Why are you being so dramatic? Why won't you just listen? You –" he broke off abruptly, snapping his fingers as if he had just solved some great riddle. "Oh! It's like that. I didn't realise."

Knox said nothing, turning his back as he reached for an upturned chair stacked on the closest table. Lifting it, he spun it up the right way and placed it on the floor. He did the same thing another three times until one table was clear. "Only twenty more to go," he muttered to himself, ignoring the silent, judgemental paladin as well as the deep ache he felt in his chest region.

"That was fast," Micah commented, as if in the middle of a conversation.

Knox glanced at him, seeing a pitying look on Micah's face. That look was worse than the anger. "I don't know what you're talking about," he replied.

"Yes, you do," Micah retorted quickly. "You don't just have a crush. You're in love with her. That's why you're so angry. You're not just pissed. You're heartbroken."

He *was* heartbroken, Knox acknowledged. More than he thought he could be after such a short period of time. But there was no denying what that pain in his chest was – unless he was about to have a heart attack. He liked that idea better than being in love with an unavailable woman.

"Aren't you going to deny it?" Micah taunted.

Knox looked at him, "What good would it do? You know, when I turned, it was fast. Like, within a week. There was no insidious voice whispering sweet nothings in my ear for months on end. It was just – *bam* – you're cursed. But in that week, I still had enough reasoning to understand what was happening – and I denied it. I didn't want to believe it. I knew that it was impossible to stop the infection. But I could have had that one last week to be truthful to my sons. To prepare them for what was to come. My denial cost me that. It cost me time with my sons. I didn't get to say goodbye." Knox paused, making eye contact with Micah so he would see the truth of his words. "When Max healed me, I promised myself I would never lie to myself again. I won't break that promise."

Micah's rigid stance relaxed, and he shook his head slowly, "So it's true – you're in love with Dawn." It was a statement.

Knox turned around and punched the wall behind him, shouting, "Gods! Yes! Yes, okay! I am in love with Dawn. Are you happy now?" He spun back around to ream Micah some more but was struck mute when he saw Dawn standing in the doorway of the bar.

"You love me?" she asked.

Knox snapped his mouth closed, looking everywhere but at Dawn. "By the Great Mother, kill me now," he muttered.

'Oh, I don't think so,' came Dana's amused reply in his head. *'All is as it should be. Go ahead. Answer her.'*

'You can't make me,' was his mature comeback. But he was forced to leave his argument with Mother Nature when Dawn began sashaying toward him.

CHAPTER TEN

Dawn's heart was pounding for a new and wholly unexpected reason as she dismissed Micah with a silent thank you. Knox looked like a cornered wild animal, all round eyes and pale skin. When she had chased after him, she had never expected to hear that he loved her. It was too soon. *Wasn't it?* she asked herself. Her head said it was, but her heart disagreed. "Is it true? Do you love me?" she asked again, needing to hear him say it to her face.

Knox shook his head, a dark frown on his handsome face as he stared her down. "Nope. That is not how this is going to work. I don't owe you jack, Dawn. You have one minute to explain yourself. If I like what I hear, then and only then, will I answer you. If I don't like it – if I don't believe you – you leave and never talk to me again."

Dawn pressed a hand to her rioting stomach. The ultimatum left her feeling ill. Still, she launched into a long-winded, and unnecessarily convoluted explanation of how she came to be kissing her paladins. It involved lots of stuttering and her trying to convey how blind she was when it came to her own appeal and picking up signals from the opposite sex. When she was done, she felt like she had run a marathon, and Knox stood staring at her like she was an alien.

"So, let me get this straight," Knox began, slowly prowling toward her. "I pour my heart out to you and admit I've been harbouring a crush on you. I then kiss you – and you kiss me back! You then go and try to sex up the Captain of your Order – who you've been best friends with for five-hundred years and have never, not once, felt an ounce of attraction to."

Dawn opened her mouth to answer but apparently Knox wasn't finished. He held up a hand for silence and came to a complete stop in front of her. So close, she could feel his body heat.

"Your poor, poor paladin humours you with a kiss, which you then see fit to bestow on Reid as well. You then declare your love for Reid – but in a purely platonic way – for me to stumble across you just at that moment, leading me to the wrong idea and causing me to flee like a teenage girl. Do I have that right?"

Dawn dropped her head in her hands, releasing a thin scream, hoping beyond hope her hands would be enough to smother herself into unconsciousness. But today was not her lucky day because Knox peeled her hands from her face, tilting her chin up to meet his pewter gaze.

"Dawn?" he prompted.

"Yes, that about sums it up," she admitted.

Knox dropped his hand, waving it about in frustration. "Seriously, Dawn. What were you thinking? How could that possibly seem like a good plan?"

"I was thinking how could I be so terrible at reading men? I mean, I'm a life warden for fuck's sake! I've spent every day with you for weeks and weeks now, and I had no idea you felt that way. I mean, you mentioned flirting that one time but when you didn't bring it up again, I figured maybe you just wanted to be friends."

Knox choked, looking incredulous, "Dawn, I flirted with you every single time I saw you."

"See!" Dawn yelled, pointing at him. "This is what I'm talking about. I had no idea. I knew I wanted you to like me the same way I liked you, but I wasn't getting any vibes. I figured it was just hope, you know? And then you kissed me last night and my heart went all pitty-pat and I got all tingly and lightheaded. It made me question everything I knew about attraction and men and signals." She snorted, "Which, it seems, is exactly nothing. I know nothing."

Knox was silent for a long time, his eyes watching her with focused regard. "Your heart went pitty-pat, huh?"

Dawn peered at him, fearful and hopeful at the same time. "Yes."

"Why do you suppose it did that?" he then asked.

Dawn chewed her lip, wanting to get the answer correct. It was too important to get wrong. "Because I like you?" she ventured.

"Is that a statement or a question?" Knox demanded, crossing his arms over his chest and causing his biceps to flex appealingly.

Dawn straightened her spine. "A statement. I like you, Knox."

"Like me as in …?" he asked, repeating Dawn's question from the day before.

Taking a chance, Dawn took a few steps closer to him. "As in, *like you*, like you. I like you as a man, Knox. I like you as a chaden. I like the way your grey eyes darken like thunderstorms when you're angry. I like the love you show for your sons. I like the way you look at me when I talk as if what I have to say is the most important thing in the world. I like the way your butt looks in jeans. I like *you*, Knox."

"Now, that, is the right answer," Knox said, snatching Dawn close and taking siege to her lips.

Dawn moaned, wrapping her arms around Knox's head and holding onto his ears so he couldn't escape. The kiss spun out of control, both of them fighting for dominance. Dawn managed to pull back, giving his top lip a small bite before soothing it with her tongue. Her hands roamed across Knox's broad chest, slipping under the hem of his shirt and discovering hot skin covered in a fine smattering of hair. Knox allowed her to explore and she decided to take advantage of his kind nature. She dropped to her knees.

"What are you doing?" Knox asked breathlessly, eyes round as saucers as his chest rose and fell rapidly.

Dawn smiled up at him from her new position, squeezing his hardness through his jeans. The thick fabric was definitely a hindrance and she reached up to unbutton them and pull down the zipper amid a flurry of curses. She hummed happily when his hard cock was instantly revealed. He wasn't wearing underwear. Pushing his jeans down to his ankles, she jacked his length a couple of times, learning the shape and texture, before she looked up at him. "Do you mind?"

Knox vigorously shook his head, "No. Nope. Nuh-uh. I don't mind at all."

Dawn smirked, "I didn't think so."

Getting a good grip, Dawn held Knox's flushed dick still as she rubbed it across her mouth, his pre-cum painting her lips like lipstick. She then looked directly into Knox's eyes and licked her lips, moaning at the taste. Knox's breath wheezed out as he begged and pleaded. Heady with her powers of seduction, and horny as hell, Dawn sucked the tip of Knox's dick into her mouth. She stopped, carefully fitting her teeth under the cap of his foreskin and swirled her tongue around his slit. Knox grabbed her hair in a punishing grip – just the kind Dawn liked – and thrust his hips forward, forcing her to take more of him. It had been a long time since she had given anyone head, but she did her best to relax her throat as Knox did his best to fuck her face. Dawn loved it. She clutched his arse cheeks, drawing him in closer and bobbed her head in counterpoint to his hips. Reaching down, she fondled his balls, feeling them roll around before they pulled up tighter to his body.

Knox swore creatively, pulling back and grabbing the base of his dick. "Enough. Mercy. Holy shit, I'm gonna blow."

Dawn reached for him, swatting his hand out of the way and stroking his spit-slicked cock. It was long and thick, and red and shiny from her mouth. "It's delicious," she stated, more to herself than Knox.

"Sweet heaven, Dawn," Knox groaned, dragging her to her feet and practically bending her backwards from the ferocity of his kiss.

Dawn lifted one leg and locked it around his waist, pulling their groins into alignment. She gasped, feeling wetness flood between her thighs and wanting nothing more than to feel Knox inside of her. She ripped off his shirt before doing the same to her own. "Take me," she commanded. "Take me now."

Knox looked a little dazed as he set her away from him. "You are so perfect," he declared, only to ruin it by adding, "We can't do this here."

"What are you talking about? Of course we can," Dawn challenged, trying to grab him by his hard dick and show him the way.

Knox's chuckle was dark as he shook his head, "You're an animal. Why am I not surprised? It's always the quiet ones. But seriously, Dawn, anyone could walk in. And the first time I have you is not going to be on the floor of some pub."

Dawn felt her lip extend in a pout, not liking what she was hearing at all. She liked that he respected her and wanted to take time with her, but she was horny and Knox had said he loved her. *Her.* She wanted her man and she wanted him *now*. She looked over at the scarred bar. "If not the floor, how about the bar?"

Knox sputtered, "What? Huh? Yes! Fuck, yes! Wait, no. I mean no. Not happening."

Dawn tsked and started to walk backwards, reaching behind her back to unhook her black cotton bra. Had she known she was going to be getting laid, she would have worn something racier. But Knox didn't seem to mind if his bobbing erection was anything to go by. Pulling the straps down her arms, she held the bra up from the tips of her fingers for a moment before tossing it across the room. She then pushed her pants down her legs, trying to channel her inner stripper as she moved her hips to a soundless beat. Knox looked entranced and he watched avidly as she pushed her pants away, taking her knickers with them. She was wearing beige, high-rise, underwear and she didn't want to ruin the illusion of Dawn, The Sex Siren. She felt behind her for the bar and then used her hands to leverage herself up. She winced. "Damn, this is cold on my butt. You can be on the bottom," she informed Knox.

Apparently, that was the last straw because he charged across the room after removing his shoes and flinging his jeans aside. He stepped between her legs and pulled her face to his, kissing her with all the passion and frustration she knew he was feeling. And she knew because she felt the same way. It took some manoeuvring, but she soon had Knox flat on his back on the bar and she threw her leg over him, straddling him and keeping him at her mercy. He reached up and cupped her breast, massaging the fleshy mound even as his other hand ventured between her thighs.

Knox groaned when he found her slick and wet. "Perfect," he muttered. "So perfect." He then waved his hand at the front door and Dawn heard a rush of wind right before a loud click. "I locked the door," Knox said.

"Perfect," Dawn repeated. She kissed him one last time, more than ready for him. She knew she was being wanton and impatient, but it felt like she had been waiting for this moment forever. For a man who finally saw every part of her and gave himself to *her* selflessly, rather than demanding she give herself to *him*.

Lowering herself onto his length, she threw her head back, rejoicing in the feeling of being filled. For all her time spent declining offers of sex, she really did enjoy it. Her body stretched to accommodate Knox's impressive girth and she tightened her inner muscles experimentally. Knox groaned and thrust up into her, almost causing her to lose her balance. His hands quickly came up to grip her hips as he set a fast pace, thrusting up from underneath her and pulling her down to meet the hard jabs at the same time.

"Look at you," Knox panted, voice filled with the grit of lust. "You look like a naughty cowgirl up there." He moaned, pumping into her a few more times before saying, "Gods, your tits."

Dawn looked down, taking note of the way her breasts bounced with every motion. Her breasts were large, but she liked to think they were balanced out by her hips. She had always loved her hourglass figure and was gratified to see Knox approved as well. She snaked her hand up to tweak a nipple, gasping when it shot sensation straight to her clit. Knox released her hips to pull her down and kiss her breathless. She stayed where she was working her hips against Knox, the position putting pressure on her clit every couple of thrusts. It wasn't long after that before she felt a tingling in her clit and her internal muscles began tightening rhythmically over and over again as she was flung into an orgasm that had her screaming Knox's name. Knox's shout of completion reached her ears and he lost his rhythm, pistoning into her crazily as he worked to wring out every drop of pleasure for them both.

CHAPTER ELEVEN

Knox stared stupidly at the ceiling, his body struggling to breathe as he came down from an orgasm that, by rights, should have killed him. Dawn was sprawled boneless on his chest, her panting breaths hot against his skin. He lifted his heavy arms, stroking them down Dawn's back, and finding it slick with sweat. When he got to her butt, he gave it a small pinch, holding her tight when she jumped so she wouldn't fall.

Pushing her hair out of her face, Dawn scowled up at him. "What are you doing?"

"Just checking to see if you're still conscious," he grinned down at her. Dawn giggled and Knox basked in the sound. He tucked some hair behind her ear, asking, "Are you okay?"

Dawn searched his face for a moment, asking a question of her own in return. "Do you still love me?"

Knox gripped her tighter, feeling her generous breasts squish against his chest and causing his exhausted dick to make a heroic twitch. "Yes. Of course, I still love you." He squeezed her arse, "In fact, I think I love you even more now."

Dawn laughed, kissing his chin. "Then, yes. I am very okay."

Knox sighed, relaxing back against his bar, and wondering how he was ever going to be able to serve drinks to his customers without replaying sex with Dawn every single time. It would be damned inconvenient to pop wood every time he wiped down the bar top. Still, he was content to hold her there for a while longer yet. The outside world could wait.

"What do we do now?" Dawn asked after a few minutes. She propped herself up on his chest so she could see him better.

"Now we put the closed sign on the door and give me a breather of say, ten minutes, before we start all over again. I was thinking … reverse cowgirl?" Knox's grin was as cheeky as it was raunchy.

Dawn pinched his nipple, making him yelp. "That's not what I meant, and you know it."

Knox did know. He also knew exactly how to answer her. "Now we date."

"Date?" Dawn looked surprised.

Knox bopped her on the nose, smiling at her cute frown. "Yes, date. We continue to see each other for recreational activities as well as conversation. We continue to touch and kiss and cuddle. And we most definitely continue to have sex." He paused, holding her close and moving his lips to the shell of her ear, before he whispered, "We do all that until it happens."

Dawn smiled, laughing a little. Then she asked, "Until what happens?"

Knox kissed her mouth, tangling his tongue lazily with hers until they were panting again. "Until you fall in love with me in return," he finally answered. Dawn tried to move off him, but Knox wouldn't let her. Instead he held her tighter. "Quit wiggling or we'll fall off here. It's a miracle we didn't break our necks as it is."

Dawn was biting her lip, looking anxious. "I'm sorry I can't say it back. I –"

Knox shook his head, stopping her. "Don't apologise, I understand. Trust me, I know this is fast. I don't really know when or how I fell in love with you. I didn't realise until I saw you kissing your paladins – naughty, naughty, by the way. Remind me to spank you for that later. But I made a vow to myself, after Max healed me and made me a man again. I'm not sure if you overheard that part, but I vowed I would never lie to myself. Even if I could go against my own promise, I wouldn't want to. I like loving you. It feels good. I want to keep loving you. Is that okay?" he asked, suddenly feeling unsure.

"It's definitely okay," Dawn breathed, pushing up to kiss him again.

Knox kissed her back, joy filling his heart. He grinned cockily at his lover, "Besides, if watching you fumble through our initial courtship was anything to go by, watching you fall in love with me is going to be hysterical."

Dawn gasped, "You arsehole!" She mock growled, pushing herself up and straddling his waist.

Knox laughed, spanning her hips with his hands. "It's going to be a fun ride."

Dawn's expression turned sultry and downright naughty causing his dick to plump a little. "If you think that is a fun ride, you're going to love this." Then she turned around and straddled him in reverse.

He groaned, slapping her rump. "Giddy up."

Dawn's laugh was music to his ears and a balm to his soul. And her hand was like magic to his dick, he mused as she stroked him back to full hardness. All in all, it was the best ending to a misunderstanding he had ever had.

BOOK THREE

SUNSHINE

CHAPTER ONE

"You know, your mummy has all these swirling stars in her eyes – like an entire galaxy! She is my star and my moon. And you, you are going to be my little Sunshine," Ryker told his daughter, whispering against Max's stomach. His hand followed the kicks and punches as he hummed *You Are My Sunshine*, the vibrations making Max giggle. Ryker looked up at Max. "Stay still, mummy. Daddy is bonding here."

Max was reclining in bed with a bunch of pillows behind her – because laying flat was out of the question now. Her stomach was just too heavy and she was only able to take shallow breaths when she was on her back. She smiled at Ryker as she ran her hands through his silky, long locks. His hair was now long enough to tie back in a band, though not as long as Beyden's had been when Max had first met him. Still, Ryker was learning the ways of the man-bun from Sensei Bey and Max loved it. Her father, on the other hand, teased Ryker ruthlessly about it. Max thought the love/hate relationship Mordecai and Ryker had built was beyond adorable, and their daily bantering always made her laugh.

"What are you giggling about?" Ryker asked, giving her tummy a final kiss before reclining next to her.

"You and my father. You two are so cute together," Max replied.

Ryker grunted, "I hate him."

"You love him," Max corrected.

"I love to hate him. How about that? See, I can compromise." He smiled winningly at her.

Max shook her head, completely melting from that smile. Which, she knew was entirely his intention. "Come here," Max gestured him closer with her finger. He looked a little smug, but still he obeyed, and Max kissed him lazily for a delicious few minutes.

It was a Sunday morning, later than they would usually linger in bed, but there was nothing pressing on the schedule and her Order had things well in hand anyway. She now only had a little over four weeks to go before she could hold her daughter in her arms and she was getting impatient. Both to be able to kiss her and cuddle her, and also because she felt huge. She hadn't been able to see her feet in weeks, nor shave her legs. Which meant, who knows what was going on between her legs. *Not that it mattered*, Max thought. Ryker had put a stop to their lovemaking a good six weeks ago. He was simply too aware his kid was in her belly. Max thought he was hysterical, but she couldn't blame him really. Their daughter moved a lot. Max patted her stomach, only to get a solid nudge in return. She sighed, the sound filled with happiness and contentment. She was in bed with the man of her dreams as he sang to their unborn daughter and promised her the world. What more could she ask for?

Everything was perfect.

Just then, a cloud obscured the sun, causing the sky to darken and their room to dim. Max felt a shiver go through her body and she frowned, her gaze searching the horizon out the window. She rubbed her arms, trying to force the goosebumps away. "What was that?" she wondered.

"What was what?" Ryker asked, levering himself up to look at her. He followed her gaze out the window, watching as the cloud moved on and the bright sun returned. "You okay?"

Max nodded her head, feeling silly. She hadn't had a vision or anything, but she still had a funny feeling that something was coming.

She just hoped it wasn't the baby, she thought, rubbing her hands over her tummy. She still had a few things to take care of before that happened. Making a mental note to see Jazz for a check-up that day, Max pushed the incident out of her mind. It was just a cloud, after all. Then she finally answered Ryker, "I'm fine. Nothing to worry about here. Your Sunshine is just fine too."

Ryker had started referring to the baby as Sunshine when Max was around five months pregnant. Not only did he think the nickname was fitting for what his daughter would bring to them – pure sunshine, light, and love – but every now and then, Max's stomach would heat up. Max hadn't been at all concerned about it. Her baby only did it whenever she or Ryker patted her or talked to her. Ryker, of course, had flipped his shit when his hand had warmed up one night when they had been fooling around. Thinking about it now, Max realised that was the exact moment Ryker had put a hiatus on their sex life. Jazz and Max's mother had checked the baby out and assured them there was nothing wrong. Max herself had done a little snooping around with her own special sight and found her daughter's body and soul to be perfectly healthy. For some reason, she just liked to light up like the sun whenever her mummy or daddy talked to her. Max had no problem with that, and Ryker had thus, bestowed the nickname Sunshine. It had stuck, and most of her family now greeted her tummy with *'hello Sunshine'* whenever they saw her.

"Are you sure?" Ryker pressed, placing his palm over Max's forehead.

Max allowed it, smiling in reassurance. "I am positive. All good here. What are the plans for today?"

Ryker rearranged himself – and Max – so he was spooning her from the side, every part of his hard, muscled body touching hers. "My plans consist mainly of this."

"Hmm, I like your plan," Max agreed. Then, figuring it was worth a shot, she grabbed his hand and moulded it to her very full breast. "You know what would be a better plan?"

Ryker groaned, his warm breath tickling the back of her neck as he burrowed his head there. He squeezed her breast, causing Max to gasp and arch because she was super sensitive. "Max, stop being naughty," Ryker complained – but he didn't remove his hand.

Max smiled and began to think her plans of seduction were working for once when Ryker nibbled on her earlobe. She could feel his hardness pressing into her backside and she began to rock against him. Ryker groaned, using his free hand to tilt her head back and deliver a searing kiss. The angle was awkward but Max didn't care. She was just getting prepared for the mammoth task of rolling over when Sunshine chose that moment to punch her right in the vag. At least, that's what it felt like to Max. Like an internal uppercut. Max gasped and began swearing, the lingering heaviness between her legs that always accompanied such jabs making her want to sit up. Ryker, of course, let go of her like she was a hot potato. But he did help her sit up straighter.

"Uh, sorry. I got a little carried away," Ryker said, looking sheepish and gorgeous with his dark eyes and rumpled hair. He was now standing beside the bed, rubbing her shoulders.

Max licked her lips, eyes darting to the erection outlined in his boxer briefs. "Not carried away enough."

Ryker pointed a finger at her. "No. Stop it, you minx. No orgasms for you."

"How about an orgasm for you then?" Max suggested, before reaching out and cupping her man's heavy dick. She got away with a few strokes over the fabric of his underwear before he stepped back, breathing hard.

"Max …" Ryker warned, his bare chest rising and falling rapidly with his quick breaths.

Max pouted. "You and your stupid rules." When they had stopped having intercourse, Ryker had also banned all orgasms of all sorts. Even for himself. Something about solidarity and not asking Max to do anything he wasn't willing to do himself. Thinking about it now, Max decided it was the most romantic thing he had ever done for her. The thought made her laugh and shake her head. She held up her hands in surrender. "Fine. You win."

"You're still the most beautiful vision I have ever seen in my life. I love you very much," Ryker told her, the sunlight at his back making him look like a hero from mythology.

Max felt her eyes tear up – she was far more emotional than she used to be. "I love you very much too."

Ryker bent down, kissing away the two tears that escaped before nibbling on her lips, coaxing them open. Max opened willingly and allowed the sensual kiss to spin out, creating tension but also satisfaction. So that when Ryker finally pulled back with a final kiss to her forehead, Max didn't feel horny. She felt cherished. "What am I going to do with you?" she asked.

Ryker winked at her, "Ask me that again a couple of months after Sunshine is born."

Max grinned. "Deal."

After waddling her way to the bathroom and peeing an embarrassingly small amount considering how full her bladder felt, she felt the Order link flare up. The voices were muffled, which meant someone was talking to Ryker. Max could have easily listened in, but she always respected the privacy of her friends. She may be their liege, but sometimes what they had to say was for Ryker only. Ryker didn't look concerned as he absently scratched at his wriggling coat of arms, so Max continued to get dressed. Sure, a lazy Sunday was planned. But she was up and moving now, so she may as well put pants on. She had taken to sleeping in Ryker's t-shirts, which even at eight months pregnant, were still roomy on her. They were fast moving into spring and although most days were clear and sunny, the air was still sometimes cool. As such, she dressed in maternity leggings, a maternity singlet that had a built-in self-bra, and left an unbuttoned light flannel shirt on over the top. She hadn't been able to wear a bra with underwire since she was fourteen weeks along and it had been an adjustment to wear wireless maternity bras. With her breast size, she just didn't feel supported without wire. But that wasn't really an issue now because her baby bump did a pretty good job of acting as a ledge for her tits.

Moving out of the walk-in, she found Ryker pulling on cargo pants and a t-shirt. She watched him cover up that amazing chest of his with a small sigh. He really was amazing to look at. And he was all hers.

Sometimes she could still hardly believe it. Moving closer to him, she saw a small frown on his face. Thinking of her Order, she asked, "Problem?"

Ryker shook his head, "No. I don't think so. That was Darius, your mother and father called to say they were on the way."

"They called?" Mac repeated. Her parents never called. They just showed up. "That's weird."

Ryker shrugged, clearly unconcerned. He pulled on his boots and laced them up. "Maybe your father is starting to respect my boundaries."

Max snorted, "Yeah. I'm sure that's it."

Ryker grinned at her, and she knew he had been joking. Holding out his hand for her to take, he helped her from the room. "Come on. Let's go find out what they want."

Max shivered again, a quick glance behind her showing another cloud covering the sun. *It's an omen,* she thought, sure of it now. But she held her tongue – and Ryker's hand tighter – as she went to see her parents.

CHAPTER TWO

Ryker thought it was a little off that Dana and Mordecai had announced their visit rather than just showing up, but he didn't think on it too much because he was just too damned content. He had the love of his life holding his hand and his daughter was nestled all safe and happy inside her mother's womb. As he walked into the kitchen, he found all six of his knights there, and about half of their lovers. Despite the fact Cali and Axel had moved out of the main house and made new homes for their families in the cabins on the property, they still ate most of their meals there. Ryker didn't mind. In fact, he loved it. He had made it clear that his home would always be a home for his entire Order, and he had an open-door policy any time of the day or night. It was nice to see Dex and Cali have space for Maxwell – who was growing like a weed and now seven months old and just starting to crawl. Likewise, for Axel and Celeste with Spiro. Dex's three paladins had taken up residence in the third cabin and Ryker had enjoyed getting to know the three men better over the past few weeks. The fourth cabin remained empty at this stage, even though it had been earmarked for Lark and Ivy.

When they had first spoken of building more cabins, Max had offered each member one of their own. It made sense that those with kids move out, but it hadn't been mandatory. Dex and Cali, as well as Axel and Celeste had graciously agreed. Some of the others, on the other hand, had declined stubbornly. Darius had been very blunt when he had informed Max he would not be leaving – even if it was just metres away. He and Diana would stay in their extended rooms quite happily. Beyden and Jasminka had likewise refused to leave, though, Jazz had a bedroom at her clinic in HQ if it was ever required. Lark and Ivy had been happy to stay on in the house as well. That was, until Max dropped her bombshell on them. Ryker smiled to himself, recalling Max's words.

"That cabin is for you, Lark. Trust me, Ivy is going to be a baby-making machine and you guys will need the privacy as well as the space for all those cots."

Ivy had been suitably horrified and since then, had steadfastly refused to move into the cabin. Ryker couldn't be happier for them. For *all* of them, including himself. Shuffling Max to a seat next to Dex so she could coo over Maxwell seated in his highchair, Ryker went and put some bread in the toaster and made Max a hot Milo. Max smiled at him in thanks when he handed it to her, but it was in an absent way. He began to ask her if anything was wrong when he heard the toast pop. Zombie's ears pricked up – one of them at least. Despite being fully grown, one of his ears refused to stand upright and was still soft and floppy. The other was ruler-straight though, causing the lopsided, bi-coloured, stripy, spotty dog to look even cuter in Ryker's estimation. Not that he told the dog that. Zombie got up from his position under the dining room table and looked at Ryker hopefully. Ryker shook his head, telling the dog a firm "no". Zombie whined pitifully before retreating to Ivy, who glared at Ryker for being mean and proceeded to scratch Zombie's tummy until he forgot all about the toast.

Ignoring the damn dog and leaving his woman to the tender mercies of their Order for the time being – they were all fighting over feeling Max's tummy – he went and got the butter out of the fridge. Just as he was about to butter his toast, Mordecai and Dana walked in. "Morning," he threw over his shoulder.

"Good morning, Ryker," Dana's voice sounded a little formal, but Ryker shrugged it off.

"You guys want anything? Coffee? Food?" he asked.

Dana shook her head, glancing between Max and Ryker. "No, thank you. Mordecai and I were hoping we could talk with you and Max."

Ryker looked at her over his shoulder once more, giving her a smile before he turned back to finish buttering his toast. "Go ahead," he invited.

Dana cleared her throat, "Alone."

Ryker stiffened. Turning around, he noticed his entire Order was staring at Dana in concern. Although Max was big on privacy, they didn't keep any secrets from each other. Especially not big, important information as it appeared Dana wanted to talk about. Ryker looked to Max, who had gone decidedly pale and he felt anger flash through him. With one word, Dana had caused Max fear. He frowned at Dana, "What the hell? You're scaring Max."

He made it to Max in three long strides, tugging her against his side. He was relieved and satisfied when he felt his daughter give a little tumble underneath his seeking palm. His Order all stood, lining themselves up beside him, showing support as well as a united front. Ryker felt so proud of them all. They truly were a unit now. "Talk," he demanded.

Mordecai stepped forward, raising a calming hand. "There's no need to gang up on us here. We just want to have a quiet word with you and Max. You can rush back in and inform your Order immediately afterwards if you want."

Ryker was about to tell Mordecai that he didn't get to tell Ryker what to do with his Order, but Max squeezed his hand, silencing him. "Ryker, it's okay. We should listen." Max let go of him, walking to her parents without hesitation and leading them from the room.

"What the hell was that all about?" Cali demanded, glancing over her shoulder to check on Maxwell.

"I have no idea. But I will find out," Ryker vowed, his mind reeling with all kinds of scenarios. And not one of them was good. "Stay here.

Be ready," he commanded. His Order all nodded, murmuring supportive words and reaching out to pat his back or arm. He flashed them a small smile of thanks before he hurried after Max.

He found them in the library – no great surprise there. Although Ryker had the area fitted out specifically for Lark years ago, it was a favourite of Max's. If she wasn't in the kitchen and dining area, or out by the sea, she could be found curled up on the comfy chairs or in front of the fireplace with a book in her hands. Mordecai and Dana had taken a seat on the lounge and Max was still standing. He hurried over to her, drawing her down to an overstuffed chair and making sure she was comfortable before paying his in-laws any attention.

Max smiled at him, "Everything will be okay."

"It damn well better be," he told her, kissing her lips quickly. He then stood up and looked at their guests. He had no intention of sitting down until he knew what was going on.

"Max. I am sorry. It was not my intention to scare you or Ryker. I have been meaning to talk with you about something for a while now, and I confess, I kept putting it off. I was hoping you might come to me of your own accord. That you might have had a premonition or some feelings …"

Ryker noted the way Max looked out at the now cloudy sky before he frowned at Dana. Max didn't say anything, so Ryker did. "Premonitions? Feelings? What are you talking about? Is something going to happen to the baby?"

Dana shook her head, rushing to answer. "No. Not at all. I promise."

Ryker's fierce frown remained in place as he looked at Mordecai. "Mordecai, will you just spit it out. You obviously know what Dana is talking about. One of you get on with it already."

"I do know, yes. Only because I could see something was weighing on Dana and I made her tell me last night. That's why we're here now," Mordecai responded. His arm was around Dana's back in clear support.

"It's okay, mum. Just talk to us," Max finally urged, her eyes directly on her parents.

"It is about the Triumvirate. Things are shifting ..." Dana began, before stopping and biting her bottom lip nervously.

Ryker nodded. "Sure, what with Gaias and everything." Learning Max essentially had a brother was a big surprise. Throw in he was the custodian Emmanuel had eaten, and was now going to be taking over Mother Nature's role in Otherworld so Dana could be free to love Mordecai, and it had been mind-blowing. But Ryker had met him twice now and very much liked the guy. He had an innocence about him that made Ryker feel all brotherly toward him. Ryker knew Max felt the same way.

"Right. Gaias. He is the reason I was able to step aside – because there was already a replacement waiting in the wings for me. Not that I knew that. Such knowledge had been kept from me. But the fact that the Triumvirate was changing was not news to me. You see, I had believed another member would be the first to step down." Dana paused, glancing at Mordecai before her eyes locked onto her daughter's. "Because I knew of his replacement."

Ryker felt his eyebrows hit new heights. "Father Time or Death will be retiring as well?" That was interesting information, but Ryker still had no idea why Dana felt the need to share it privately with them.

Dana nodded. "Yes. Tempus has no such replacement yet – that any of us know about anyway. None of us have foreseen a protégé for Time. But Tanda, on the other hand ..."

"Death is going to have an apprentice? That could be the coolest thing I've ever heard," Ryker said, amused by the idea of a miniature Grim Reaper.

Dana's smile was stiff and held no humour. "Yes. It will be years before the newest Death deity will be able to replace Tanda, but ... they have already been chosen."

Dana then looked directly at Max's very round stomach and Ryker felt the blood freeze in his veins. "Please tell me you're not alluding to what I think you are," Ryker said, voice low as he stared daggers at Dana.

Dana sighed, eyes darting to Mordecai, who swiftly took her hand.

"I am saying that your daughter will one day be the replacement for Tanda."

"Fuck you!" The words were out before he could even think. But even if he had time to consider his words, he wouldn't change them – or take them back.

"Ryker ..." Max began, tugging on his arm.

"Don't *Ryker* me! Don't tell me to be calm about this, Max. There is no way our baby is going to become some kind of Death God!"

Max ignored his outburst for a moment, instead turning to Dana. "Are you sure?"

Dana nodded, "Yes. Positive. I saw it the moment we discovered your pregnancy in Otherworld. Both Tanda and Tempus have since confirmed it."

Max drew in a deep, slow breath, all the while rubbing concentric circles over her abdomen. She looked across the room at nothing and her eyes swirled like an aurora a couple of times before returning to their usual turquoise. "Okay."

Ryker looked down at Max in astonishment. "What the fuck do you mean, *okay*?! This is not okay, Max."

Max turned beseeching eyes to him, tugging on his hand. "We already knew she was going to be the first of her kind – a Spirit Goddess. The details about the role she'll play don't make any difference."

Ryker saw red and pulled his hand free. He paced away from Max, glaring at her, as well as Dana and Mordecai. "The role she'll play? Are you listening to yourself? This is our baby we're talking about. Not some candidate for a job. And how is a Spirit Goddess the same as Death?" Ryker demanded.

"It is not exactly the same," Dana admitted. "Your daughter will still be the first of her kind, she will still be known as a Spirit Goddess. Death and Spirit go hand in hand. It is all about the souls. The souls are what she will be in charge of," Dana informed him.

Ryker turned his back on the room, thoroughly disgusted with all of them – including Max. The thought had bile rushing to his throat and he swallowed quickly. The blasé attitude of Max when it came to their daughter was unacceptable to him. "No," he said, looking at the ground. "No," he repeated, turning around. "No, Max." He looked down at the woman he loved and the sizeable bulge that was evidence of his daughter. "She's not even born yet, and you all have her life planned out. I refuse to let my daughter be used as some kind of pawn in the fucked-up game of the universe. Her life is what she chooses to make of it. In thirty years if she comes to me and tells me she wants to be one of the Four Horsemen of the apocalypse, then I will write her a cover letter addressed to the Devil himself. But until then, the only thing she is, is our daughter. That is her job."

Max stood up, understanding in her eyes. "Of course, Ryker. She will always be our daughter. No matter what fate has in store for her. I'm sure Tanda isn't planning to step down anytime soon –"

Ryker cut her off, unable to believe his ears. "Are you seriously okay with this?" he could see that she was, and he rushed on to speak before she could answer and piss him off further. "Of course, you are. I mean, only you, Max. Only you could spawn the next fucking Grim Reaper!"

Max recoiled as if he had slapped her, her face becoming an expressionless mask. She then turned and left the room without a further word.

"Fuck!" Ryker yelled, yanking on his hair, and looking around for something to throw.

"Ryker –" Mordecai began.

"Don't. Seriously, Mordecai. Just … don't." Then he fled.

CHAPTER THREE

*M*ax moved as fast as she dared to considering how her balance was affected by the weight of her belly. Tears flowed unchecked down her cheeks as Ryker's words replayed inside her head. She didn't realise where she had been headed until she stopped and found herself in the nursery. She and Ryker, with the input of everyone in her Order, had decided to go with a sky theme for their baby's room. Each wall depicted a different view of the sky, from fluffy clouds and sunbeams, to a dark and stormy day filled with lightning. The night sky took up the better part of two walls and was densely filled with stars, planets and galaxies. A cute moon lightshade hung from the centre of the room, and the plain white furniture was the perfect complement to the busyness of the walls. Max had spent hours designing and painting the walls herself. It was perfect.

The sight of all the perfection made her cry harder and she clung to the numerous pairs of arms that suddenly wrapped around her. Cali, Diana, Lark, Beyden, Darius, and Axel stroked her hair, patted her back and held her close as she cried herself out. Nobody said anything. Nobody asked why. And nobody tried to find out by peeking via the Order link.

Eventually, Max pulled back, mustering a smile when Beyden used the sleeve of his shirt to wipe her face. "Tell us," he said.

And so, she did.

"The thing is, I agree with Ryker. Hell, I'm proud of him for standing up to my parents. I know what he's like – his temper is like a flashfire that strikes hot but burns itself out quickly. I figured I would give him some time to think about everything," Max said, looking at all the nodding heads. They were now standing around her in a semi-circle as she sat in the rocker. "But the way he said that last part, about it being typical for me to spawn the Grim Reaper? I didn't know he felt that way about me."

"What way?" Darius asked, looking ready to do some damage to his Captain.

Max looked down at her hands, unable to look any of them in the eyes as she responded. "Like I was a burden. Like I deliberately cause chaos to everyone's lives. Like I *want* all this crap to follow me around; life on the streets, the chade attacks, disrupting the council, causing a civil war, blowing myself up, making a baby destined to reap souls."

"Max, he doesn't think that. Nobody thinks that," Diana assured her.

Max shook her head. "You didn't hear him. It wasn't the words he said, it was the tone."

"Max, Ryker loves you more than anything else in the whole world. You should have seen him when he thought you were dead. He simply stopped existing. His heart continued to beat, and air filled his lungs, but he was a dead man walking." Lark paused, reaching out and placing a hand on Max's bump. "And now he has this. This little girl who he loves just as much. This little girl who is fragile and can't fight her own battles yet. He was protecting her the only way he knows how. As well as protecting himself."

"Himself?" Max questioned, knowing in her heart that everything Lark said was true. She knew Ryker's love for her was all-consuming. But that didn't mean there wasn't some parts about her he maybe didn't like.

The corner of Lark's mouth kicked up in a sardonic smile. "Max, a scared Ryker is a loud Ryker. And a terrified Ryker is a man who lashes out at everyone. Especially those he loves the most. Because you are the most convenient."

Max thought about it for a moment, deciding Lark was right. Ryker had been terrified. Still ... "We've never really had a proper fight. I mean, we argue all the time and we piss each other off of course. But we've never had serious words before. Never thrown hurtful words at each other since we became a couple." She looked at her friends. "He hurt me."

"Right," Axel said, cracking his knuckles. He walked quickly to the door, followed by Darius.

"Will you two macho men stand down?" Lark halted them. "Beating Ryker up won't fix anything."

"The hell you say!" Axel growled, Darius nodding his head in agreement.

Lark rolled his eyes, "We want the best for Max, right? So just wait. Now, Max. Tell us how *you* felt when Dana told you the baby was going to become a part of the Triumvirate one day?"

Max shrugged, chewing her lip. "It was a surprise, but also not really at the same time. I mean, there are a lot of details I want to know and clarify. I want to speak to Tanda as soon as possible. But overall? I'm okay with it, I guess. I mean, how could I not be? I felt the truth of mum's words as soon as she uttered them," she revealed.

"Exactly," Lark said, as if he had solved all of Max's problems.

Max glared up at him, "Is that supposed to make sense to me?"

Diana patted Lark on the arm, gently pushing him aside so she could take his place in front of Max. "What Lark is trying to get at is that you feel secure in the information because you can feel your daughter and see the future. Ryker can't do that. He doesn't have the powers you do. He doesn't have the innate knowledge that everything is going the way it is supposed to. All he knows is that someone is telling him his daughter is going to be extra special – to more than just him – and he has to believe them. Max, he was just told he is going to have to share his precious baby with the whole world."

"The same information doesn't cause you to have a nervous breakdown because you were born knowing you would belong to the world. You're desensitised to it," Cali pointed out.

"Oh," Max said, finally understanding what they were saying to her. Yes, she supposed it was easy to accept that everything was going to be okay when she could already see her daughter laughing and playing in the shallow waves with her daddy. Max hadn't ever seen her daughter's face, but she kept having recurrent dreams about Ryker helping their toddler daughter jump over the waves, her black curly hair shining in the sun and her innocent giggles floating back to Max where she sat on the sand. When Max said she knew her daughter was going to be safe and happy, she meant it literally. It wasn't just a mother's hope or wish. She knew it because she felt it with her very soul. Which, now knowing her daughter was going to be like the Queen of souls, raised a whole new bunch of questions.

Max groaned, dropping her head into her hands. "What am I supposed to do?"

"First," Darius said sternly, still looking like he wanted to punch Ryker. "Get an apology."

"A big one," Axel added.

"And then talk about what this all means to you both. Not just what it means to Ryker. And not just what it means to you. But what it means to both of you as parents. You're in this together," Beyden pointed out quietly, so unassuming in his wisdom.

Max felt her chin tremble and water flooded her eyes again. "You guys are the best," she yelled, before bursting into tears once more. Her Order simply smiled and wiped them away.

CHAPTER FOUR

"Stupid, stupid, stupid!" Ryker cursed himself as he paced back and forth along the sand. He was the first to admit he was a miserable bastard and often flippant with his words. When he had first met Max, he had made the mistake of flinging cruel words at her. But he had never consciously hurt her since then – until today. His carelessness had been born from shock and it was a defence mechanism to be sure, but that was no excuse. He had truly fucked up and if he was going to fix it, he needed the help of his entire Order. *If* they were still speaking to him. He knew for a fact they were all currently ensconced with Max in the nursery, no doubt cursing his name. He deserved it, and more. Still, he wasn't ready to back down where his daughter was concerned. If Tanda thought he could swoop in and steal his baby, he had another think coming.

"I have no intentions of stealing your baby."

Ryker spun around, his duel sickles singing as they left their harnesses. Tanda was standing before him in ripped jeans and a t-shirt, looking cool, calm, and collected. Ryker wanted to take his head off. "What the fuck do you want?"

Tanda held his hands out to the sides. "I simply want to speak with you. I was going to tell you and Max myself, but Dana thought it would be better coming from her." Tanda's lips twitched. "I see that it wasn't."

"Do you think this is funny?" Ryker asked, incredulous. His grip tightened on his weapons.

Tanda's face fell flat, his black eyes looking straight through Ryker. "No. I do not."

"She's mine. Mine and Max's. She is not a tool to be used," Ryker gritted out.

"We are all tools to be used," Tanda replied. "But why would you think that precludes your daughter being yours? She will always be yours, no matter what duty she has."

Ryker pointed a sickle at the god. "Don't play your word games with me. I refuse to accept this."

Tanda shook his head. "Your acceptance doesn't change the facts. Your daughter is who she is."

"She's a baby! Not even born yet!" Ryker yelled, furious once more.

Tanda didn't respond to Ryker's outburst other than to raise a dark eyebrow. "And? It's not as if I'm going to snatch her from the birthing bed and put the Spear of Destiny into her hands or anything."

"The Spear of what?" Ryker asked before he could stop himself. He then slashed a sickle through the air. "Stop trying to distract me. You cannot have my daughter."

Tanda frowned now, taking a step closer to Ryker. "Why do you keep harping on about me taking your baby? I have already said that is not how it works. Dana has said it will be years before any of this comes to fruition. Even your woman has said she is okay with it. Why do you insist on being wilfully ignorant?"

"It doesn't matter if it happens one week after she's born or one hundred years into the future. She's still going to have to go to Otherworld, isn't she?" Ryker yelled, giving voice to his biggest fear.

"Ah," Tanda said, nodding his head. "I see now. You do not want to lose your daughter to the rules of the Triumvirate."

Ryker turned his back on Death, unable to look at him as his heart began beating furiously in his chest. Dana, Max, and Mordecai had already lost so much – and given up so much – thanks to the stupid rules of Otherworld and the veil. Dana had been virtually imprisoned, unable to take action to save her beloved daughter. Max had lost her memory – twice – crossing the veil. Mordecai had been faced with spending only captured moments of time with his woman because of the stupid visitation rules. So, yeah, Ryker was petrified his daughter would one day cross the veil – and never return.

"It is true the veil is a law of nature unto itself. And so are the Triumvirate. But with every new Triumvirate comes new rules. Gaias, for example, will be a completely different ruler of nature than Dana. As such, your daughter, will be completely different with how she handles death than me. That is already evident in what she is."

"What is she?" Ryker asked, feeling an ember of hope as he turned back around.

"A Spirit Goddess," Tanda dutifully answered. "Remember?"

Ryker eyed the man sceptically. "But you're not a Spirit God?"

"No. I am a Death God."

"But my daughter is supposed to take over your role?" Ryker was trying his best to understand.

"She is. But she will still be her own person. Just as Gaias is his own person. Together – with their third – they will form their own Triumvirate," Tanda stated.

"So, she won't be subject to the same restrictions as you?" Ryker wanted further clarification, even though he was beginning to lose some of the sharp razor's edge of panic.

Tanda shrugged, "In a way she will be subject to more than me. She requires vitality, after all. I do not."

"Spiro," Ryker murmured. "Spiro is a Sprit Paladin and is supposed to be her knight."

"That is true," Tanda allowed, but said nothing further.

Ryker blew out a breath, eyeing the literal Grim Reaper. *My life is so weird,* he thought – not for the first time since he had met Max. Speaking of Max, he now had an urgent need to see her. "I still want to punch you in the head," he informed Tanda.

Tanda smiled, his dark eyes swirling silver and gold for a moment.

"I do not blame you. But, Ryker, do remember we are going to be spending a lot of time with one another as I mentor your daughter over the next couple of hundred years."

"Hundreds of years?!" Ryker yelled to a now empty beach. Tanda had disappeared as quickly as he had come. Ryker could care less, he had more important things to worry about than Death itself.

Sheathing his sickles, he spun around and was brought to a hasty stop when he discovered his Order lined up in front of him on the beach, blocking his way into the house. "I'm not going to argue with you," he told them. "Take your shot." They stared at him in silence for a few beats before Axel pushed Darius in his direction.

"Go on, punch him," Axel prompted.

Darius looked at Ryker askance, before glaring at Axel. "You hit him!"

Axel tsked and shook his head. "You're all talk, my man. I knew it. That's just sad."

Darius growled and made a grab for Axel, who dodged and laughed. And that was when Ryker knew his Order had forgiven him. Still, he made sure they knew. "I didn't mean it."

Cali rolled her eyes, "We know that. But you were still a male idiot."

"What does me being male have to do with it?" he asked, frowning at Cali.

"Trust me, being a male always has something to do with idiocy," Cali replied dryly.

Ryker wanted very badly to defend his sex but figured it was a losing battle. Especially considering the predicament he currently found himself in. "I'm going to need your help," he confessed.

His Order looked at each other, communicating as close friends did without the need for a telepathic link, before they all nodded at him. "What do you need?" Beyden asked.

Ryker thought of a certain object he had been concealing for months, and for the first time in an hour, he smiled.

CHAPTER FIVE

Three hours later, Ryker's hands were sweating as he watched Max humming to their daughter on their bed. It had taken longer than he intended to get things organised and in all that time, he had not sought out Max to apologise. It had been a gamble – he knew how upset and unsure she must be. But he was counting on it being worth it. Still, he felt his eyes begin to water as he watched Max dash at a rogue tear on her cheek, even as she continued to hum, her pitch as pure as an angel's. The last of his nerves evaporated however, when he realised what song she was singing; *You Are My Sunshine*. It hadn't been much of a leap for that song to become their thing, not after Ryker decided Sunshine was the perfect nickname for their baby. A gentle nudge through the link from Diana had him remembering the time and he cleared his throat.

Max's head swung to his and her chin quivered, "Ryker."

"Max," He rushed into the room, still too afraid to touch her just yet. His love was crying. And he was the reason. "Max, sweetheart. I'm so sorry." His voice cracked but he forged ahead, "Please forgive me. I didn't mean any of that the way it sounded. I just got so scared when Dana said –" he stopped, clearing his throat from the lump threatening to block his ability to speak. "She's my little girl," he finished, unsure what else there was to say. Because to him, that was all that mattered. She was his little girl and he could not care less what the gods and goddesses wanted of her – despite his little chat with Tanda.

Max let out a huge sniff before jumping up and flinging herself into his arms. He wrapped his arms around her as she sobbed into his chest, murmuring gibberish and promises and apologies over and over again until she quieted. Pushing the hair back from her face, he tipped her chin up so her red-rimmed eyes met his own, before wiping the remaining tears away with his thumbs. "I am so, so sorry," he repeated.

Max shook her head, "It's okay. I understand."

Ryker blew out a breath, feeling relief, amusement, and frustration in equal portions. "Of course you understand. You're damn perfect. But that doesn't make it okay. I took out my fear on you and that is unacceptable."

Max sighed, circling his neck with her arms. She pushed up onto her tippy toes to gain a little more height – even though it still only brought her to his chest. Smiling a little, he bent his head down at her urging, nearly crumbling when she bestowed a sweet, chaste kiss to his lips before whispering in his ear; "You are going to be the best father in the whole world. I love you so much."

Groaning, Ryker captured her lips in a searing kiss that was messy in a satisfying way as they each tried to vent some of their frustrations, pain, and anger. They were both breathing hard when they came up for air, and their daughter chose that moment to give a solid kick. Ryker felt it easily given how close he was still plastered to Max. It caused him to pull back – because feeling his daughter move whenever he and Max were doing anything sexual still creeped him the hell out. He gave the bump a little pat, apologising. Max's giggle was like music to his ears.

"How many times do I have to tell you that she doesn't know when we're getting jiggy with it?" Max asked.

Ryker looked at Max seriously. "I didn't believe you when you said that when you were only three months pregnant and I certainly don't believe you now when you're eight months pregnant. Especially now I know she's —" he stopped abruptly.

"The next Grim Reaper?" Max asked, archly.

Ryker grimaced, "Yeah, really sorry about that."

Max patted his chest before taking his hand in hers and leading him to the bed to sit. "It's okay. I honestly do understand. You hurt my feelings – not gonna lie. But I was also reminded about the advantage I have."

Ryker winced when Max admitted he had hurt her. But still asked, "What advantage?"

"My powers. And the fact that I'm currently a mobile home for our daughter. I can feel things you can't. I have knowledge you don't. You have a distinct handicap," Max informed him.

Ryker thought about that for a moment and it actually went a long way to validating his fears. It also helped him understand Max's side of things as well. "You weren't blasé about the information, were you? You simply knew more than I did."

Max shook her head, "I promise you, I would never be blasé about anything that came to our daughter's health or happiness. It was a shock to me as well. I promise. The thing is, as soon as mum said those words, I got a feeling of supreme *rightness* and I knew what she was saying was true – as well as *right*. I don't know how to explain it. That probably sounds like a cop-out."

"It doesn't," Ryker promised her. "It sounds like the appropriate response from someone born of Mother Nature, who is a goddess in her own right." Ryker was relived to see the genuine smile light up Max's face and he couldn't resist kissing her once more. "Now, about the spawning comment ..."

Max arched a perfectly shaped brow at him, "Yes?"

"That was me lashing out and being childish. I adore and respect everything about you. I love you. There is nothing about you I would change. Including spawning death babies."

Max laughed, throwing her head back. "Okay, okay, I believe you. You are forgiven. But why the change of heart? You don't have to pretend with me. You're entitled to your feelings."

Ryker shook his head, "I'm not pretending. I took some time to pull my head out of my arse. The conversation with Tanda helped too, not gonna lie," he added.

Max sat up straighter. "Tanda? You spoke with Tanda?"

"I did," Ryker said, then went on to relay the entire conversation to Max.

"Wow," Max said, chewing on a fingernail before Ryker gently removed her finger from her mouth.

"Yeah. Wow," Ryker agreed. "So, it sounds like we have plenty of time to figure all this out. And we *will* figure it out," he vowed.

Max nodded, still looking a little concerned. "He hinted she wasn't going to have to stay in Otherworld? I didn't even think of that. No wonder you were so upset. I'm sorry."

"Hey, no more sorries, okay? We're all good now. And yes, I think that is what he was alluding to. In an annoying cryptic way," Ryker then muttered.

Max snorted, "Tanda is the king of cryptic, I'll give you that. And you're right, no more apologies. We are most definitely good." She pulled Ryker's face down to hers for a deep kiss.

Ryker pulled back, sternly telling his dick to quit the dirty thoughts it was thinking. They still had a few months before Max was going to be up to any kind of hanky panky. Resolutely pushing all thoughts of how blue his balls already were, he stood up and held a hand out to Max. "I know you've forgiven me, but I was still hoping you'd let me make it up to you."

"There's nothing to make up for. You were standing up for your daughter," Max replied, taking his hand and allowing him to pull her to her feet.

Ryker shook his head, "I made you cry. That's a *lot* to make up for. Nobody gets to make you cry – even me. *Especially* me."

Max smiled, eyes bright once more, even as she shook her head. "You can't protect me from everything." Ryker simply grunted in disgust over that comment, causing Max to laugh outright. "Fine then, ancient knight. How do you propose to make it up to me?"

Ryker felt nerves skitter along his spine before he revealed, "I'm taking you on a babymoon."

Max stilled, eyes wide. "I'm sorry. I could have sworn you said *babymoon*?"

Ryker tipped Max's face up to his, looking into her eyes. "I did. Max, this past twenty months have been insane. Insanely good because I met you and we made a baby and saved the world and the chades and all that shit. But also insanely bad, because, well, we saved the world and the chades and all that shit. You haven't had a moment's downtime since you stepped into this world – literally stepped into this world – decades ago. Pretty sure there's no one out there that could use a vacation more than you."

Max was eyeing him with suspicion and not the excitement he had been aiming for. "Every time I've asked for a holiday with you, you've tried to turn it into a mission, and I always end up caving and saying I changed my mind because that is *not* my idea of a good time."

Ryker cringed. "I know. And I'm kind of sorry about that."

"Only kind of?" Max sputtered.

Ryker shrugged, "Yeah, kind of. Because we were living in different times with the threat of chades trying to suck out your life force at every turn. But times are different now. We have an even bigger support group, no more evil entities – mostly," he quickly amended, thinking of the few sick paladins that kept popping up. "And we have a literal goddess here who can hold down the fort."

Max contemplated his words for a moment. "A babymoon?" she asked again for clarification.

"Yes," Ryker confirmed.

"Just the Order? Or should I expect a full chaden entourage on this relaxing getaway?" she then asked wryly.

Ryker shook his head, starting to grin. "No Order. No entourage. Just you and me."

Max gaped at him. "Now I know you're joking."

Ryker picked up Max's hand, kissing the back of her knuckles. "I'm not joking, baby. We've never really had any time to ourselves. I figured it might be nice to be just the two of us before it becomes three of us." To his dismay, Max burst into tears again. He patted her back helplessly. "Max?"

"I'm sorry. I just –" she sniffed loudly, "I just would love that so much."

Ryker blew out a relieved breath. "So, is that a yes?"

"Yes!' Max shouted, grinning widely. "What were you thinking?"

"Road trip," Ryker stated.

"Road trip? We're going to have to stop every hour for me to pee," Max warned.

"I'm aware," Ryker said, knowing that Max's bladder was now the size of a pea apparently. She got up at least four times to pee during the night. "But it's not like you can fly either."

"Where would we be roadtripping to?" Max asked, looking more and more excited.

"The Blue Mountains. I know you love the ocean, but I figure it's been a long time since you visited the mountains." He paused, feeling uncertain. "Does that sound okay?"

"That sounds absolutely perfect." Max sighed, "I love the mountains."

"Perfect." Ryker let out a pleased breath. "Now, come with me. We have a bunch to do today if we want to leave tomorrow morning."

CHAPTER SIX

Max was so excited! She hadn't been anywhere other than an hour in either direction of where they lived since she had stumbled upon Dave's just a couple of months shy of two years ago now. She hadn't realised how long it had been, and how she had not paid much attention to the fact she was fairly well cooped-up. Sure, she had asked Ryker for a few trips here and there, but she hadn't pursued them seriously because her idea of a romantic getaway with her guy did not include a dozen other armed individuals accompanying them. For someone who had spent a lifetime moving from place to place, her home now was the longest she had ever spent in one place. It was wonderful and it was a blessing, but now that the idea of getting away was in her head, she simply couldn't shake it. She wanted the impromptu babymoon so badly. She was so focused on her thoughts as she stepped out of the back door, following where Ryker led, that she didn't notice the crowd at first. She had no idea how that was possible, but the huge crowd was only brought to her attention when Ryker stopped abruptly in front of her.

"Ryker, why did you stop?" Max trailed off, taking in the dozens of paladins, wardens, and chadens lined up along the beach. As well as her mother, Tanda, Tempus, and even Gaias. What was more bizarre was the hundreds of fairy lights sparkling in the back garden and forming an aisle of sorts onto the sand. She turned around to ask Ryker what the hell was going on – and damn near choked on her own spit when she found Ryker on bended knee.

"Max," Ryker began, lifting one of Max's lax hands. "I love you. Will you marry me?"

Such simple words, Max thought. *I love you* and *will you marry me?* No long flowery prose, no big poetic declaration. But those few words meant more to her than any sonnet possibly could. *And of course, Ryker knows that,* Max thought. *Because Ryker knows me. He knows the direct route to my heart.* And she knew the fastest way to his heart as well. So her answer, when she could finally speak, was simple and true. "Yes. I will marry you. I love you."

Ryker's grin lit up his dark eyes and he pushed a ring onto her finger. Max gasped when she felt power rush up her arm. *No, not power,* she corrected. *Spirit.* Looking down, she saw a simple gold band holding a single stone in place. It looked like a white opal, with an opaque white background, slashed through with pinks, purples, oranges, greens and blues. It flashed with life every time the sun hit it and Max knew it was more than just a simple stone. "Where did you get this?" she asked.

Ryker jumped to his feet, hugging her and murmuring into her neck. "I found it. When I was digging around Eden a few months ago. I showed Slate and he said opals are not endemic to this part of Australia but that he had no doubt that's what it was. He also said it was no regular opal, but I have no idea what that means. I just know when I found it, it was destined to go on your finger. Slate agreed to set it for me. Do you like it?"

Max pulled back, admiring the ring again. "It is beautiful. I can't believe you found this!"

Ryker shrugged, looking so happy and earnest, it made him look younger than his years. "It's the only one I found and no one else mentioned finding anything more of the sort. Just one of those things, I guess."

"I guess," Max agreed, shaking her head. She was about to kiss her new fiancé again when the presence of all those souls registered again. "Um, Ryker? What are all these people doing here?"

Ryker smirked, "Well, you know that babymoon I mentioned? I figured we could call it a honeymoon as well."

Max thought for sure she was hearing things. "Honeymoon?"

"Yep," Ryker confirmed cheerily. "We're getting married. Now."

~

Max looked into the full-length mirror and couldn't believe the vision staring back at her. After Ryker had dropped his latest surprise, they had been overrun with congratulations, hugs, and kisses. Apparently, while Max had been crying her eyes out and questioning her relationship with her baby-daddy, Ryker had been arranging a flippin' wedding. Eventually, her mother had managed to whisk her away and they had spent the better part of an hour in Max's bedroom. Cali, Diana, and Celeste had gone to work on her hair and makeup, while Ivy and Jasminka had stood and offered commentary. They had both steadfastly denied any skill over such things and left the other three women to play. Max, being still somewhat stunned, had allowed them to do what they willed until her mother had returned from a quick jaunt to Otherworld. Dana had promised she would only be a few minutes – able to keep such promises now that she was no longer tied to the Triumvirate. When she had popped back in carrying what looked like a set of robes, Max had adamantly shaken her head. "Nope. No way."

"Hush. Trust me," her mother had responded.

Max had closed her eyes, pretending there weren't six other women in the room when her mother magically stripped her naked, before tugging the voluminous folds of fabric over her head. Max had pointedly kept her eyes shut as six pairs of hands tugged and rearranged the robes, tying something around her ribcage, until they were all seemingly satisfied. Now, standing in front of the mirror, the only thing holding back her tears, was all the mascara her friends had put on her lashes. Max didn't want to mess up the great job they did. But, oh, she looked like a bride. And it was the one thing she had never, not in her entire existence, ever thought she would be.

The white robe was an all-in-one piece with holes for her head and arms. That should have made it look like a muumuu, but the gold braided rope high around her ribs, and under her breasts gave the robe shape. It also allowed room for her pregnant belly, highlighting the perfectly round bump beautifully. The robe itself was not a simple white, but was threaded through with extremely fine threads of colour. Blues, pinks, greens, reds, purples, greys, and golds. Every colour of her Order was represented in the shimmery threads. They could only be seen when the light hit them just right, and they were subtle. But the overall effect was magical. And beautiful. "I look like a bride," she finally voiced.

"You do!" Cali exclaimed.

"A very beautiful bride," her mother said, coming to stand beside her. "I am so happy for you, my daughter."

Max hugged her mother hard, thanking her for all her sacrifices so Max could be exactly where she was now. Now that she was pregnant with her own child, she fully understood the depth of agony her mother must have felt when she had been locked away from her all those years. Max remembered her wilful arguments when she had been barely more than a child herself. She had been so sure of herself and her path. But she had been selfish, not caring about what would happen to her mother once she was gone. "I'm sorry."

Dana frowned, cupping Max's cheek. "Why are you sorry?"

Max couldn't speak, instead she opened up her mind for her mother to see, only to receive a sharp tug on her expertly curled hair. "Ouch," she yelped, reaching up to make sure everything was still in place.

"That was for being silly. Max, you were right to leave when you did. Yes, it was hard – torturous even. But when I stop and think about how even one small deviation from your path would have changed this present, right here and right now … Well, it was worth it," Dana ended with a small smile.

Max looked at herself in the mirror one last time before smiling at her friends and family. "Definitely worth it." They all stared, a little misty-eyed for a few more minutes before Max finally laughed, "Well, am I going to get married or what?"

She was then rushed from the room amid lots of giggles, only to come to a shy stop when she found her father at the bottom of the stairs waiting for her. "Dad …"

"Oh, Max, you look so beautiful," Mordecai said.

She threw herself into his arms and they shared their first, full-on hug, complete with a few tears. Pulling back, she told him, "Thank you for never giving up on finding me all those years. I didn't know you were out there, I honestly never thought about it. But I am so glad a good portion of my stubbornness comes from you. I'm so glad, out of all of the men in the world, that you're the one who is my father."

Mordecai sniffed once before clearing his throat. "You are very welcome. I am so glad, out of all the women in the world, that you're the one who is my daughter." Max laughed and accepted the elbow Mordecai held out for her. "I am here to walk you down the aisle," he explained.

Max nodded her head and allowed her father to lead her out the back door and down the aisle outlined in friends, family and fairy lights. It was only mid-afternoon, but with the clouds covering the sun, the lights were very pretty. Rounding the slight bend, she got her first eyeful of Ryker. He looked unbearably handsome in white linen slacks and a matching shirt with no buttons. In fact, it had a rather robe-like quality to it, almost like a tunic. Max didn't care what it was called. All she knew was that he looked damn sexy in it. And he was wearing it as he married her. Because they were getting married. Max's steps faltered and she wondered why she couldn't draw enough breath into her lungs. Before she completely freaked out and embarrassed herself, Zombie jumped up against her, butting his head under hers and licking her face. It wasn't exactly hard for him to do now, given he was almost the size of a Great Dane and she was barefoot. Laughing, she looked into his bi-coloured eyes, feeling the unconditional love he had for her – as well as the confidence. She patted his head in thanks and continued her journey, gripping Ryker's hand painfully tight when she reached him.

Tempus was standing next to Ryker and he winked at her. "I hope you do not mind me officiating. I promise, it's all very legal."

Max laughed, knowing nothing could be more official than Father Time marrying you. "I would love that, Uncle Tempus," she replied, reminding him of their affectionate relationship. As much as Dana had broken the rules all those years ago, Tempus and Tanda had still loved Max and were true uncles in her eyes. It was another reason why she was not too afraid for her daughter – because she trusted her Uncle Tanda unconditionally.

Ryker pulled her in as close as the baby allowed, wrapping his arms around her waist and locking his hands in the small of her back. He bent down to kiss her sweetly on the lips, whispering, "You take my breath away."

Max's breath shuddered out, "You take mine away," she whispered back.

And then Tempus began. The ceremony was a mixture of a traditional human wedding as well as a handfasting. Max loved the part where she and Ryker placed coloured ribbons over their interlocked hands as they spoke words and promises special to them and their growing family. It had been even better when each and every one of her paladins, along with Jazz, her mother and father, had also stepped up to tie ribbons and add their own hopes, well-wishes and promises.

What jolted Max was when Tempus asked her to place her ring on Ryker's finger. "I don't –" she began, only to be gently nudged by Slate of all people. Looking down at his open palm, she saw a perfectly smooth, white opal ring, streaked through with the same riot of colours as her own stone. Picking it up, she felt the power – and the protection – that were forged into the very atoms of the stone. The ring appeared to have no beginning and no end – there was no obvious join. Max knew without being told that Slate had fashioned the ring by hand using his domain.

"Thank you," she told Slate sincerely, before turning and pushing the ring onto Ryker's finger. Ryker then did the same to her with her ring, grinning as they seemed to flash magically in the light.

"I now pronounce you husband and wife," Tempus declared.

And just like that, Max thought, *I'm married.* All other thoughts were lost however, under the onslaught of Ryker's mouth against her own. She gave herself up to the promises and the passion of her new husband, feeling nothing but joy.

CHAPTER SEVEN

Ryker grunted as he lifted Max and carried her over the threshold of their rental property. He knew it was a human tradition, but he had gotten a kick out of the idea and had surprised Max by sweeping her into his arms as soon as she unlocked the door. He was experiencing second thoughts now though, as his back protested to carrying Max and the added weight of the baby. Who knew pregnant women could weigh so much? he thought, wisely shutting down their mental connection first. Taking a quick look around, he saw a dark brown leather lounge in the living area and quickly deposited his wife there.

"Do you need more time in the gym? Maybe more time on the mats?" Max teased, smiling up at him.

Ryker mock growled, "Quiet, you." Then he kissed her. A lot.

"Mmm-mmm," Max murmured, licking her lips when they parted. "Are we really not going to have sex on our honeymoon? We already didn't have sex on our wedding night."

"Max …" he warned.

Max pouted, "Fine. You're lucky I have a healthy body image. Otherwise a girl might get a complex thinking she was no longer desirable to her man now that she's pregnant."

Ryker looked at her askance. She was looking particularly lovely in a long maternity dress with skinny little straps and some kind of cute half-sized cardigan over the top that tied up in a knot just under her generous breasts. Not only was her fabulous cleavage on display, but her baby bump was accentuated. She had happy, healthy colour in her cheeks and to cap it all off, she was wearing his wedding ring. He had never seen a more beautiful sight in all of his life. She had never been more appealing to him. He wanted very much to make love to her, all night long, but he also had read that orgasms could bring on labour. And with only four weeks until her due date and them being so far from home, there was no way he was taking chances.

"Gods, you are so adorable," Max said abruptly, smooshing his cheeks.

"I am not adorable," Ryker grumbled, realising his wife had been reading his mind. It didn't really bother him. At least she knew how much he wanted her.

Max smiled, eyes going soft. "I do know. You love me very much."

"So much," Ryker promised. He kissed her one last time before patting her stomach. "And I love my little ray of sunshine too. Now, shall we explore? Are you too tired? We can just chill out on the lounge for the rest of the evening."

"Explore! At least in here. It is super cute. I can't believe we get to stay here a whole week," Max exclaimed, hopping up and exploring their accommodation.

Ryker smiled, looking around for himself. He had rented a converted barn overlooking the Megalong Valley in the Blue Mountains. They were still in New South Wales, about four-and-a-half hours drive from their home. At least, it should have taken that long, Ryker amended. Instead, it had taken closer to seven hours and it was now close to five in the evening. Max had been correct with her prediction – lots of pee stops. But Ryker didn't mind. He was on his honeymoon. With his wife. Max's chuckle caught his attention and he focused on her.

"How often are you going to refer to me as your wife?"

Ryker didn't reply at first, he was too busy taking in her flushed cheeks with her solo dimple and her sparkling eyes, alight with happiness and love. When Max smirked at him, he cleared his throat and answered, "As many times as I can reasonably work it into a sentence for the foreseeable future."

Max sighed happily before heading from the small kitchenette off the living room into what he assumed was the bedroom. "I don't blame you. I love thinking of you as my husband as well." She startled him by laughing loudly from the other room. "Especially considering when I woke up yesterday morning I wasn't even engaged."

Ryker laughed a little at that himself. When he had first found the uncut semi-precious gemstone, he knew it was no ordinary stone. Nor had it been pure luck. He couldn't put his finger on how he knew, but he knew it was destined to be Max's wedding ring. He had been intending to pop the question after the baby was born and figured they would not be in any hurry for the actual wedding. It had been a spontaneous decision to get married the day before, but it had worked out perfectly. The ceremony had been amazing and even the reception – organised at the very last minute – had been no less fun than one planned a year in advance in Ryker's estimation. Thanks to Knox, they had managed to secure enough alcohol for Darius to get drunk. And that, right there, was enough said. Any party where Sir Darius consumed copious amounts of liquor was a good party.

Ryker followed Max as she poked around and discovered a well-appointed, rustic yet modern barn conversion with a very spacious bathroom with a giant clawfoot tub, a huge, four poster king sized bed in the bedroom and a spectacular view of the valley from their private back porch. That was where he found Max, staring out at the dense trees and the rolling mountains in the valley below. Coming up behind her, he wrapped her in his arms and kissed the side of her neck, hugging his wife and child close. Their rings flashed like fire in the evening sun and he shook his head, still unable to believe Slate had found an identical stone and had turned it into a ring for Ryker in secret.

"Does this mean you forgive him?" Max asked, leaning back and settling in.

"I guess I'm going to have to," Ryker replied. He knew Max was referring to Slate's poor welcome of Max to their society. Slate had treated Max as if she were shit he scraped off the bottom of his shoe. And he had treated Ryker and his fellow paladins the same over the years. But it seemed the new IDC representative had undergone a change of heart.

"He's a good man," Max assured Ryker. "Just not as good as the one I married."

Ryker kissed her. "I couldn't agree more."

CHAPTER EIGHT

"Are you okay?"

Max looked up at Ryker from where she had been glaring at her legs for the last few minutes. "Yes, it's just this stupid cramping in my upper thighs," Max mumbled, rubbing the offending ache.

"They're back?" Ryker asked, setting aside the Thai food he had been dishing up for dinner.

After spending another wonderful day sightseeing and driving from one lookout to the next, as well as some easy walking along some trails, they had decided to have a casual dinner in their rental instead of going out. Most of that had to do with how tired Max was, as well as the damn cramps she kept getting in her legs all day. Not to mention the sporadic backpain as well. To say she was now feeling a little grumpy was an understatement. Max looked at Ryker as he squatted down in front of her, his big, warm hands rubbing over her thighs. Max sighed, enjoying the feel of her man's hands on her as always. They also helped alleviate some of the shooting pain. Bonus.

"They never really went away," Max admitted.

"What? Why didn't you tell me?" Ryker demanded, looking concerned.

Max laughed a little and tugged on a strand of his hair. "Because it's just leg cramps. They're common in pregnancy." Although, she thought they were usually more in the calf region rather than the thigh. But what the hell did she know? It wasn't like she was an expert.

Ryker was still frowning and looking unconvinced. "Maybe spending a whole week away was a bad idea. Maybe we should head back tomorrow instead of the day after."

"No way," Max was adamant. "This is our honeymoon, and I am having a wonderful time. It's perfect, truly, Ryker. I love you so much." It didn't take much encouragement to get him to lean forward and kiss her. She sighed into his mouth, happier and more content than she had ever been. They had spent the last five days exploring, eating, and sleeping. Just the two of them. It had been pure bliss, and she was determined they would vacation together more regularly in the future.

"I love you too," Ryker murmured, kissing her cheeks. "But I don't want our daughter getting any ideas to come out early."

"I still have three weeks until my due date. We'll be home in two more days. Don't worry, she's not going anywhere," Max promised. Although, the feeling of heaviness between her legs was a little disconcerting. Not to mention uncomfortable. The baby was definitely head down and she felt as big and as hard as a bowling ball.

"Uh-huh," Ryker said, standing up again. "Famous last words. Cali thought she had more time too, remember?"

Max remembered. She had known about the early arrival of baby Maxwell months before it happened. She had done her best to make sure one of her best friends was looked after during her time in need. Max wasn't going to lie, she could use a phone call with her doctor friend herself. She was just standing up to find her phone when a sharp pain tightened her belly, hard enough to make her gasp. Wrapping her arms over her distended stomach, she rocked back and forth a few times trying to breathe through the pain.

"Max? What's happening?"

Ryker's concerned voice penetrated her single-minded focus and she was able to look at him as he rushed over to her. The pain held on for a good minute before it finally eased enough for her to draw in a deep breath and sit back down in the chair. "Oh boy. I think that was a contraction."

"A contraction?" Ryker practically yelled from where he was once more kneeling in front of her. "A labour contraction?"

Max smiled, though she was sure it was smaller than her usual ones. "Yes, a labour contraction. Don't worry, I'm sure we have ti –" Max broke off, sucking in a quick breath and holding it as her uterus tried to turn itself inside out. *Or perhaps the baby is trying to eat her way out,* she thought. The pain was certainly bad enough for Max to believe it. Panting, Max gripped Ryker's hand hard. "Okay. I take that back. I don't think we have time."

Ryker's eyes were wide and he looked terrified, still he held her close and spoke logically. "Your mother. Contact your mother. She can come and poof us right out of here and back home. Back to Jasminka and the clinic. Right?"

Max nodded, relaxing a little. Yes, she would simply call her Goddess mother. Fumbling for the connection that was usually front and centre in her mind, Max's eyes widened and her mouth fell open in shock. It wasn't there. The intrinsic link she shared with her mother ever since she had used her spirit domain to heal Eden, Beyden and her own memory was no longer there. It was just ... gone. "Uh-oh," she muttered, right before another contraction hit her hard.

Ryker stroked Max's tight stomach in soothing circular motions, instructing her to breathe with him and telling her everything was going to be okay. A full minute later, when the contraction eased, he said, "What did you mean *uh-oh*? What did Dana say? Where is she?"

Max bit her lip, trying to stifle the panic threatening to bubble to the surface. "She's not coming."

"What the fuck do you mean she's not coming?!" Ryker yelled, jumping to his feet.

Max winced, knowing he wasn't going to take the rest of the information well. "I can't contact her. The connection is gone. Like I have no telepathy anymore."

"How is that possible?" Ryker demanded.

"I don't know. It just is," Max said, voice shaky.

Ryker quickly crouched down again, pushing the hair back from Max's face. "I'm sorry. It's okay, sweetheart. Call the Order instead."

Max nodded her head and reached for the soul-bond that connected her to every member of her Order ... only to find it just as absent as the one she shared with her mother. Frantically calling up her other powers, she tried to call the air, the earth, even the water in the damn toilet bowl. Nothing. Nada. Zip. She was completely powerless. She was about to flip her shit when another contraction hit her, and she was forced to breathe through another minute of torture. Panting she said, "You call the Order. Use your potentate abilities. Do it now."

Ryker didn't question her, instead he immediately closed his eyes, snapping them open a few seconds later. His face was incredulous as he shouted, "I can't reach them. The link – it's not there!"

Max patted her very hard stomach, trying to calm herself as well as the baby who was kicking quite forcefully. "I can't access it, either. I think ..." she snagged Ryker's eyes with her own. "I think we're on our own."

"On our own?" Ryker looked positively horrified. "Fuck that. I'm calling an ambulance. That's what a human would do." Ryker fumbled for the phone he rarely used – because he had a mental link with all the people that really mattered – but it was dead and no amount of shouting and hitting the damn thing would turn it back on. "What the fuck is going on?"

"I don't know," Max replied, eyeing the front door. "The car? Hospital?" She wasn't overly afraid anything bad would happen to her or her daughter. She had it on good authority that her little girl was destined for big things, after all. Still, Max had no intentions of pushing the baby out without a shitload of drugs. She was only experiencing early contractions and they were truly horrible. What would they be like an hour from now? *Nope*, Max decided. *Drugs*.

Ryker went to the front door of their accommodation and found it to be stuck. Not only stuck, but the handle wouldn't even move. He turned disbelieving eyes on Max, "We're locked in."

Max watched helplessly as Ryker tried the side door, and then all the windows. Even going so far as to throw a chair at a window. It didn't so much as crack the glass, let alone smash it. Max felt a hysterical laugh bubble up, but it quickly morphed into a groan when pain tore across her abdomen once more. Forcing all thoughts of being trapped inside a converted barn, hours from her friends and family as she laboured with her first child with no pain relief aside, she breathed and counted her way through the intense contraction.

"Max," Ryker said, wiping the sweat off her forehead. "What are we going to do? Why is this happening?"

Max took his hand, leaning her flushed face into the coolness of his palm. "I don't know. It's like I have no powers at all. Like I'm a regular human. But what is keeping us from getting out? It's like ..." she trailed off, her eyes widening when she saw a translucent, shimmery waterfall covering all the walls and windows. It hadn't been there moments before but unless she was hallucinating, the veil was now inside their holiday rental.

"Uh, Max? I don't mean to add more to your plate, but do you see that?" Ryker pointed to the walls.

Max looked at him, surprised. "You can see it?"

Ryker nodded. "It looks like the place has been wrapped in rainbow clingwrap. What the fuck is it?"

"It's the veil," Max replied, still shocked Ryker could see it.

Ryker whipped his head around to face her. "The veil? The doorway between worlds? That veil?"

Max nodded. "Yes, that veil. I mean, I've never seen it like this. It's usually a doorway like you said. This, this is huge. It's more like a dome. No wonder you can't open the doors or windows. I think ..." Max broke off, biting her lip.

"You think what? Max? Honey, don't go silent on me now. I'm trying really hard not to freak the fuck out here," Ryker revealed, cupping her face in his hands.

Max gripped his wrists and looked straight into the chocolate depths of his eyes. "I think we're between worlds."

Ryker sat back so fast that he fell on his arse. "Between worlds? But how?"

The question gave Max something to focus on as she cursed her way through another contraction. If she was timing it correctly, her contractions were lasting for a minute, give or take, and were less than five minutes apart already. She had a feeling she was going to be holding her daughter in her arms in less than an hour. When she could talk again, she asked Ryker to help her to a more comfortable position, which ended up being on the floor in the living area on the thick, plush rug with a stack of pillows piled up behind her. Her poor husband looked a fright, with his hair a tangled mess from his constant tugging on it, his wide eyes, and his unnaturally pale face. Reaching out a hand to him, she urged him to sit next to her. She felt some tension leave her when Ryker immediately drew her close and placed his big hands on her tummy.

"I think it's the baby," Max then started verbalising what she intuitively understood – now that she had stopped panicking and started thinking. "I think she's the one doing this with the veil. I believe she needs to be born straddling both worlds. And that is why we can't communicate with anyone."

Ryker looked down at the mound that was his soon-to-be-born daughter and frowned. "She's not even born yet. How can she be doing this? And 'straddling both worlds'? I don't understand."

"One of our biggest concerns for her future role was that she would have to abide by the same rules as the Triumvirate, right? She would have to spend more time in Otherworld than here? And given she is being born like a regular human from largely human parents, albeit immortal ones with powers, who knows if she can even cross the veil with ease. Well, I think maybe she's creating a loophole," Max explained.

"A loophole," Ryker repeated, wheels clearly spinning in his brain. "By creating this veil bubble, she will be born in both worlds and therefore able to live in both?" There was both worry and hope in his eyes.

Max shrugged, covering Ryker's hands with her own. "I guess so. It's the only thing that makes sense."

Ryker finally grinned, his eyes lighting up with what could only be called pride. "Our daughter is a genius."

Max grinned with him, giving him a moment of happiness before dropping her next bombshell on him. "You know what this means, don't you?"

Ryker shrugged, "She's already powerful?" he guessed.

"That she is," Max agreed, her body tensing up for another contraction. "But I meant in terms of her delivery. You're going to have to do it."

CHAPTER NINE

*R*yker went so still he was sure even the blood in his veins stopped moving. Him? Deliver a baby? And not just any baby? *His* baby. "Nope. No way. That is not happening, Max. You just tell her to wait or to drop her bubble or something." He knew he sounded like a moron, but he couldn't help it. Max clearly thought he sounded like one too, because she glared at him through red hair fast becoming slick with sweat.

"I don't think she's listening to either one of us, Ryker," Max said through gritted teeth, before slumping back against the pillows.

"Max, I'm sorry. I really am. I'm not trying to make this harder than it already is. But I can't do this," Ryker ended on a whisper, pushing the hair back from Max's forehead.

Max searched his face for a moment before sighing. "You're really scared," she noted.

"Babe, I am bone-deep, piss my pants terrified." He wasn't ashamed to admit it.

Max smiled at him, "You know, that makes me feel better. I feel better knowing you're more scared than I am."

Ryker chuckled darkly. "Really? I'm glad to help any way I can.

But I gotta say, it should not be a comfort that the man who has to catch your baby is about to hyperventilate."

"You've always been a comfort to me. From the very first time we met, with you lurking in the shadows of your kitchen and telling me I looked like shit," Max told him.

Ryker shook his head. "I was scared then too. Scared of the way my body reacted to yours. Scared of the way I wanted to touch you and keep you safe. I was scared of what you represented, even in my repressed state."

Max reached out and touched his face lightly with her fingertips. "What did I represent?"

"My future," he responded with simply eloquence. "I didn't want a reason to come out of the dark hole I had buried myself in. But I knew, just from one look at you, that you were my future."

"And now we've created a new future together," Max said, linking her fingers with Ryker's and placing them over her stomach. "So, how about you help get her out?"

Ryker blew out a sharp breath, feeling his daughter move under Max's very tight abdomen. There was no doubt his baby wanted out and she wanted out now. There was not going to be any Great Mother or Order running to the rescue. The sooner he accepted that, the sooner he could be there for Max and his child. "Okay. I'm going to boil water and get some towels and the sheets off the bed."

"Boil water?" Max looked amused as she raised her eyebrows.

"Hey, I may not be immersed in human society, but I've watched my fair share of movies. Boiling water is always integral to an impromptu birth." He winked at Max, telling her to call for him if she needed him.

He then went to the small kitchenette and filled up the kettle, turning it on. Next, he got a few bottles of cold water out of the fridge and checked the freezer. He was relieved to find ice cube trays already filled and frozen, so he tipped the cubes into a bowl before getting all the towels from the bathroom and stripping the sheets from the bed. By the time he went back into the living room, it was obvious Max had just gone through another contraction. He hadn't exactly been counting but he knew they were close together. Really close. He took off his watch and placed it next to Max, telling her to press the stopwatch function when her next contraction hit. He wanted to know precisely how far apart they were as well as how long they were lasting. Running back into the bedroom, he got one of his t-shirts, Max's hairbrush, and a hairband. He picked up the bowl of ice on the way through the kitchen and knelt down beside his frazzled-looking wife.

"Come on, let's get you undressed and into something more comfortable," he urged, helping Max out of her maternity shirt and leggings. He stripped her bra and underwear off, kissing her naked belly once before pulling his shirt down over her head. He eyed the mound that was Max's stomach warily, wondering how it was possible for her to look bigger than she had just minutes before.

"She's not going to burst out like in *Aliens*," Max said, voice dry.

Ryker whipped his head up. "I wasn't thinking that!" he said quickly and guiltily. Because, yeah, that was definitely where his thoughts were headed. "Here, let me braid your hair." He sat on the lounge behind where Max was on the floor and performed a quick braid before tying the band at the bottom. Hopefully, it would stop Max's thick hair from getting in her face and overheating her.

Max reached around and fingered the braid, before turning her head. Her voice was filled with surprise when she asked, "Where did you learn to braid?"

Ryker ordered himself not to blush and tried for casual when he shrugged. "I'm about to have a daughter. I figured I should learn how to do girl hair. Diana and Cali have been letting me practice on them."

Max's eyes turned watery and she whispered, "Oh, Ryker. You really are the sweetest man."

Ryker scowled, pushing to his feet. "I am not sweet, woman. Mean. I am mean – and don't you forget it."

Max giggled, the sound like music to Ryker's ears. "Oh, yes. So mean. Yooooou –" Any further teasing was lost to a groan as pain gripped her once more.

Ryker was quick to start the timer and then he simply coached Max with her breathing. Wiping her forehead with a damp cloth and mumbling a bunch of crap into her ear he hoped helped her in some way. "Okay, that lasted seventy-two seconds and was about two-and-a-half minutes since the last one. What does that mean?"

Max grimaced, "That means I'm likely in the transition phase where your cervix dilates from eight to ten centimetres."

Ryker thought back to the birthing books he had read and also to the birthing video Jasminka had seen fit to force him to watch. Although his mind was fragile from the trauma of both things, he still retained some of the information. "There's no way, Max. That is the final stage of labour. That would mean you've been in labour a lot longer than twenty minutes."

Max nodded wearily, "I think I've been in labour all day."

"All day? What the fuck?!" Ryker exclaimed.

Max snorted, "You know those 'thigh cramps'? I think they were signs of early labour. Plus, I've had a sore back most of the day too."

"Thigh contractions? There's no such thing," his voice was firm, but his insides were shaking. Yes, he had resigned himself to helping Max deliver the baby, but he had believed they still had hours yet. And in that time, his Order was sure to wonder why they weren't checking in and they would send Dana their way. Ryker was sure of it.

"Ever heard of referred pain?" Max cocked an eyebrow at him. "Look, I'm no expert, but I know these contractions are already really intense. They are long and they are close together. I think I'm already in the homestretch."

Ryker blew out a breath. "Okay. Okay, that's cool. I can deal. At least your water hasn't broken yet. I mean, that's the point of no return, right?" And just like that, Ryker watched as the towels underneath Max turned very, very wet.

Max looked down between her legs before glaring back at him. "You just had to say it, didn't you?"

After that, Ryker kept his stupid fucking mouth shut.

∼

"This sucks!" Max yelled thirty minutes later. "I'm serious! This is just fucking awful. I am going to have a talk with my mother and every other motherfucking god responsible for fertility and childbirth. They are clearly a bunch of sadists. I mean, who would make this up? Pushing a literal human being from a body orifice! It's pure insanity."

While Ryker agreed with Max, he also found her rant funny as hell and a single chuckle got loose before he could stop it. Max whipped her head around from her position on all fours – a position she had deemed more comfortable three contractions ago. The glare he received contained enough heat to rival the sun and he quickly apologised. "Sorry. I completely agree with you."

"Damn fucking right you agree with me," Max grumbled, hanging her head once more. "I swear, I better not rip from hole to hole. That's a thing you know!"

Considering Ryker was currently at the same end as said holes, he really, really did not need that visual. He wasn't sure anyone could hear them in their weird little dome, but he still prayed to any god listening to leave Max's holes separate. He didn't claim to be an expert on female anatomy, but he knew those holes were supposed to be like eyebrows – there should always be two. "How are you feeling?" he asked, changing the subject and rubbing the small of Max's back. Her contractions were now coming practically on top of one another and Max was beginning to show signs of fatigue.

"I feel like I need to push."

It was the third time Max had told him as much and although he knew a lot of childbirth was instinctual and automatic, he also knew it could be a bad thing to push too soon. After the first time, Ryker had warily checked between Max's legs. The transformation down there brought tears to his eyes, but he let that go and tried to focus on what Max said he should be seeing – and feeling. Yes, Max had made him check how much of his hand he could fit and also if he could feel the baby's head. He knew he was going to need a lot of therapy after this and only prayed he would develop amnesia for certain portions of the delivery process. After his initial investigations, it was deemed Max should wait a bit more before giving in to her body's urge to push. Taking a deep breath, Ryker prepared himself to check the situation again, only to rear back in panic a second later.

"What? What is it?" Max screeched at him over her shoulder.

Ryker swallowed with difficulty. "I can see the head."

Max went startlingly white, causing her turquoise eyes to appear even more vibrant. "You can see her?"

Ryker nodded. "I, ah, I think it's time to push with your next contraction."

"Really? You think?"

Sarcasm dripped from Max's mouth like molasses, but Ryker didn't take offence. Instead he smiled and rubbed her back. "Come on, sweetheart. You got this."

Max's breath exploded in a burst of air and tears rushed to her eyes. She nodded once with determination. "I got this."

The following seven minutes were a blur of noise and fluids, but three long contractions later, Ryker was finally holding his squalling daughter in his arms. She was very pink and very slippery, covered in all sorts of goop and blood. Her dark hair was stuck to her scalp and she was arching her back, screaming her displeasure to the world. And Ryker fell in love instantly, irrevocably, and without prejudice. Tears ran from his eyes as he kissed her angry little brow before helping Max turn over and placing their daughter on her chest. Max gasped, cradling the baby, her eyes eating up every single detail while Ryker did his best to tie off the umbilical cord in three places – twice closest to Max and once close to the baby. When it came time to cut that lifeline between mother and baby though, he finally hesitated. His hand shook and he was terrified of cutting that last and vital connection.

"It's okay. She's okay," Max told him, clearly reading his hesitation. The baby let out another angry mewl, causing them both to laugh. "See?"

Ryker nodded, quickly cutting the cord now. He then wrapped his daughter up, put clean bedding underneath Max, and coaxed her through birthing the placenta. He was horrified at what the life-sustaining organ looked like and he quickly wrapped it up, pushing it aside. That thing was going to give him nightmares, he thought. But what was sure to make up for it, was the now quiet baby in her mother's arms. After cleaning up Max as best he could, he took her at her word when she said she was feeling as best as could be expected and her bleeding was normal. Then he sat down beside Max and stared at his daughter.

"Here she is, daddy. Your little Sunshine," Max whispered, handing him the baby.

Ryker completely melted when the baby opened her eyes and looked at him. Her eyelids were still swollen, so it was kind of like looking through slits, but it was enough for Ryker to see the colour. "Turquoise," he said, grinning at Max. "She has your eyes."

"And your hair," Max said, stroking the black strands. The baby scrunched up her face before crying once again, causing Max to laugh. "As well as your temperament."

Ryker kissed the baby on her forehead, followed by her cheeks. "Don't listen to mummy, precious. Daddy likes to be heard too." He then passed the babe back to Max and they both held their breath as she rooted around for a few minutes before finally latching on to a nipple and beginning to suck.

"So," Ryker said softly, loathe to interrupt the priceless moment. "About her name …"

CHAPTER TEN

The following day dawned bright and clear. Looking out the window, Max could see the early morning sky was free from clouds and was a lovely mix of pink and blue. It was going to be a beautiful day. But that was to be expected, considering her husband was currently sitting on the lounge completely transfixed with their newborn daughter. Max shook her head, moving gingerly across the room. She was sore as hell, as well as feeling all loose and wobbly in the stomach area. It was gross. Which was why she had spent a solid fifteen minutes under the warm spray of the shower, leaving her baby in the capable arms of her daddy. Ryker was in the exact same position she had left him in – staring at and stroking a sleeping baby.

"She's so beautiful," Ryker whispered, patting Max on the leg when she lowered herself down next to him.

"I have to agree with you." Max reached out to touch the soft, warm cheek. "Holy crap, Ryker. We have a baby. You delivered our baby," she suddenly said, the past twelve hours rushing back to her.

Ryker looked up and snorted, shaking his head. "I know. Hella fucking crazy." His eyes widened and he quickly looked at the sleeping baby. "Shit, sorry. I know I can't say words like that anymore."

Max laughed softly before leaning in and kissing Ryker with all the love and pride she felt for him in that moment. He had been a true rock for her during the labour and delivery. It may have been super quick, but it had hurt like hell, and she had been very scared. She knew Ryker had been just as scared. And he was probably never going to look at her vagina in the same way ever again. But, she supposed, some things were worth the sacrifice. Their daughter chose that moment to mewl like a little kitten before nuzzling at Ryker's chest. They both smiled, kissing her tiny fingers and perfect hands as Ryker transferred her with great care into Max's arms. Max opened her robe and fiddled around for a few minutes until her daughter finally achieved a decent latch. Max tried not to cringe, but it wasn't easy. She'd had the baby on her breast pretty much every hour for twenty minutes at a time since she was born, trying to get her milk to come in as quickly as possible. She wasn't sure how long they were going to be trapped inside and she didn't want her daughter to get dehydrated. But the baby seemed to be getting what she needed if Ryker's wet nappy-shirts were any indication. Max's nipples, however, felt like one big bruise. Breast feeding was hard. She hoped they would be able to leave soon …

Max whipped her head up, only just realising that the lovely sunrise she had just observed had not been through a pearly, translucent veil. She whacked Ryker on the shoulder, and his head shot up from where he had been drifting off. He had gotten no sleep the night before. Max herself had managed three fifteen-minute catnaps. "Ryker! The veil is gone."

Ryker jumped up and went to the front door. He turned the knob and the door opened instantly. "Looks like Little Miss did what she needed to do. I'll call the others."

"Wait," Max spoke quickly, halting Ryker before he could use his phone or tap into the Order link. "Will you wait five more minutes? I just want a little bit more time with just us."

Ryker's eyes softened and he walked back over to the lounge. Bending down he kissed Max's forehead. "Of course. How do you think they're going to react?"

"Are you kidding?" Max rolled her eyes. "They are going to go absolutely crazy."

"We missed a scheduled check-in," Ryker pointed out. "They're probably already going crazy."

Max bit her lip, suddenly feeling guilty for wanting more time alone with just the three of them. "Maybe we should –"

"Nope," Ryker cut her off, slinging his arm across her shoulders and hugging her close. "They'll be fine. Five minutes with just us sounds perfect to me."

Max sighed, gazing in wonder at her black-headed daughter as she sucked voraciously. "This really is a beautiful spot. We should come back again, don't you think?" Max asked Ryker, looking around the converted barn with affection. It would forever hold a special place in her heart.

Ryker made a grunt of agreement. Then he snickered. "You realise we just had our daughter in a barn, don't you?"

Max frowned at him, "What's got you so amused? I do know, I was there when it happened."

Ryker laughed, looking more at peace than Max had ever seen him. "She's a deity, right? A goddess?"

"Yeeesss," Max drew the word out, unsure what Ryker was getting at.

"I'm just saying; a barn, an unexpected birth of a god's – or in this case – a goddess's child?"

Max finally clued into what Ryker was suggesting and she was so startled that she jumped, before bursting into laughter. Thankfully, the baby was too busy to notice and kept right on feeding. "You're ridiculous, you know that?"

Ryker held up his hands in surrender, "Hey, don't blame me. I was simply pointing out the parallels."

"Hmm," Max allowed, saying no more on the subject.

Ten minutes later, Max was holding a now sleeping baby when she felt the Order link light up like a Christmas tree. Ryker snapped to attention and held up his arm. His coat of arms was writhing and his symbol for life was shining brightly. They both shared a wince when six voices began echoing in their heads at the same time. Before either of them could respond, Max felt a rush of power close by that could only be her mother. Several other familiar life forces were with her, and Max knew her mother must have poofed her entire Order there, as well as her father if Max wasn't mistaken. It sounded like a stampede outside their door, and Max rocked the baby, telling Ryker to hurry.

Ryker yanked the door open, scowling at the army on the doorstep. "Will you keep it down? You'll wake the baby."

Max couldn't see any faces, but the sheer silence was telling.

"Baby? What baby?" The question came from Darius.

Ryker sighed and stepped back from the door. He gestured them all inside, saying harshly, "I mean it. Be quiet. And calm."

Max stayed where she was, watching in amusement as the small living area became overrun with paladins, a warden, and a goddess. Her mother was there along with Mordecai, plus her entire Order, as she had known. All the partners were missing, as was Maxwell, but that was okay with Max for now. In fact, it was kind of perfect.

"Hi, guys. Meet Souline."

WHAT'S NEXT IN THE PALADIN WORLD?

Coming up in *The Elemental Collective: Volume Two* – three more novellas featuring, Nikolai (plus one), Kai (plus one), and Caspian (plus Leo) 😊

ALSO BY MONTANA ASH

The Elemental Paladins Series (paranormal/urban fantasy romance MF)
COMPLETE SERIES

WARDEN

PALADIN

CHADE

RANGER

CUSTODIAN

REVOLUTION

RECKONING

The Reluctant Royals series (paranormal/urban fantasy romance MF)

RELUCTANT KING

Haven (paranormal Ménage MMF, dystopian, shifters, fated mates)

HAVEN

The Familiars Series (paranormal reverse harem/polyamorous romance MMMF)

IVORY'S FAMILIARS

The Forbidden Series (paranormal, mystery reverse harem/polyamorous romance MMMF)

FORBIDDEN HYBRID

FORBIDDEN HEX

Standalone (paranormal reverse harem/polyamorous romance MMMF)

TINK AND THE LOST BOYS

MEET MONTANA

Montana is an Aussie, self-confessed book junkie. Although she loves reading absolutely everything, her not-so-guilty pleasure is paranormal romance. Alpha men – just a little bit damaged – and feisty women – strong yet vulnerable – are a favourite combination of hers. Throw in some steamy sex scenes, a touch of humour, and a little violence and she is in heaven! She is a scientist by day, a writer by night, and a reader always!

FOLLOW MONTANA

Follow Montana!
Join Montana's Facebook Group - Montana's Maniacs
Email: montanaash.author@yahoo.com
Website: http://www.montanaash.com/
Facebook: https://www.facebook.com/montana.ash.author/
Twitter: @ReadMontanaAsh

Printed in Great Britain
by Amazon